DATE DUE

DOCTORED EVIDENCE

DOCTORED EVIDENCE

A SUSPENSE NOVEL

MICHAEL BIEHL

BRIDGE WORKS PUBLISHING COMPANY

Bridgehampton, New York

Published by Bridge Works Publishing Company, Bridgehampton, New York, a member of the Rowman & Littlefield Publishing Group.

Distributed in the United States by National Book Network, Lanham, Maryland. For descriptions of this and other Bridge Works books, visit the National Book Network website at www.nbnbooks.com

FIRST EDITION

The characters and events in this book are fictitious. Any similarity to actual persons, living or dead is coincidental and not intended by the author.

Library of Congress Cataloging-in-Publication Data

Biehl, Michael M., 1951–
     Doctored evidence : a novel / Michael Biehl.—1st edition
        p.   cm
     ISBN 1-882593-55-3 (alk. paper)
     1. Medicare fraud—Fiction.   2. Women lawyers—Fiction.   3. Hospitals—Fiction.   I. Title

PS3602.I34 D63   2002
813'.6—dc21   2001052895

10 9 8 7 6 5 4 3 2 1

∞™ The paper used in this publication meets the minimum requirements of American National Standard for Information Sciences–Permanence of Paper for Printed Library Materials, ANSI/NISO Z39.48-1992.
Manufactured in the United States of America.

To Cathleen

ACKNOWLEDGMENTS

I wish to express my appreciation to Robin Hathaway and Barbara Phillips for their excellent and valuable editorial advice. Likewise to Warren Phillips for his generous efforts in bringing this book to publication.

Thanks and warm regards to my dear friends Jim Wood and Sonja Rein for their encouraging and helpful comments on the initial draft. To my son Michael: you're the best.

Most of all, I am forever grateful to my wife, Cathleen, who not only made it possible for me to write this, she made it fun.

DOCTORED
EVIDENCE

PROLOGUE

"**O**h, my God."

These are not words a patient wants to hear from his doctor during a medical procedure. Larry Conkel was undergoing a myocardial biopsy. He was sedated, strapped to a padded table, and surrounded by people in masks. A long plastic tube, which minutes before had been inserted in a vein in Larry's neck, was being delicately coaxed by his doctor through a valve in Larry's heart.

"Jugular intercourse," Larry had joked nervously when the catheter was inserted. Dr. Bernard had politely chuckled. Now, the doctor's mild oath transformed the relatively carefree atmosphere of the early minutes of the procedure to one of alarm and confusion. The remark was muttered under the doctor's breath, whispered, but it was enough to send a whiplash of fear through everyone in the room, including the patient, despite the sedation he was under. Then Bernard said it again, much louder.

"Oh, my God!"

Something had gone dreadfully wrong, something that had never happened before in Dr. Edward Bernard's twenty years as a cardiologist. The catheter had broken up. The plastic tube in Larry Conkel's vein had fallen to pieces. Shards of various shapes

1

and sizes bounced and spun inside his flaccid, oversized ventricle and went shooting through his pulmonary valve toward his innocent lungs.

"I don't believe it. I don't fucking believe it."

The nurses and technicians assisting Dr. Bernard in the cath lab cast stiff sideways glances at each other, as if to say, "Bernard's losing it." A doctor was never supposed to lose control in the presence of a patient. But Dr. Bernard was overtly, exaggeratedly upset.

"I don't believe it. We've lost the fucking thing. Jesus!"

For several long seconds, Dr. Bernard watched the angiogram, his brow furrowed like a bulldog's. The lab was hushed, save for the treacherous murmurs and chirps of a multitude of steely monitors. Larry broke the silence, sputtering through a mist of cooling water being sprayed in his face to relieve the horrible flushing caused by the radiopaque dye coursing through his bloodstream.

"What's happening?" Larry tentatively asked, sounding as if he was not quite sure he wanted to know.

Dr. Bernard shoved a short, red-haired nurse aside with his forearm and leaned over the patient. The doctor's bulging eyes were bloodshot, and his sweaty upper lip twitched as he spoke, stale cigar smoke on his breath.

"We have an unanticipated problem with the catheter. It's very unusual. We may have to move you to an operating suite. Excuse me."

Dr. Bernard turned and stepped quickly out of the cath lab. Another long silence ensued, as the cath lab staff looked at one another, making small shrugging gestures, rolling their eyes toward the ceiling. The giant X-ray camera hovered menacingly over the patient, as if threatening to collapse and crush him. The room seemed to grow hotter and more stifling by the second, as the harsh overhead lights beat against the hard, sterile surfaces of the lab like sun on desert sand, and the tension grew more palpable. Again, Larry was the first to speak.

"So," he asked the red-haired nurse holding the misting device, a tremor in his voice, "do you know the difference between a hematologist and a urologist?"

"Go ahead, Mr. Conkel. Tell me."

"A hematologist pricks your finger."

Outside the cath lab, Dr. Bernard ordered a nurse to contact Dr. Herwitz, a surgeon who was the Chief of the Medical Staff at Shoreview Memorial Hospital. Dr. Bernard said to tell Herwitz he needed a consultation, stat. Within ten minutes, Bernard and Herwitz were huddled outside the cath lab, talking rapidly to each other in low tones.

Bernard was tall and bulky, with short dark hair and a deeply lined face. He had a neck that projected forward from his husky torso, rather than up, as if it were collapsing under the weight of his massive head. His blue surgical scrubs were wrinkled and damp with perspiration. Herwitz was a much handsomer man, sleek as a greyhound, with silver hair and intense blue eyes. His patrician features were composed, and he exuded an air of self-assurance. Herwitz's lab coat was starched white and crisp, his black dress pants neatly creased. The men concluded their discussion and walked off in opposite directions.

Twenty minutes later, Larry Conkel was in an operating room, prepped for surgery, with his hand on the wrist of a thin, middle-aged nurse holding an anesthesia mask. The nurse knew who Larry Conkel was. He worked at Shoreview Memorial, as the hospital's chief financial officer. He had a wife and two children. He also had an enlarged heart, the reason he was in the hospital as a patient that day, which happened to be his fortieth birthday. Just before he was anesthetized, Larry looked up into the kind, concerned eyes of the nurse, and spoke.

"Nurse," he said quietly.

She leaned forward to hear him. "Yes, Mr. Conkel?"

"If I don't make it out of surgery, tell Karen Hayes in the Legal Department to look in on Walter."

The nurse smiled and patted the back of Larry's hand.

"You'll be fine, Mr. Conkel," she said.

Four hours later, Larry Conkel was pronounced dead. Within another hour, every person working at Shoreview Memorial knew what had happened to Larry.

Only one knew why.

PART I

You know, there's always somebody playin' with dynamite.

—MOSE ALLISON

CHAPTER
1

"No, Jake, not the Cabernet Sauvignon again," Karen Hayes said, doing a deliberately bad imitation of a bored, affected socialite. She curled the telephone cord flirtatiously around her index finger and leaned back in her black leather swivel chair, surveying the spartan furnishings of her office.

The office was of modest size, about ten by twelve. It contained a simple walnut desk, behind which Karen sat. The surface was empty save for one neat pile of work papers held firmly in place by a heavy, cut-crystal paperweight. Spread out on the matching walnut credenza behind her desk chair were a personal computer, a telephone console and a five-volume set of statute books. Two plain, modern guest chairs covered in practical gray cloth faced the desk. Behind the guest chairs a single window looked out through the branches of a small sugar maple to the front steps of the main entrance to Shoreview Memorial Hospital. The walls of the office were adorned by two small diplomas and two large steel-framed modern art prints of stark, geometric shapes.

Karen propped one foot on the clean surface of her desk and the other on the bare hardwood floor. The skirt of her prim navy blue suit rode up to the middle of her thighs.

"I rather feel like a Pinot Noir tonight," she said.

"I plan on spending the rest of the afternoon thinking about what you'll feel like tonight, sweetheart," replied Karen's husband, Jake, in a husky baritone, "but I'm not sure Pinot Noir goes with the entrée."

"And that would be?"

"Cheese pizza, reheated from last night."

"You're right as always, dahling," she conceded. "Cabernet it is. You've such a flair for these things. Pick up some oven cleaner while you're at it."

"I don't think we're going to have time to clean the oven tonight," said Jake. "I've got a long agenda."

Karen dropped the telephone cord and twisted her finger through a lock of her long, straight black hair. "A long agenda again? Tut, tut. You and your long agenda," she teased, tilting her head back and rotating in her swivel chair far enough to see her secretary, Margaret, standing in the doorway.

Margaret was twenty-five years old, had waist-length brown hair and was excessively thin. She wore a snug ribbed-knit sweater that showed all of her ribs. Large hoop earrings dangled from her earlobes and too many bangle bracelets clanged about her bony wrists. Karen blushed, uncertain how long Margaret had been standing there or how silly her conversation with her husband might have sounded to an outsider. The embarrassment passed and irritation at being interrupted took its place.

"Hold on, Jake," she said, not bothering to cover the receiver or push the hold button. "What is it, Margaret?"

Karen's secretary was flustered. "I told Dr. Bernard you were on the phone, but he insisted on talking to you right away. He said nothing could be more important; he said there was a disaster in the cath lab, big trouble for the hospital, he said . . ."

"Margaret," Karen blurted abruptly, "stop. Take a deep breath. Now, slowly, what am I supposed to do? Where is Dr. Bernard?"

"He's on my line. You have to talk to him right now or he's going to raise hell with Mr. Grimes. That's what he said."

"Okay," sighed Karen, "put the call through on my line. Jake? Gotta go."

"Adios, Ms. Bigshot Lawyer," said Jake.

"Dosvidoniya, comrade," said Karen, reluctantly pushing the reset button on her telephone console. Reluctantly, because she believed Edward Bernard, M.D., to be vulgar and vexatious. He was also unabashed about throwing his weight around at the hospital. He had plenty to throw. Dr. Bernard admitted a lot of patients, and therefore brought a lot of money, to Shoreview Memorial. He was what was known in hospital parlance as a "big admitter." With two hospitals in town competing for the same patients, big admitters were treated like royalty by hospital executives. Karen knew she was expected to bow and scrape to the big admitters.

In less than a second the phone chirped and she lifted her finger, releasing the reset button.

"Karen Hayes."

Dr. Bernard sounded exhausted. "I had a catheter break up on me. It's a bad outcome. Christ. There's gonna be a lawsuit, and the hospital had better fucking protect me. This wasn't my fault. The goddamn thing just dissolved. I did nothing wrong. I did nothing wrong. Nothing."

Karen pulled a pen and a pad of yellow lined paper from the center drawer of her desk. "Excuse me, Dr. Bernard," she said with forced patience, "but I'm not following. When and where did this happen?"

"About four hours ago in the cath lab. Herwitz had to crack his chest. Pieces of the catheter lodged in his lungs and God knows where else. Herwitz put him on heart-lung bypass and spent almost four hours trying to dig chunks of plastic out of his lungs, but they were too hard to locate. He finally gave up. Then they couldn't get him off bypass. His cardiomyopathy was too advanced. His heart was too weak."

Karen remained calm. This was what she called an "incident," and she had managed hundreds of incidents of varying severity in her twelve years at Shoreview Memorial, some of them much more bizarre than a defective catheter.

Karen was the "in-house" attorney for the hospital; she was an employee of Shoreview Memorial, and it was her only client. Little happened at the hospital that she had not previously seen. Even before Dr. Bernard got to the punch line, Karen had the legal situation pretty well sorted out: the hospital was not liable for Dr. Bernard's mistakes, if he had made any. Like most physicians, Dr. Bernard was not an employee of the hospital; he was an independent professional and as such was responsible for his own mistakes. If Dr. Bernard truly had done nothing wrong, this was an injury caused by a defective product. The manufacturer of the catheter would be responsible.

"What's the status of the patient?" she asked.

"The patient expired just after 1300 hours. Shit, I haven't even had lunch yet."

"Doctor," said Karen, trying to strike a business-like and confident tone, "as of now, this isn't really a legal matter. We don't even know if a claim will be made, do we? Other than having the Risk Manager prepare to talk to the patient's family, there's not much I can do at this point. I don't get involved with the coroner or do the paperwork to transport the corpse."

"Don't kid yourself, counselor," sneered Dr. Bernard, "that little bitch will sue us all."

Karen suddenly felt a sinking, heavy sensation in her lower abdomen, and had a toxic, metallic taste in the back of her mouth. Her blue eyes darted around the office as she tried to figure out why she had this sick feeling. Something clicked.

She closed her eyes tightly. "Dr. Bernard, weren't you scheduled to do Larry Conkel's biopsy this morning?"

"This was Larry Conkel," said Dr. Bernard.

Was Larry Conkel. Past tense. Karen wanted no more conversation with Dr. Bernard. "Gotta go," she said without expression, and put the receiver down, not waiting for a reply.

Larry was dead. Someone Karen knew personally, someone with whom she worked, ate lunch, shared grievances, fought, and made up. Someone she genuinely liked. Someone who talked about politics and religion with her, showed her pictures of his kids, exchanged birthday presents, complained about his marriage. She momentarily felt a little involuntary exhilaration that something exciting was happening in the hospital. There would be gossip and drama, a break in the routine.

Then she saw an image of big, sweet Larry in her mind, with his perpetually disheveled brown hair and rumpled suit, laughing at one of his own corny jokes, which he told incessantly, and Karen started to weep, quietly. She got up, walked with deliberation to her office door, and closed it. She walked slowly back to her desk chair, sat down, put her hands over her face, and sobbed. She rocked to and fro in her chair as sadness washed over her. When, after several minutes, her composure returned, a feeling darker and grimmer than sadness began to gnaw inside her. She dropped her arms to her sides and stared blankly across the surface of her desk.

"This was my fault," she said.

CHAPTER 2

That evening, Jake and Karen Hayes sat in unfinished oak chairs in the kitchen of their small Victorian house. They faced each other, their knees touching, Karen still in her navy blue suit from work and Jake in a pair of old jeans and a gray sweatshirt. Karen was short and slight, with deep dimples, a thin, straight nose and exceptionally fair, freckled skin. Her usually bright eyes looked dolefully at Jake as he leaned over her protectively. Jake held one of Karen's small hands in each of his own. He was over six feet tall and weighed two hundred pounds—roughly twice Karen's size. Her vulnerable mood made their size difference seem even greater.

"It's not your fault. Not in any respect," said Jake, with gentle intensity.

"Why didn't I let him go to St. Peter's for the biopsy? That's where he wanted to go. What business was it of mine? When was I appointed Marketing Director for Shoreview Memorial? That bunch of assassins!"

"It was still his decision," said Jake, "and somebody else's screw-up."

"I know," said Karen glumly. "But I had to put in my two cents."

A slice of cold pizza with a single bite out of it and an unread newspaper sat on the round oak kitchen table next to an empty bottle of inexpensive red wine and a full pack of menthol cigarettes. On the worn, faded kitchen counter several pieces of unopened mail were scattered haphazardly amid an assortment of harmonicas, which Jake, a professional blues musician, called harps. Two days' accumulation of unwashed dishes was piled in the sink.

"I bet you weren't the only one at Shoreview Memorial who got on Larry's case about going to St. Pete's for his own operation. He's supposed to be one of the boosters for Shoreview."

Karen realized Jake was right. When Larry Conkel was told he needed a biopsy on his enlarged heart to determine the cause of his cardiomyopathy, he had scheduled the procedure to be done at the other hospital in the city, St. Peter's, by a physician not on the Shoreview Memorial medical staff. Larry confided to Karen that he had taken heat from his coworkers at Shoreview about being a "traitor." The hospital CEO, Joseph Grimes, had spoken to him quite seriously about how it would look if one of Shoreview's own executives went to "our competitor's facility." Grimes considered the city of Jefferson to be the battlefield of a great "holy war" in which only one of the city's two hospitals would survive. Because HMOs and medical technology were shortening or eliminating hospital stays and the population of Jefferson had not grown in twenty years, there were not enough patients to keep two hospitals viable. So, the hospitals fought for patients like two packs of jackals having a tug-of-war over an antelope carcass. Grimes made sure all the executives knew that filling the beds at Shoreview Memorial was the top priority. And Karen knew Grimes would hold it against Larry if Larry went to St. Pete's for his biopsy.

Karen had not ridiculed Larry about his choice of hospital, nor had she preached loyalty. Out of genuine concern, she had simply asked him why he was going to St. Peter's Hospital. Larry had given an unconvincing explanation about being embarrassed to have Shoreview employees, whom he knew personally and worked with, see him in a hospital gown, strapped to a table. Karen found Larry's reasoning weak and told him so. She had suggested that Larry weigh the short-term embarrassment against the long-term effect on his career as a result of ticking off Grimes. A week later, Larry had made an appointment with Ed Bernard at Shoreview.

"I should have stayed out of it," Karen groaned. "Why am I always handing out advice like I'm so smart?"

"Because you *are* so smart," said Jake, "and you hand out great advice." He checked the clock on the outdated avocado-colored oven and continued. "Hey, if you're done eating, are we going to do anything about my long agenda?"

Karen cocked her head and forced a smile. "Could your agenda wait until tomorrow, Jake? I'm wiped, and I still have the creeps about all this."

Jake shrugged good-naturedly, but Karen could see disappointment in his eyes. "Sure, no importa," he said, "but tomorrow, I'll need help relaxing." Tapping the pack of cigarettes on the table meaningfully, he said, "Remember, next week I'm going to quit smoking."

Karen just looked at him with a tolerant, knowing smile that said, "Sure you are."

Shoreview Memorial Hospital was a mid-sized hospital in a mid-sized city named Jefferson about twenty miles too far from Chicago to be considered a suburb. The hospital's name was a lie. Although it was within walking distance of a murky, man-made lake formed by a dam on the polluted Weyawega River, there was no view of the shore from Shoreview.

14

The structure had been built in two phases seventy years apart. The original building was a homely, two-story box of dirty red brick, full of yellowing linoleum, noisy radiators and asbestos. The new "wing," as it was called, was actually an envelope, surrounding the original building on three sides. The new wing was four stories high and modern in design—steel, plate glass, and concrete—giving the hospital, as a whole, the appearance of an Atlantic City hotel encircling a hold-out rooming house. The surgical suites, physicians' offices, and patient rooms were in the new section. The old building housed the administrative offices, including the Legal Department.

At 8:15 A.M. the next morning—Tuesday—Karen Hayes entered her office, feeling weary after a fitful night's sleep. She tossed her khaki trench coat on a chair, flopped down behind her desk, picked up the telephone and pushed the blinking red "Message Waiting" button on the console.

"*Enter your code number now,*" said a mechanically recorded female voice. Karen pushed 0-6-1-8, the first four digits of Jake's birthday.

"*You have four new messages in your mailbox,*" said the voice.

"Damn, how could I have four messages already?" Karen asked the recording.

"*Message one, received Monday at 6:50 P.M. To hear the message, press 2.*"

"This is Dr. Bernard. Look, Hayes, I don't appreciate being hung up on. It really pisses me off. So if I've committed any malpractice this afternoon, it's your fault for upsetting me. Anyway, I didn't get a chance to tell you, you better take control of this Conkel case right away, get the records fixed up, whatever. Just keep me out of any legal shit. I don't need to remind you or Joe Grimes what my admissions are worth to this hospital. St. Pete's would be glad to have me on staff any day of the week."

15

"If you would like to hear the message again, press 2. To hear the next message, press 3. To erase the message, press 4." Karen saw no reason to save Bernard's repulsive message. She had never "fixed up" a medical record and had no intention of fixing up Larry's in order to protect Bernard. She did, however, jot a note to remind herself to have Larry's record put in safekeeping. Records damaging to the physician had been known to "disappear," leaving the hospital in an embarrassing and indefensible position. She pressed 4 to erase, and 3 to hear the next message.

"Message 2, received Tuesday at 7:45 A.M. To hear the message, press 2." Karen did so.

"Karen, Joe." It was Joe Grimes, the hospital CEO. "Stop by and give me a report on what we're doing to avoid a lawsuit on this thing with Larry. We can talk about other business with the Jefferson Clinic, too. Oh, and have your secretary send Larry's wife some flowers."

Not waiting for the prompt, Karen pressed 4 to erase, then 3 and 2 for the next message.

"Hi there. My name is Dean Williams. I'm a stockbroker at Jackson, DeSalle. From time to time, we have exceptionally attractive investment opportunities . . ."

Karen quickly pushed 4, then 3, and then 2.

"Hello, Mrs. Hayes. This is Deb Jazinski from the surgical nursing team. I don't know if I should leave this on your voice mail or call you in person, but, well, Larry Conkel gave me a message for you yesterday."

Karen sat bolt upright in her chair. A chill passed through her as she stared out through the one window in her office at the denuded branches of the sugar maple, shuddering in the damp November wind.

"Just before he . . . well, you know, before . . . before his surgery, he told me that if he didn't make it . . ." the digital tape hissed while she paused, "out of surgery . . ." She paused again.

16

"Spit it out!" snapped Karen into the receiver.

"Mr. Conkel told me if he didn't make it, to tell you to look in on Walter. That's all. Have a nice day." Karen's eyes dropped to her lap.

"*If you would like to hear the message again . . .*" Karen pushed the reset button, and dialed her home number.

"Y-y-yello," Jake's baritone voice answered, a Sonny Boy Williamson record playing in the background.

"Jake, it's me. I just got a message that has me totally weirded out."

"Tell me, tell me."

"Some nurse named . . . I forget, a Polish name, called and said she had a message for me from Larry, before he died."

"Heavy, heavy. At least it wasn't from him after he died."

"Don't make fun, smart-ass. I'm a little scared."

"Sorry."

Karen described the message, and after a thirty-five-minute discussion of acquaintances and relations all the way back to when they met each other in college, Karen and Jake concluded that they knew no one named Walter to whom Larry Conkel could have been referring. They considered whether the nurse might have heard the name wrong. Larry's wife's name was Paula. Sounds a little like Walter; could Larry have said, "Look in on Paula"? Maybe Larry was delirious, what with everything he was going through; maybe the nurse was a schizo; maybe it was a sick prank. Or maybe Karen heard the message wrong. She used the conferencing feature on her phone to play the message back so Jake could hear it. But after another twenty-five minutes of theorizing, they gave up.

"'There was the door to which I found no key'," quoted Jake, "'there was the veil through which I might not see.' Omar Khayyam."

"Oh, thanks awfully for the literary reference, guy with a bachelor's degree," Karen retorted.

17

"It was magna cum laude," he said with mock pride.

"It was in music. You know, my parents still can't believe what you do for a living, considering that you have a college degree."

Karen and Jake, married for fourteen years, often joked about what was a real sore point with Jake's in-laws, namely Jake's occupation. Karen's father was a cost accountant at a company that made industrial blades and a registered Republican. He listened only to classical music. Karen imitated her father's deep voice: "A grown man playing a child's harmonica."

"Harp," corrected Jake.

"And you play it like an angel," she gushed, "but my daddy still thinks it's a joke."

Jake sighed with feigned despair. "I guess dat's why dey call it 'da blues'."

CHAPTER
3

Karen Decker had met Jake Hayes in the winter of her junior year in college, when she was twenty years old. Jake was twenty-two at the time, but only a sophomore.

Karen had been a disciplined, well-organized student, majoring in history, who chose her courses with careful consideration of what each would contribute to her degree requirements, grade point average, and chances for admission to graduate school. Jake, on the other hand, took only what seemed interesting.

Karen had made one and only one attempt to take a college course strictly for the fun of it, a foray into spontaneity and self-indulgence that would last all of ten mortifying minutes. It would be years before it occurred to Karen how well the course had actually worked out.

It was a music appreciation course, introductory level. She thought it would be a lot of listening to records and reading about composers. The first day of the class, the professor distributed songbooks containing vocal parts for Gregorian chants and other pre-Baroque choral works. The students divided themselves into sopranos, altos, tenors, baritones and basses. Karen was not sure where she belonged. She stood with the altos because it seemed safe, not too extreme.

The professor had the class singing within the first five minutes of the course. Karen had no idea how to sight-read vocal music and was astonished that everybody else in the class did. After two and one-half years at Hartford College, Karen remained unaware that the school was a magnet for serious music students.

She tried to get through the first piece by simply mouthing the words, relying on the four other altos and eighteen other voices in the room to conceal her ignorance. The professor silenced the class with a wave of his arm. He was an austere, middle-aged man with steel-rimmed glasses and a military bearing, who always wore a dark suit and tie to class. He pointed his baton directly at Karen.

"You. I can't hear you. Sing out."

The class repeated the chant, from the beginning. To Karen, the other students sounded like the Mormon Tabernacle Choir. They all seemed to have confidence and beautiful voices. She attempted to duplicate the notes being sung by the other altos. The professor waved the class silent again and aimed the baton at Karen.

"Sing a descending major scale," he ordered. "Start here." He blew a note on his pitch pipe. Karen sang five notes. "You're not an alto," the professor declared. He took her songbook away and handed her another. Karen moved to the soprano section while the class watched silently. When the singing started again, Karen put her songbook on her chair and walked quickly out of the classroom. She broke into a run as soon as she was out the door. She wanted to find a deserted restroom and cry. Then she heard a man's voice call out behind her.

"Hey! Alto!" She stopped and turned around. It was a tall, broad-shouldered boy in a green plaid flannel shirt and blue jeans. He had long brown hair, a droopy mustache, and wide-set, friendly eyes. She had noticed him in the baritone section, smiling at her. He trotted up to her.

"Dull class, eh? Good decision to bolt. I'm giving that one a miss, too. I mean, Gregorian chants? Talk about your oldies." He sang a few notes from the chant. "Remember that one? Big hit

20

for Thelonius the Monk in 1302."

By the time the boy paused for breath, Karen had lost the urge to cry. The two talked about course alternatives as they walked across the snow-covered campus to a small diner for coffee, which turned into a long lunch. Karen was charmed and intrigued by the young man, who had introduced himself as Jake Hayes, and who was so different from the other men she knew, especially the pre-med student she was dating at the time. She wondered if Jake had just taken pity on her. She was, however, less charmed when she awoke that night, violently ill from the salmonella bacteria in the greasy diner's roast beef sandwich.

She spent three days in the college infirmary recuperating. Jake visited her every day, always managing to avoid arriving when Carl Gellhorn, the pre-med Karen was dating, was there. During those three days, Karen learned that Jake was born in Canada, neither of his parents was alive, and he was a devotee of Eastern philosophies. He had once lived in an ashram in India where he learned to play the sitar and the tabla. He had visited the ashram on a lark, along with a number of his musician friends in the '70s, but ended up staying for two years. While there, he met and had a love affair with a woman from Crete who spoke no English. Jake spoke no Greek. They had to communicate non-verbally.

"We were both studying Hindi," Jake explained. "And over a period of months, we both learned to speak it better and better, until we were able finally to communicate well enough to figure out that we couldn't stand each other."

Karen also learned that before he had entered Hartford College, Jake held a variety of jobs, including piano tuner (he had perfect pitch), instrumental instructor at a boarding school (he was fired for smoking pot with the students), and forklift operator (he "needed the scratch"). He played several musical instruments, and wherever he was and whatever his day job, he usually "played

21

for pay," as he put it, somewhere, even if it was just ragtime piano at an ice cream parlor.

Karen came to realize that Jake was a much more attentive listener than Carl, the pre-med student, warmer, funnier, and about eighty percent more physically attractive. She also learned that Jake had just switched majors, from philosophy to music. She was a little disturbed when she deduced that Jake had skipped out on the first day of a required course just to spare the feelings of a stranger. It seemed so frivolous.

All these years later, Karen knew that Jake was the least frivolous, the most centered, and the most compassionate person she had ever met. How sad, how frustrating, she thought, that her parents still weren't able to see or appreciate that. But they just couldn't get past their doubts about the financial security of a blues musician.

CHAPTER

4

Returning from a late lunch on Tuesday afternoon, Karen Hayes paused outside the threshold of her office. Anne Delaney was there, apparently waiting for her. Karen watched as Anne bit futilely at the hangnail on her thumb, having already chewed her fingernails all the way down, and gazed intently out the window. Although she appeared to be blankly staring, Karen knew Anne was checking to see if the first light snow of the season was accumulating on the front steps of the hospital. She would be relieved to see that it was melting on contact. Slips and falls on the sidewalk were the city's responsibility. But the stairs were the hospital's and, therefore, Anne's.

Anne Delaney was the Risk Manager at Shoreview Memorial, a job that combined a high level of responsibility with a low level of authority, similar to an air traffic controller for the Luftwaffe. It was her duty to keep as little money as possible from leaving Shoreview coffers to pay for injuries suffered by the hospital's patients, employees, and guests. She arranged for insurance coverage, investigated claims, and constantly scanned the campus for hazardous conditions that could lead to lawsuits. She also met with persons injured on the hospital campus and their families in an attempt to persuade them not to sue.

Karen noted that Anne was wearing a black suit—her uniform for meeting with bereaved families—a detail intended to suggest that she respected and shared their pain. Anne paid attention to such details; she was careful and thorough and, consequently, very effective in her job. Today her meeting had been with Paula Conkel, Larry's widow.

Anne had an attractive, slightly plump face and curly brown hair. The black suit fit her snugly. Anne's weight fluctuated, the result of persistent binge eating that also aggravated her chronic heartburn. Karen suspected that Anne's binge eating and heartburn were symptoms of job-related stress and had even spoken to her about it. But Anne, who was completely devoted to her job and derived great satisfaction from it, dismissed the notion. She lived alone, without pets, boyfriends, or other distractions. She had begun her career in hospital risk management at one of the largest hospitals in Chicago, Raasch Evangelical Medical Center. One evening after work, she was attacked in the hospital parking lot, in a corner of the lot where a burnt-out lightbulb had created a darkened area. Anne's pugnacity and a powerful set of vocal cords had saved her from becoming a rape victim, but it took ten stitches to close the wound she suffered when her head struck the asphalt.

When Anne told Karen her story, Karen realized that the burnt-out lightbulb in the parking lot was probably the seed of Anne's compulsiveness about making certain the hospital premises were free of hazards. After the attack, Anne left Chicago for the safer, if duller, confines of Jefferson. Raasch Evangelical's loss, our gain, thought Karen. If Anne Delaney, instead of being paid her modest salary, received a fraction of a percent of the money she saved the hospital, she'd be a millionaire.

When Karen saw Anne waiting for her, she hesitated, uncertain whether she and Anne were obliged to hug and console each other over the death of their coworker. Karen deeply respected Anne's competence and diligence and was very fond of her personally. Nevertheless, she was uncomfortable with displays of emotion in the workplace, finding it difficult to resume a crisp, professional demeanor afterward. She decided to avoid senti-mentalism if possible.

"Hi, Annie," she said with little expression.

Anne turned from the window with her arms crossed and pressed against her body, as if she were chilled. "Oh, Karen," she said with obvious mournfulness. Anne's instinctive empathy and will-ingness to share the emotional pain of others were valuable qualities since she had to meet regularly with families over-whelmed by some calamity.

Karen's hand shot up, palm out. "I won't cry if you don't. Deal?"

The right corner of Anne's mouth drew up slightly. Part of being a professional sympathizer was knowing when to back off. And like Karen, Anne was always pressed for time and preferred to get right down to work. "Deal," she said. From the desk table she picked up a reddish brown folder already labeled "Larry Conkel—Wrongful Death Claim," and sat down in one of the two guest chairs facing Karen. "Got a couple of problems with this one," she said, opening the folder.

"Why am I not surprised?" Karen mused, grabbing a yellow legal pad and a ballpoint pen and taking her place behind the desk. The high-backed chair made her look even smaller than her 108 pounds. She held the yellow pad on her lap and tapped on it with the ballpoint. "Fire away."

"I met with Paula this morning," said Anne, stressing the name "Paula" with mild derision.

"And how is the merry widow?" Karen plucked the cap of the ballpoint off with her teeth.

"She had Ben McCormick with her."

"What!" exclaimed Karen, bouncing forward in her chair and spitting out the plastic cap of the pen. "You're kidding me. Boy, she doesn't waste much time, does she? The body's not even cold. I wonder how she got an appointment with McCormick so fast? I wouldn't have thought that was possible."

Ben McCormick was the most well-known, most successful, and most feared plaintiff's personal injury attorney in the county. His incessant television ads trumpeted that he held the state records for the largest malpractice verdict, $50 million, as well as the highest number of verdicts over $1 million. His one-third share of the money awarded to his clientele of amputees, widows, and basket cases had enabled him to live in Babylonian opulence, acquiring the largest, most expensively decorated home in Jefferson, and a twenty percent ownership of an NFL franchise. Ben had also acquired a succession of stunning wives, each one more junior in age to Ben than her predecessor, no small accomplishment for a man who, although tall and imposing, walked with the aid of a cane and had the face of a gargoyle. He owned a vintage Ferrari that was older than any of his wives. Although his ethics were sometimes questioned, no one doubted his effectiveness. The letter advising an insurance company that Ben McCormick represented someone making a claim doubled the amount of money the liability insurer would reserve to pay that claim.

"So, Annie," said Karen, "I suppose your attempt at goodwill ambassadorship didn't exactly leave the bereaved Mrs. Conkel with the warm fuzzies."

"Paula didn't say more than two words the whole time," said Anne. "McCormick handed me a retainer letter and he did all the talking. I laid it on about how sorry the administration and staff are about what happened. Which in this case is absolutely true. Everybody here liked Larry. I told her we were all devastated. I even offered to have the hospital pick up the cost of grief counseling in our Psych Department for her and the children, even though the accident was not the hospital's fault in light of the defective catheter."

"Did McCormick have anything to say about that?" asked Karen.

"Oh, yes," said Anne. "He said he was certain there was plenty of fault to go around. He said that he expected St. Francis Medical

Supply, which sold us the catheter, to be involved, as well as both Bernard and Herwitz. And he said the hospital, as the ultimate vendor of the catheter, could not wash its hands. Those were his words. He said the hospital had a duty to inspect and test the supplies and equipment it uses. He also said the hospital had probably been negligent in granting Dr. Bernard privileges to do the procedure."

Karen sat back and rocked in her swivel chair. A flash of red drew her eyes to the window. A male cardinal alit on a branch of the sugar maple tree, nodded his head twice for no apparent reason, and streaked away.

"Good old Ben," Karen said, shaking her head. "He goes into attack mode right out of the blocks. He'll come at us with everything he's got." She smiled with bemused admiration. "How does he already know the manufacturer of the catheter?"

"He asked, I told him," admitted Anne.

"Well, that's the last free information he's going to get."

Karen made a note to arrange for a letter from Shoreview's law firm to be faxed to McCormick, advising him that the hospital had retained counsel on the claim. Under the canons of legal ethics, receipt of such a letter would require McCormick to go through those lawyers before contacting anyone at Shoreview, and thus protect the employees from further probing. "Did he say anything else?"

"Yes," said Anne, "he declined my offer on the counseling. He said he would arrange for *competent* therapists to treat Mrs. Conkel and the children, and would retain psychiatric and other experts not affiliated with us to evaluate the children's emotional damage and Paula's damages for loss of consortium."

"Ha!" erupted Karen. "That's a good one. From what I know about the Conkels' marriage, Paula will wear dancing shoes to the burial. According to Larry, there was no consortium to be lost, not for years."

"Lucky for Larry," observed Anne. Both women laughed. Years of dealing with tragedy and loss on a recurring basis had given each of them a well-developed sense of gallows humor.

The cardinal returned to the maple tree and hopped from branch to branch. Snow was beginning to accumulate on the steps below. Karen gazed out the window.

"Well, I'm not going to get too worked up about this thing yet, at least as far as our liability is concerned. We'll cross-claim St. Francis Medical Supply. Whatever McCormick does, we'll get indemnification on the manufacturer's warranty. So, Annie, you said you had a couple of problems. What's the other one?"

"The manufacturer's warranty," said Anne.

Karen frowned. "Oh? Don't tell me the product was expired."

"No, but it contains a caveat that might be relevant. Take a look at this." Anne took a long sheet of white paper out of her claim folder and handed it to Karen. It was a package insert from St. Francis Medical Supply Corporation for the type of catheter used in Larry Conkel's biopsy. Anne had highlighted a portion of it in yellow. She chewed a strand of her hair while Karen read:

CATHETER MAY BE USED ONLY ONCE. DO NOT REUSE. DO NOT RESTERILIZE. RESTERILIZATION MAY RESULT IN FAILURE OF CATHETER AND VOIDS ALL WARRANTIES, EXPRESS OR IMPLIED.

Karen looked up with a weary expression in her eyes. She realized the hospital's legal position would be jeopardized if the warning had been ignored. She also realized that at Shoreview Memorial and other hospitals, single-use medical devices were sometimes reused, either to save money or to save the trouble of restocking, or just because somebody forgot to reorder and let the supply run out. She propped her elbow on the arm of the desk chair and cradled her chin in the heel of her hand. "Now you're going to tell me some bozo resterilized the damn thing."

"We don't know for sure yet," said Anne. "Central Supply tells me we have resterilized catheters in the past, but the practice was stopped. I'm having tests done on what's left of the one they used on Larry. We may have a report by tomorrow, and it will be here on Friday at the latest."

"I won't be in on Friday," said Karen. "I don't work the Friday after Thanksgiving. But have the report addressed to me, anyway. It can't hurt to preserve the argument that it is a privileged attorney-client communication. Make no copies, and put what's left of the catheter in safekeeping. I'll arrange for an outside expert to review the medical record and the angiogram." Karen sighed. "If worse comes to worst, the hospital will only go down for the $50,000 deductible. Anything above that will be covered by our malpractice insurance. Thank God for the malpractice insurance! Any other problems, Annie?"

"Just one," Anne mumbled.

"And that would be?"

"The malpractice insurance." Anne cast her eyes down to the folder in her lap. She picked up a one-page letter and handed it across the desk without comment and without looking up.

The letter was addressed to Joseph P. Grimes, CEO, Shoreview Memorial Hospital. It was from the State Mutual Insurance Company, which provided the hospital's malpractice insurance. It stated that Shoreview's quality control program did not meet state requirements, and hence, the hospital's malpractice insurance was void retroactive to the first of the year. If correct, this meant that Shoreview Memorial had no insurance coverage for a large malpractice claim.

"This letter is almost three weeks old. Why don't I know about it?" Karen demanded.

"Mr. Grimes claims he didn't receive it until last Wednesday. He sent me a copy Friday. I didn't want to ruin your weekend. Then Monday, this thing with Larry . . ."

"I see. Well, maybe this won't hold up." Karen flipped the letter in the air. Both women had heard Larry's last report to administration on the hospital's financial condition: nearly $2 million of red ink expected for the fiscal year. At that rate, Shoreview would have to close its doors in less than six years. An uninsured, multimillion-dollar judgment would be the coup de grace. The survival of the hospital now appeared to depend on Karen's ability to successfully defend her late friend Larry Conkel's lawsuit.

Karen pinched her chin between her thumb and forefinger and gazed out the window again. The front steps of the hospital were blanketed with snow. The cardinal was nowhere in sight.

"If State Mutual is right and we're bare on this," she said, "we better hope nobody cooked that catheter, or we're all unemployed."

CHAPTER
5

Karen and Jake made love that night. Most couples would have considered it a mutually satisfactory union, each doing what the other expected with warmth, openness, and a deftness that was the cherished result of years of steadfast practice and attention, the two hurrying to a deep and unrestrained simultaneous climax. But by their standards, Jake and Karen knew that the rite lacked ardor and spontaneity. Karen was anxious and tense, and Jake would have taken another rain check but for Karen's temperature chart, which indicated that eros was mandated, lest a month's fertility medication go to waste. Karen and Jake had not used birth control for half of their fourteen years of marriage. After thousands of acts of unprotected intercourse, they remained childless. They had tried virtually every medically accepted treatment short of major surgery to remedy the situation, without results. Karen was forty years old; time was running out. Now, the onset of each menstrual period was interpreted by the couple as a defeat, an occasion for despair and the recalculation of increasingly long odds.

Afterward, they lay apart, each aware that the other had noticed it was not one of their better efforts. "I'm sorry, Jake," Karen apologized. "Larry's death has everybody at work neurotic. Me, too, I guess."

"No importa, we'll bounce back," consoled Jake. "Speaking of Larry, did you already give him his birthday present?" Jake sounded sheepish. A few days before Larry's death, Jake had suggested to Karen that they do something special for Larry's fortieth birthday. Knowing that Larry collected beer mugs, Jake had proposed giving Larry one of his and Karen's most prized possessions, a souvenir beer mug with a hand painting of the great blues harp player, Little Walter. Little Walter had written the song that Jake and Karen considered "their" song, "Blues with a Feeling." It embarrassed Jake to admit that, with Larry's sudden passing, he now regretted this act of generosity.

"I was wondering when you'd ask about that," said Karen. "Yeah, unfortunately, I gave it to him Friday. He loved it." She poked Jake in the ribs with a knuckle. "Remember, it was your idea to give away our hand-painted, one-of-a-kind souvenir beer mug from the Chicago Blues Festival, the one with the name of our song on it, the one you spent all the money you had to buy."

"I know. But how many people do we know who collect beer mugs? What'd he have, a hundred? The guy was a stein fetishist."

Karen laughed. "Jake, you're generous to a fault."

"I always thought of Larry as generous to a fault," said Jake. "He was always giving people things. Just last week, he gave me those Bulls tickets."

"The Bulls aren't what they used to be."

"Who is?"

"Anyway, you were right to give him the mug. Maybe we can buy it back from Paula."

"Or steal it back," said Jake.

Wednesday morning, Karen called Carl Gellhorn, M.D., the former pre-med student she was dating when she met Jake and with whom she had remained friendly over the years. Carl was now a professor of cardiovascular medicine at Johns Hopkins University, so Karen asked him if he would review a case from Shoreview Memorial that appeared to be headed to court and give her his candid impressions of the care rendered. Carl agreed, and she obtained a copy of Larry Conkel's medical record and the tape of the angiogram, which she had earlier placed in safekeeping, from the Director of Medical Records. She instructed her secretary, Margaret, to package the copy of the medical record and the tape and to send the package via Federal Express to Dr. Gellhorn, without a cover letter. Karen noticed that Margaret, who usually showed a touch of irritation whenever Karen asked her to do any work, demonstrated an unusual level of interest in the medical record of the recently deceased hospital CFO.

In spite of Karen's intuition that Joe Grimes would not under any circumstances allow her to implicate Shoreview Memorial doctors—especially not any "big admitters"—she was determined to get an objective opinion about the performance of Bernard and Herwitz. It was her job to defend Shoreview Memorial, and she couldn't do it without knowing the truth. Besides, she felt a compulsion to learn whether her interference in Larry's choice of hospital had really caused his death. She could keep her friend Carl's opinion to herself, if necessary.

Karen then reviewed the voice-mail message she had received from the surgical nurse who relayed Larry's final message. She listened to it twice and then called the nurses' station in surgery and asked for Deb Jazinski.

"This is Deb."

"This is Karen Hayes in the Legal Department. About that message you left on my voice mail."

"Oh. Yes. I suppose that seemed sort of strange."

"Putting it mildly."

"Yes. But that's what Mr. Conkel said to tell you. Look in on Walter."

"Is that all he said?"

"Yes."

"But your message said he prefaced it with, 'if I don't make it' or words to that effect."

"Oh. Right. He did say that."

"Were those his exact words?"

"I'm not sure I remember his *exact* words. Something like, 'If I don't make it out of surgery, tell Karen Hayes to look in on Walter'."

Karen suppressed a growing impatience. She did not want to say anything to make Nurse Jazinski defensive or nervous. She wanted the most accurate view possible of Larry's message. Friendly voice now, she told herself, friendly voice.

"Did Larry say anything else?"

"No, not to me. But I heard he told a dirty joke in the cath lab."

Typical Larry. Already, in retrospect his constant joking seemed more endearing and funnier than it did when he was alive. But the fact that Larry joked in the cath lab told Karen nothing. He would have joked regardless of what he thought was happening.

"What was Larry's mood like when he gave you the message?" asked Karen.

"His mood? Bad, I would guess. He was about to have emergency surgery."

"I don't want you to guess." Karen paused. Was that unfriendly? "I'm sorry," she said, "but this is really important. How was Larry acting when he said 'if I don't make it out of surgery'? Did he seem confused about what was happening to him?"

"Confused? No."

"Was he . . ." Karen felt a fullness well up in her throat and behind her eyes. "Was he frightened?"

34

The line was silent for a moment. "No," said the nurse. "Now that you mention it, he didn't seem frightened. Actually, now I remember thinking at the time that Mr. Conkel didn't seem scared, or even like he was covering up being scared, like you'd expect a patient to be in a situation like that."

Karen sensed that her witness was now back in the moment, where she might yield a glimpse of the event as she had perceived it at the time, clear of the distortions of recollection.

"How did he seem?"

"He seemed . . . *determined*."

When she returned from lunch, Karen found an envelope on her desk, addressed to her and marked "Confidential." It displayed no postage, so Karen figured it had been hand-delivered. Inside was a memorandum from Gilbert Austin, a consultant at Jefferson Engineering, Inc., the company Anne Delaney had hired to test the catheter that had dissolved in Larry Conkel's veins and killed him. After the date, November 24, the report read:

RE: ANALYSIS OF FOUR INCHES OF PLASTIC CATHETER.

WE TESTED SUBJECT CATHETER MATERIAL FORWARDED BY MS. ANNE DELANEY, RISK MANAGER, SHOREVIEW MEMORIAL HOSPITAL. TESTS WERE PERFORMED FOR TENSILE STRENGTH, PUNCTURE RESISTANCE, BENDING AND COMPRESSION. PIECES OF THE SUBJECT CATHETER WERE EXAMINED USING INFRARED SPECTROSCOPY AND DIFFERENTIAL SCANNING CALORIMETRY. THE SAMPLE MATERIAL WAS COMPARED TO NEW MATERIAL FURNISHED BY THE

CUSTOMER. WE FOUND THE MATERIAL TO BE BRIT-
TLE AND LACKING ELASTICITY COMPARED TO THE
NEW SAMPLE. OUR CONCLUSION IS THAT THE SAM-
PLE MATERIAL HAS BEEN SUBJECTED TO HIGH
TEMPERATURES RESULTING IN A BREAKDOWN OF
POLYMERS.

An invoice for $550 was enclosed.

It certainly looked as if someone had resterilized the catheter,
in violation of the manufacturer's warning. Thus her defense of
the malpractice case was in jeopardy, along with the survival of
Shoreview Memorial and, therefore, her job. But something else
bothered Karen about the report, something she couldn't put her
finger on, that made her feel frightened and somber. She reread
it. No question about it, she felt fear. It was the way the conclusion was phrased that bothered her. Could there possibly be
something more to the Larry Conkel incident than an inap-
propriate but otherwise innocent resterilization of the catheter?

That night, Karen sat ringside at the Caledonia Club listening
to Jake's band, which was named Code Blue. Karen had given
Jake the idea for the name of his band. "Code Blue" was jargon used at many hospitals, including Shoreview Memorial,
that when announced over the hospital's public address system
generated a coordinated response by the staff. The codes were
designated by various colors—blue, red, pink, gray—that in
many instances suggested the condition for which they were
used. For example, a "Code Red" advised the staff that there
was a fire at the designated location, "Code Gray" indicated
that a tornado or severe storm was in the area, and "Code
Pink" was used to activate the plan for handling an infant ab-

duction. "Code Blue," the most commonly used, meant that a patient had suffered a cardio-respiratory arrest, that is, had no heartbeat and was not breathing. A split-second response from physicians, nurses, respiratory therapists, pharmacists and other technical staff, as well as a certain amount of good luck, was needed to save the life of the patient.

Jake said Code Blue was a good name for a blues band. Grim, black-humor names for bands were in vogue. Plus, Jake thought it an apt description of the dire condition of live blues music in the midwest and most of the rest of the country. With blues in one of its periodic downswings, Karen knew Jake and the other members of Code Blue considered themselves lucky to have a regular engagement at a place like the Caledonia Club. Most blues acts were relegated to shot-and-a-beer taverns that paid peanuts. The Caledonia Club was one of the classier places in Jefferson, clean, trendy and well decorated. It served a relatively upscale clientele and paid its live acts pretty well.

Karen watched Code Blue perform, Jake down on one knee, head bowed, playing a melancholy solo from "Blues with a Feeling." It was Jake and Karen's "song." Karen remembered the first time she heard the song. It was the night she had discovered the right half of her own brain.

CHAPTER
6

The first time Jake asked Karen for a date she wasn't quite sure that he had. As she was leaving the college infirmary after her bout with food poisoning, he nonchalantly remarked, "Okay if I swing by Friday, we can catch some dinner, maybe some music after?"

When Friday evening came, Karen was annoyed. Dinner and music. Could be a French restaurant and the symphony. Could be the salmonella diner and LPs in a dorm room. What to wear? Maybe Jake wasn't so wonderful. Carl would have given her more information. Having observed Jake's lumberjack wardrobe, she figured gray slacks and a white sweater covered the possibilities. It turned out not to matter. Nothing she owned would have fit with Jake's outfit.

At 7:00 P.M. the housemother informed Karen that she had a visitor in the common room. When she entered, Jake was seated at an old upright piano, a cigarette dangling from his mouth, playing an atonal modern jazz piece, full of incredibly rapid scales and angular arpeggios that seemed all but random to Karen. Jake was dressed entirely in black and was wearing a beret. On the front and back of his long-sleeved black jersey were gaudy silkscreens of eight-armed Hindu gods sitting in lotus position. He looked like a '50s beatnik who had been exiled to Woodstock. Karen walked over to the piano.

"Know any classical?" she asked. Jake put his cigarette in an ashtray on top of the piano and launched into a Beethoven sonata. While Jake, were he asked, would have said his interpretation was tasteless and unoriginal, to Karen it sounded like Horowitz. When he finished, she applauded vigorously, as did a small audience that had been drawn into the common room. Jake stood and draped Karen's down jacket over her shoulders, offered her his arm, and the two strolled out.

Sitting in Jake's Volkswagen, Karen had been enthusiastic. "You play beautifully. No wonder you're a music major. Are you preparing for a career as a pianist? You should, you know."

"I'll never be a jazz or classical concert pianist," Jake said matter-of-factly. "I don't have what it takes."

"What do you mean? You never make a single mistake. You play with feeling and sensitivity. You've obviously worked hard at it. What don't you have?"

Jake looked at her apologetically, his eyebrows cocked out like quotation marks around his brown eyes. He raised his left hand in front of his face. Karen felt a small shock in her throat and a twinge of nausea. Jake was missing most of the little finger on his left hand and the tip of his fourth finger.

"Dad left his saber saw plugged in," said Jake. "My concert piano career was over when I was five years old. Guitar, too." Karen was astonished she had not noticed the disfigurement before. In retrospect, his piano playing seemed impossible. "On the plus side," said Jake, "you just might be in the presence of the world's best eight-fingered Canadian sitar player. Now, if you've still got an appetite, what say we chow down?"

He took her to a small Jamaican restaurant that served spicy pumpkin soup, fried plantains, yucca, and broiled grouper with root vegetables. Karen tried ginger beer for the first time. The Rastafarian waiter flirted with Karen, who found the whole experience exciting, but a little frightening. Carl Gellhorn's idea of an exotic restaurant was Hong's Chinese Palace.

Adding to her nervousness, in the VW after dinner Jake lit a joint and offered it to her. She politely and somewhat reluctantly tried a couple of tokes and was feeling disoriented and anxious when Jake parked the car in an unlit parking lot in a run-down neighborhood, in front of a place called "The Mineshaft."

Inside The Mineshaft, it was noisy, warm, smoky, and smelled of stale beer. The walls and ceilings were painted black, and the dirty wood floor was littered with cigarette butts. Large black and white photos of black men Karen assumed were musicians of some kind hung haphazardly around the main room, which was jammed with small battered tables and chairs. Jake led Karen by the arm through the boisterous crowd, which was near capacity and mixed racially. The audience, for the most part, was noticeably older than Karen—not a student crowd. Karen felt out of place and apprehensive.

Jake led her to a table with a piece of paper folded like a pup tent sitting in the middle of it, on which someone had printed "Reserved" in pencil. He helped her off with her coat and held her chair. Karen excused herself to go to the restroom, which was the size of a broom closet, smelly and stifling. Her claustrophobia, combined with the marijuana, made her heart pound so intensely she was afraid it would fibrillate. She decided to risk bladder injury instead and returned immediately to the table.

"Would you care for a drink?" Jake asked. "I recommend a Stinger." Karen did not know what a Stinger was, but she said "Okay" and Jake headed for the bar.

Alone at the table, her apprehension intensified. She held her purse on her lap, her knees tight together, and squeezed the handles. "What am I doing here?" she said to herself. "This is too weird. I don't know this guy that well, why would I trust his judgment? If I'd gone out with Carl, I'd be in a safe suburban movie theater right now. Instead, I'm in some seedy dive where people probably get stabbed. For all I know, he lost his fingers in a knife fight. Why is he taking so long?" She felt short of breath, panicky.

The crowd got suddenly quiet and eyes turned toward a small stage on which two scruffy-looking men with guitars and an even scruffier guy with a set of drums had set up. A thin, bald man with a gray beard and several garish tattoos stood at a microphone in the middle of the stage. He spoke in a gravelly, alcohol-soaked voice.

"Good evening, and welcome to The Mineshaft. I want to remind you cats to tip the waitresses generously because I don't pay 'em for shit. And now, let's get it together for the best blues in the middle west. Ladies and gents, The Mineshaft is proud to present Buddha and the Lowdown Polecats!"

The man disappeared behind a shabby velvet curtain. Karen thought she heard four gunshots, and she jumped in her chair, but it was just the snare drum setting the quick tempo. The bass guitar kicked in at such a volume she could feel the vibrations on her skin. The lead guitar started playing a bright, effervescent solo and voices in the crowd began to shout out encouragement. In the back of Karen's anxiety-gripped mind, something said: "Hey. These guys are *good*."

A waitress came up from behind and put a drink on the table. Karen opened her purse.

"It's taken care of," shouted the waitress. Karen spun around and scanned the bar. No Jake. Great. He goes to the men's room and misses the start of the show.

Next, a vocalist joined in, exhorting the audience:

"Aw, mercy! You know it ain't no crime,
C'mon now, get down y'all
And have a good time.
Gonna rock this joint

41

Yeah, gonna rock this joint
Now I know we can do it,
So let's get down to it!"

The singer leapt from behind the curtain. It was Jake. He slid sideways across the stage to the microphone, cupped a small rectangular piece of metal to his mouth, and suddenly the room was filled with a wailing, soaring sound and a blast of applause. Jake spun on his heels and dropped into the splits. The audience whooped.

Oh my, thought Karen. I was worried he'd miss the show. Jake's in the show. Jake *is* the show. She began to get angry with him for tricking her. "Show-off," she said out loud. "Bastard." But something remote in her mind said, "I'm having *fun*." By the end of the opening number, she was on her feet with the rest, whistling through her teeth.

Without patter, the band went right into the next number, a slow one, "Blues with a Feeling." Karen relaxed and savored the conviction in Jake's soulful rendition of the ballad. As she watched and listened, she felt herself sexually lubricating. Her limbs and face were suffused with a warm, sweet feeling. Jake closed his eyes tightly as he played, absorbed in the sound of the harp, as if in a trance. Karen said softly, "This guy is insane." But that small voice in the back of her mind said, "This guy is the one."

Karen still retained some of that feeling twenty years later as she sat listening to Code Blue at the Caledonia Club. Jake's hair was shorter now and his waist a tad thicker. His mustache was neatly trimmed and starting to show some gray. He wore a plain black jersey, without psychedelic adornment. But he still appeared to be transported to another world when he was deep into a song, especially a slow one. Over the years, his playing had acquired the simplicity and elegance of a mature virtuoso. A patron at the next table, a regular who knew who Karen was, leaned over and shouted to her, "He sure plays the hell out of this one, don't he? He write it?" About half of the songs Jake's band played were original, the other half were covers of songs performed by pioneers of the genre.

"No," replied Karen. "This is a classic. By Little Walter."

At her own mention of the name, Karen felt a tingling sensation at the back of her neck. The expression dropped from her face. She grabbed her jacket and hurried across the small dance floor to the stage. With a nod of his head, Jake passed the solo to the guitarist. "What's up?"

Karen shouted, "I've gotta go look in on Walter." She raised her fist to her mouth, thumb up, and pantomimed drinking. She looked at Jake out of the corner of her eye, eyebrows raised as if to say, "Get it?" Jake watched as Karen snaked her way toward the door, a smile of admiration and gratitude spreading across his broad face.

CHAPTER
7

Just after midnight Karen slipped into Larry Conkel's office on the second floor in the old section of Shoreview Memorial. Larry's office was approximately the same size as hers, but that was where the similarity ended, she thought. Whereas her office was sparely furnished and orderly, with just one neat pile of work papers on the desk under the heavy cut-crystal paperweight, Larry's office was chaos in bloom. Deep, crooked piles of documents, letters, computer printouts, junk mail and trade publications covered every square inch of his desk and file cabinet, as well as the top of the radiator and much of the floor. His tables and wall shelves were full of knickknacks, travel souvenirs, houseplants, empty soda cans and opened packages of breath mints and hard candy. While Karen had two steel-framed modern art prints of clean, geometric shapes on the walls of her office, Larry had dozens of variously sized, framed photos of himself with friends, family members, medical staff members, local politicians, and a plethora of scaly game fish.

On one huge bookcase, he had nothing but mugs. Karen knew people who collected stamps, coins, matchbooks, anything having to do with owls, and one who collected antique eggbeaters. Larry collected beer mugs. He had pewter mugs, glass-bottomed mugs, ceramic mugs with the logos of imported beers and ales from Europe, Latin America and the Far East, and mugs in the shapes of faces, with little hats that tipped up when you pressed a thumb lever. He had huge three-liter steins and tiny little steins that would hold only an ounce of beer. And on the top shelf he had a souvenir mug from the Chicago Blues Festival with the theme of that year's festival, "Blues with a Feeling," hand-painted in script over a caricature of the originator of the modern style of blues harp, Walter Jacobs, also known as Little Walter. "My new favorite," Larry had told Karen when she presented him with the mug as a fortieth birthday present.

Karen cleared a box of papers from a guest chair and pulled the chair over to the bookcase. Standing on the chair, she still needed to rise on tiptoe to reach the mug. She got it down and looked in the mug. Inside were a small brass key and a larger, steel key. She took the keys out, replaced the mug, stepped down from the chair, and looked around the office. Larry's desk had a lock in the center drawer, but it was unlocked. Opposite the desk was a two-drawer oak wall unit with magazines and potted cacti on top of it. The bottom drawer had a lock in it. She tested the drawer and found it locked. She inserted the small brass key and turned. It opened.

Inside were three fat reddish-brown accordion files labeled "J.C.—Fraud Investigation". Together the files were over two feet thick. The labels were numbered 1, 2 and 4. Each file contained several manila folders. She removed the file numbered 1, sat down in the guest chair and pulled out the first folder. She set the folder on her lap and opened it. She scanned a few pages of the contents. When Karen realized what she was looking at, she decided to move all the files to her own office.

It was half past midnight when she finished moving the files. Jake would be home from the gig around 3:00 A.M. She could review the documents for two hours and still be home to greet him.

In front of her was the record of an extensive investigation Larry Conkel had conducted into massive billing fraud at the Jefferson Clinic, a local medical group that supplied Shoreview many of its doctors. Much of the record was handwritten. Larry apparently did not trust even his secretary with the information contained in the file. Karen understood why.

The file revealed that three years earlier, Larry had collected data for a physician recruitment contract with the clinic. Such contracts were common: a hospital collected data showing a need for a physician in a certain specialty. A medical group, such as the Jefferson Clinic, could recruit a physician in that specialty to relocate to the hospital's service area and join the medical group. The hospital guaranteed the group that the cost of hiring the specialist, including salary, would not exceed the fees that the specialist would collect for treating patients. If it did, the hospital would make up the difference. Growth without risk for the medical group, a new source of patient admissions for the hospital. The additional patients the newly recruited physician admitted to the hospital would inevitably make the hospital much more money than it paid out to the medical group on the guarantee.

Karen knew a lot about the simple facts of hospital economics: the filling of empty beds meant more money for the hospital without much more cost. Hospital billings for the patients brought in by the new doctor were almost pure profit, so it was worth it to the hospital to guarantee the recruit a generous salary to get another big admitter on the hospital's medical staff. This sort of arrangement was only legal under federal law, however, if the hospital could prove there was a need in the community for a new doctor in a particular specialty. Without a documented need, the scheme might be viewed as just a way to increase the number of expensive treatments and therefore jack up the cost to federal programs like Medicaid and Medicare.

46

In the case of the Shoreview Memorial physician-recruitment contract three years earlier, the recruited doctor was a medical oncologist, a type of specialist who treated cancer with chemotherapy, named Norman Caswell. Dr. Caswell had always given Karen the creeps. He was gaunt and sallow and usually wore a patently insincere smile that made her think of an undertaker. Shoreview Memorial had guaranteed the Jefferson Clinic that it could hire Dr. Caswell at a salary of $300,000 per year, plus bonus, without risk if his patient revenues fell short. Because the hospital had agreed to pay any shortfall, the clinic was required to open its books to Shoreview concerning Dr. Caswell's income.

Shoreview never paid out a cent on the guarantee, Karen saw in the file, which was good. Dr. Caswell and the clinic did even better. The profits on Dr. Caswell's services to patients were nearly *four times the guarantee.*

A physician making over a million dollars a year was not unheard of in Jefferson, but Larry had personally collected and analyzed extensive data on the need for chemotherapy in the region. There was simply no way there were enough cancer patients in town to support that volume.

Larry had checked Dr. Caswell's billing records against his medical records. They matched up. Then Larry had talked to one of Dr. Caswell's patients. He told the patient he was calling to see if she was satisfied with the courtesy of the staff and the convenience of the facility when she received her chemotherapy treatments.

The patient had said, "What chemotherapy? I never had any chemotherapy."

Reading on in Larry's meticulous notes, Karen learned he had discovered dozens of cases of billing for services that had not been provided, and yet were documented in the medical records. He looked at the records more closely and discovered Dr. Caswell was up to something even worse: he had given chemotherapy to people who were not candidates for it under accepted guidelines. Patients who were legitimate chemotherapy patients had their dosages increased beyond appropriate levels, because Dr. Caswell could bill more for higher dosages. Maximizing reimbursement was the exclusive criterion on which treatment decisions had been made. That was how Norman Caswell was able to make $1.2 million a year.

Larry widened his investigation. At least four other doctors at the clinic were engaged in similar practices on just as large a scale. One of the perpetrators was Edward Bernard, the cardiologist. He had his share of documented nonexistent office visits, but much worse was his performance of cardiac catheterizations on patients with perfectly healthy hearts. Their angiograms were normal. Their medical records stated, "Patient reports chest pain." When Larry questioned them, the patients had said, "What chest pain? I never had any chest pain." On several of Dr. Bernard's cases, Larry had concluded, "The only indication for catheterization appears to have been that the patient had health insurance."

Karen could scarcely believe Larry's files. He had documented billing fraud running into the tens of millions. This was nothing compared to the unnecessary pain, anxiety, discomfort, and inconvenience scores of trusting patients had suffered. Worst of all, Larry had written, was the unnecessary risk to which they had been exposed. One recipient of an unneeded cardiac catheterization had had an adverse reaction to the radiopaque dye, gone into anaphylactic shock, and died.

Dozens of patients had been subjected to dangerous, painful, invasive procedures with horrendous side effects, for no good medical reason. Millions of dollars paid for unneeded treatments or medical care that was never even given. At least one very wrongful death.

If what she was reading ever saw the light of day, Karen knew it would destroy the Jefferson Clinic and end the medical careers of several prominent physicians.

The chirp of her telephone startled her. Feeling suddenly furtive and paranoid, she answered without giving her name.

"Legal Department."

"Legal Department? I need a lawyer. I think my wife's deserted me."

"Jake?" asked Karen.

"Y-y-y-ello," said Jake.

"What time is it?" asked Karen.

"Quarter past three. I'm home. Just checking to make sure you're okay. How's Walter?"

"Long story. I'll tell you when I get home."

"Tell me tomorrow. I'm done in."

"Busy day tomorrow. Thanksgiving."

"Gee," said Jake, "I can hardly wait."

CHAPTER
8

A winter storm slammed into the city of Jefferson on Thanksgiving Day. The shoulders of the two-lane highway that led to Karen's mother's apartment were littered with the cars of impatient drivers. Visibility was no more than thirty feet, and the wind made the wet snow look like it was falling horizontally across the flat midwestern landscape.

Karen's mother and father had divorced twelve years earlier. Ever since, Thanksgiving had been a ten-hour ordeal, with time allotted equally between mother and father to avoid offending either parent. The location of the turkey and stuffing phase of the meal, versus the pumpkin pie and coffee phase, were alternated annually like the World Series designated-hitter rule.

As Karen and Jake's eleven-year-old Volvo chugged and fishtailed through the driving snow, Karen sat in uncharacteristic silence, coiling and uncoiling a tress of her dark hair with her index finger, staring blankly at the cornfields, which were quickly turning from brown to white. She barely noticed that Jake was white-knuckled and hunched forward in his seat, struggling to keep the rear-wheel-drive car from sliding off the slick, slushy road.

"Can't believe this thing was made in Sweden," said Jake.

"What?" said Karen.

"Sweden. They make Volvos in Sweden."

"Uh-huh."

"This heap is terrible in snow. No traction at all."

"Uh-huh."

"But they have lots of snow in Sweden. It snows all the time in Sweden. With all that snow, and with cars like this, it's no wonder all the guys in Bergman movies are so dour."

"I guess."

Jake took his eyes off the road for a brief moment and glanced at Karen. "What is it?" he said.

"What is what?"

"What is 'dis trouble in mind, 'dat got you in its sway?"

"What?"

Jake looked at Karen again, more intently. "Spill it," he said.

Karen sighed. "What I found in Larry's office last night is just so awful, I don't believe it."

"What'd you find?"

"I found enough smoking guns to fill an armory. I found a malignancy growing on Shoreview. I found proof of the banality of evil."

"Could you be a little more specific?"

Karen told Jake the story—about the keys she found in the "Little Walter" mug, and how one of them unlocked the files from Larry's investigation into the Jefferson Clinic's fraudulent practices, how Larry's records showed that some of the clinic physicians routinely billed Medicare for services they never performed.

"So they're ripping off Uncle Sam," said Jake. "Shame on them. But it could be a whole lot worse. Like if they actually went ahead and operated on the old folks, when they didn't need surgery, just to get the dough."

"They did a lot of that, too," said Karen. "They did invasive diagnostic procedures like cardiac catheterizations. One of them, that creep Caswell, gave cancer patients chemotherapy they didn't need just to get the fees."

"Bummer," said Jake. He risked removing his right hand from the steering wheel and reached over to massage the back of Karen's neck. "Whoa," he said. "Lotta tension there. You're wound tighter than a four-dollar watch. That's more than just a hard day's night at your gig."

"I dread going to my mom's for Thanksgiving. You know that. And my dad's is worse. It's always the same thing. This family stuff. I hate all Pilgrims."

"Yeah, holidays can be a drag, but hey, maybe we can sort of get into the Norman Rockwell spirit. To grandmother's house we go, and all that jazz."

"That's just it," said Karen. "It's not grandmother's house if you have no grandchild to take there. Of course, Pamela will be at Mom's, exhibiting her little darlings. I hate Norman Rockwell."

Jake smiled. "Remember the true meaning of the day," he said with facetious piety. "And think of something you are thankful for."

Karen turned and stared out the car window at the blowing snow. "I'm thankful," she said, "that it comes but once a year."

The turkey was excellent, but nothing else was at Elizabeth Decker's apartment. Karen's older sister, Pamela, and her two children had flown in from Cleveland to be with their mother for Thanksgiving. Pamela's husband, Brett, an executive with a women's wear mall chain, had stayed behind. Pamela relayed her husband's excuse, the press of business on the Friday after Thanksgiving, traditionally the biggest shopping day of the year. Karen knew that Brett's absences from Decker family gatherings, which were more the rule than the exception, had long been a source of irritation to her mother. Karen wondered whether her mother suspected, as she did, that the "business" Brett was attending to was of the monkey variety.

Karen Hayes was a pretty woman, but her sister Pamela was beautiful in a wholesome, all-American way. She had high cheekbones, a small upturned nose, and mounds of artificially blonde hair. During a brief career as a fashion model she had met her husband. Both women had their mother's slender figure, but Pamela had her father's height and straight posture as well. She also had something else her sister lacked.

Fertility.

Pamela's children had been the focal point of the early afternoon, at best a dull proposition for Karen and Jake, and an unwelcome one for both children. Pamela's daughter Suzanne, an introverted adolescent, aloof and listless, acted both embarrassed and bored when her aunt, uncle or grandmother attempted to make conversation with her. Suzanne was as tall as her mother, but by slouching she managed to make her height appear to be an affliction. Karen thought she could see Pamela's good looks waiting to emerge from beneath Suzanne's glum expression and mild case of acne, and she detected in her niece's refusal to wear makeup or style her hair a callow but healthy assertion of independence. Suzanne's brother, Dante, a stocky kindergartener with black hair in a pudding-bowl cut, had difficulty sitting still for long, but had an endless capacity for orchestrating battles with his grandmother's ceramic Nativity figurines.

At dinner Elizabeth turned the conversation to Karen's children. The nonexistent ones. Karen had tried again to explain to her mother the medical possibilities, the numerous tests she and Jake had been through, the medications she had tried, the reasons for their decision not to attempt risky surgical treatment for endometriosis, which would have involved major abdominal surgery to remove fragments of endometrium, tissue growing abnormally outside of the uterus. This condition was commonly

53

suspected as a cause of infertility in women who had postponed having children until they were in their thirties.

And once more Karen tried to convince her mother that it was extremely unlikely that her infertility was the result of anything she or Jake had done in college, such as smoking marijuana, using birth control devices, or skinny-dipping in the campus pond. Pamela, as usual, offered suggestions such as doing headstands after intercourse, eating more fruit, or her favored prescription: "You're just trying too hard. Relax!" All this discussion was carried on in the presence of a sullen fourteen-year-old girl and a curious five-year-old boy.

Before Elizabeth could ask to speak with Karen privately, so she could inquire for the fourth time in as many years whether Karen had ever had an abortion, Karen leapt up. "Gotta go!" she exclaimed, and blamed their early departure on road conditions.

As it turned out, their departure was not early enough. With six inches of snow on the highway, their old Volvo did not make it above twenty miles per hour for the entire drive to Karen's father's house. The long, exhausting drive took them through the city and over the bridge below the dam on the Weyawega Flowage. Despite her tense mood, Karen couldn't help but notice that the city of Jefferson, old and tired as it was, had an undeniable charm in the winter. The dam creating the flowage was originally built for a mill. The mill had been converted into retail space for shops that sold candles, greeting cards, and antiques. A huge wooden wheel still turned on the millrace, although it was not connected to anything. The spill from the dam looked like a waterfall and caused the lights reflected on the surface of the river below the dam to shimmer in zigzag patterns.

The facades of the commercial buildings lining the main street on both sides of the bridge looked, Karen imagined, just as they must have in the nineteenth century, when the city was built. Karen appreciated the individuality of each storefront and the countless man-hours it must have taken to create the carved lintels, gargoyle gutters, and intricate brickwork with hand tools. The ornate buildings seemed to impart additional beauty to the falling snow. The generic warehouse superstores on the outskirts of town and the snow, on the other hand, seemed only to make each other uglier.

As they crossed the Weyawega bridge, Karen smiled once again at its unintentionally humorous architecture. Squat Greek-style columns embellished with carved garlands and bas-relief figures supported the massive guardrails, and the roadway was lined with rococo wrought-iron lampposts topped by flickering gaslights. At each end of the bridge sat a pair of larger-than-life concrete lions, their toothy mouths open in silent roars, apparently anticipating a grand future for Jefferson. Karen had always thought that, in the context of the city's languid pace, the lions were really yawning.

"Don't let my father bait you," she said.

"No problema," replied Jake.

"He puts you down as an indirect way of expressing his disappointment with me."

"I don't think he's disappointed with you. I think he's disappointed with me, directly."

"Nothing I ever did was good enough," said Karen.

"Oh? I remember him busting his buttons at graduation. Looking at your diploma and booming 'magna cum laude' over and over again, magna cum loudness."

Karen smiled. "Yeah, but it's been downhill ever since."

"You mean," said Jake, "ever since I came on the scene."

Karen reflected. "No, not really. I think his attitude toward us changed after Mom split. It's like he started resenting us or something. Plus, since then he's become so judgmental. He has no idea how much criticism from a father can sting."

"You ever tell him?"

"No. You don't talk about personal stuff with my dad, at least not since the divorce. He's still bitter and brittle. I don't think he'll ever get over it."

"You never told me why your parents split up."

"I never knew. My mom moved out one day. Only she knows why. All I ever got from either one of them on the subject was a lot of evasion and blather."

"Blather?"

"You know, like, 'It just didn't work out.' I'm supposed to believe two people can be together twenty-six years and raise two children, and then it just doesn't work out."

Karen reached over to the dashboard and turned up the heat.

"It's about ninety in here already," said Jake.

"I'm cold."

"That's because we're here."

Karen and Jake arrived at Gene Decker's red brick colonial forty-five minutes behind schedule, receiving a cool reception from their host. Karen's father, a stern-looking man in his tortoiseshell bifocals, wore a dark suit and a necktie and eyed with disapproval the sweaters and jeans worn by his daughter and son-in-law. Karen had known her father would look askance at their casual attire, but she figured she was asking enough of Jake to show up at these annual events without making him dress uncomfortably. Jake didn't even own a suit. And weren't they old enough to decide for themselves how to dress in their free time?

Of course, it wouldn't help that their attire would suffer even further by comparison to Pamela's. She would arrive looking chic as always in a cashmere sweater with coordinated silk pants, an ensemble by Michael Kors that Karen knew went for just under two grand at Neiman Marcus in Chicago. Pamela never failed to make Karen feel a bit down in the heels, even though she suspected that the designer creations Pamela sported had previously been worn by mannequins in Brett's stores. Still, she had to give Pamela credit for fitting into mannequin sizes after two children.

"We'd better go right to the dining room, since the evening's half shot already," Gene grumbled as his daughter and son-in-law stomped the snow off their shoes and removed their jackets. "Help yourself to the liquor cabinet, Jake. Make yourself at home, Tootsie Roll." Her father's pet name for her, which he had used since she was a child, always set Karen's teeth on edge.

Jake mixed bourbon manhattans for himself, Karen and her father, while Gene turned down the volume on the televised football game and placed platters of food on the long, formal dining room table, covered with a starched white tablecloth. Karen surveyed the decor of her childhood home, which had not changed in years. The dark wood stain, flocked brocade wallpaper and stodgy plush carpeting that had been fashionable when Elizabeth Decker picked it all out now seemed stale, tired and sad. At least the place was clean. Although he regularly used only three of the ten rooms, Gene had his cleaning service do the entire house every week, including the rooms that had been Karen's and Pamela's, still done up as girls' bedrooms.

Karen was appalled that her father had a catered turkey dinner prepared, in spite of the plans that his family come "for dessert." All that food wasted just so his grandchildren would not get something at Grandma's house that was not available at his. The three sat down in the dining room and talked about football and the weather while they waited for Pamela and the kids.

Two rounds of manhattans later, the adults drank coffee while Karen's niece and nephew dug into seconds on the pumpkin pie. Mr. Decker dug into his son-in-law.

57

"So, Jake, at some point do you think you might be getting a job?"

Karen felt a prickly sensation in her ears.

"Dad," she said, "Jake has a job. He works five nights a week, six hours a night."

"Playing jungle music in a bar."

Jake sipped his coffee calmly. Pamela giggled. Karen craned her head forward.

"He also teaches," she asserted, "saxophone and guitar."

"Don't make it sound like he's a professor," Mr. Decker responded.

"Hmm," said Jake, smoothing his brown goatee with the knuckles of his left hand, "maybe I should raise my rates."

Gene leaned back and wiped his tortoiseshell glasses on his napkin. "In my day the man went to work and the woman stayed home and raised a family."

"For one thing, Dad," said Karen, raising her index finger over the untouched cranberry sauce, "you sound ridiculous talking as if you grew up in the horse-and-buggy era. You were my age in the '70s. You're about fifteen years away from being a baby boomer, so cut the Old Time Religion crap. For another thing, Jake is a songwriter and arranger. A composer."

Karen's father put his glasses back on, slid them down the bridge of his nose, and peered over the top of them at Karen. "One song does not a songwriter make."

"Good title!" said Jake. He improvised a tune.

Gene turned to Karen. "Is he ridiculing me? Is he sitting at my table, eating my food and ridiculing me?"

"Actually," said Jake, "I didn't eat that much."

"Come on, guys," interjected Pamela, riding to her brother-in-law's rescue. "Dad, have you forgotten that the royalties from 'Disco Blues' paid off Karen's law school loans and made the down payment on their house?"

58

Jake winced at the mention of the title of his minor hit.

"Worst song I ever wrote."

Pamela continued, "Speaking of songs, want to hear Dante sing one? He learned one all the way through. The kindergarten teacher says he has excellent pitch."

"What song?" her son asked.

"The Over the River song," said Pamela.

"Forget it," whined Dante.

"Come on, now, sweetie," Pamela encouraged him, "here we go, 'Over the river and through . . .'"

"No!" yelled Dante.

Pamela arched one carefully sculpted eyebrow. "Don't you want that Lego Space Station for Christmas?"

Dante considered this for a moment. "Over the river," he began in a quavering and slightly off-key voice.

"Oh, wait," said Pamela, "stand up while you sing."

Dante stood up and ran out of the room. Gene Decker continued to examine Jake. "I would think it would bother a man to be supported by his wife. Might bother him so much he couldn't get a family started."

The remark left a tense silence in its wake. Pamela surreptitiously checked Jake's face for a reaction.

Karen smacked the table with the flat of her hand. "You know, Dad," she said, "I think you envy Jake. I think it bothers the hell out of you that he's secure about his masculinity, which you're not."

"You have a vicious tongue, young lady, just like your mother. That's why I walked out."

"Dad, please. You didn't walk out, Mom did. And it wasn't because she was vicious, it was because she was bored out of her mind, and depressed."

"It was because she was going through menopause!" shouted Mr. Decker.

Dante galloped back into the room and stuck a plastic Wrestlemania figure up to its neck in the mashed potatoes. "Mom, what's menopause?" he asked.

"You don't know anything," sneered Suzanne.

"Shut up, Suzanne," ordered Pamela. "You don't have to worry about that, sweetie," she said to Dante, "it's just something that happens to women."

"If it happens to women, why is it called *men*-opause?" asked Dante.

"That's so cute," said Pamela.

Suzanne took issue. "How come every time he says something stupid, you say it's cute?"

Karen broke in. "Mom was depressed long before she was menopausal, Dad."

"She didn't know she was depressed until you came home from college with that feminist propaganda."

Karen placed both of her hands on top of the table and took a deep breath. "So you're saying the divorce was my fault? Fact is, she never would have left if you hadn't ignored her for twenty-five years, like you did the rest of us."

Karen's father balled up his napkin and flung it on his dessert plate. He went into the family room and turned up the volume on the football game. The Bears were losing by two touchdowns. Karen stood and addressed her sister.

"Gotta go." Pamela shrugged her shoulders.

As Jake brushed the heavy, wet snow off the hood and windshield of the Volvo, Karen fumed in the passenger seat. "I hate my father," she said to herself, "I hate him!" Why does he invite us, she wondered, if all he's going to do is show disapproval? Does he lie awake at night thinking of cruel things to say? Next year, we're going to the Bahamas for Thanksgiving! Then he can sit around and insult Pammy and Brett for a change.

The car windows were nearly opaque with frost, adding to Karen's discomfort. She had been claustrophobic since childhood. She told herself that her claustrophobia was somehow her father's fault, either genetics or something he let happen to her when she was little.

Jake got in, started the engine, and turned on the windshield defroster. Two small peepholes appeared at the bottom of the windshield and grew with glacial slowness.

Karen was rigid in her seat, feet pressed against the floorboard, the back of her head hard against the headrest. As she dug her fingernails into the vinyl sides of the bucket seat, she heard Jake's baritone voice, doing a respectable imitation of Perry Como, singing, "There's noooo place like hoooome for the hol-i-days. . . ."

Karen's tension held her for a moment, then she burst into laughter. Jake joined her, and the two of them laughed until they were wheezing.

Jake pointed at the windshield, which was completely refogged. "We'd better modulate our breathing or we'll never get away from this House of Horrors!"

He shifted the transmission into first gear. Karen put her hand over his.

"Jake, what would I do without you?"

He looked at her and wiped tears from the corners of his eyes. "Probably get along with your dad," he said.

At 11:30 P.M. on Thanksgiving Day, Dietrich Heiden struggled to emerge from a disturbing dream. In the dream, he sat

on a toilet in the house where he lived as a child. His parents strode in and out of the room. He felt like he was under water. His head hurt. He was small and his feet did not reach the floor. He looked down at the pink squares of tile and saw that his toes had fallen off and were scattered on the floor. He fought to pull his eyes open to escape the dream, but the effort was painful.

His eyes opened but he did not yet remember where he was. Earlier that day, Dietrich had fallen from the roof of his house while attempting to set up a life-sized plastic reindeer decoration. He was in a patient bed on the third floor of Shoreview Memorial Hospital. An IV bag was connected by a long, serpentine tube to a needle in his left arm. He was awake, but his head still hurt.

A man with short graying hair and a port wine birthmark on his temple, wearing a white coat and khaki pants, stood by Dietrich's bed, bent over as if drinking from a water fountain. Dietrich's head was elevated, so he could see the fleshy shaft protruding from the fly of the man's pants. The man's left hand held his own penis. The thumb and index finger of the man's other hand were wrapped around the base of Dietrich's penis. And the rest of Dietrich's penis was in the man's mouth.

CHAPTER
9

The master bedroom in Jake and Karen's house faced east, making it less than ideal for sleeping when the first rays of light from the rising sun streamed through the blinds. Friday morning, the sunlight illuminated Karen's eyelids, which were dancing with the rapid eye movement of her dream state. In her dream, she was standing waist-deep in foamy, azure seawater while a warm tropical rain fell on her face and shoulders.

She opened her eyes and was startled to see a figure looming over her. It was Jake, up on one elbow, staring at her face.

"What's the matter?" she said.

"Nothing's the matter," said Jake. "I'm merely gazing with admiration upon the visage of my beloved, revirescent in the soft, morning light."

Karen noticed a familiar expression around Jake's wide-set brown eyes. She glanced at the digital alarm clock on the nightstand.

"Isn't it a little early for that?" she asked.

"For what?" he said.

"*That*," she replied.

"I object," said Jake, feigning indignation. "Can't a man merely gaze with admiration upon the visage of his beloved, revirescent in the soft morning light, without it being assumed that he's thinking about *that*?"

Karen lifted the bedsheets and peered underneath.

"The evidence strongly indicates," she said, "that you're thinking about *that*."

Jake moved closer to her. "The question is," he said, "will the evidence be admitted?"

"I'll allow it," said Karen.

"May I approach?" said Jake.

"Knock off the double entendres," said Karen, "and get to it."

Jake leaned over and kissed her on the place where her neck, earlobe, and jawline intersected. She reached down and slid her fingers under the waistband of his boxer shorts.

The telephone on the nightstand rang, jarring them both. Jake flopped on his back and groaned. Karen sat up and grabbed the phone. It was Anne Delaney.

"You know I don't work the Friday after Thanksgiving, Annie," said Karen. She yawned and flopped back on her pillow. "What can't wait until Monday?"

"An alleged sexual assault. By a doctor. On a patient."

"Ho-hum," said Karen, accustomed to such reports. "Another one of the residents give a pelvic exam to some eighteen-year-old girl with a back injury?"

"The patient was male," replied Anne.

"Ho, ho! And the doctor was . . . ?"

"Also male. Carson Weber, an emergency room physician," said Anne.

"I know him," Karen commented. "Nice guy, good-looking. What's the patient's story?"

"Patient presented at the ER at 6:50 P.M. yesterday with a head injury. Guy fell off his roof putting up a Christmas display in the dark. In that weather, can you believe it? Lucky he didn't break his neck. X-ray showed a small skull fracture. Weber examined him in the emergency room, diagnosed a concussion, admitted him to the hospital for observation. Patient calls the floor nurse in the middle of the night, says the doctor who examined him

64

in the ER came into his patient room and, uh . . . performed fellatio on him."

"Wow!" Karen exclaimed. "That's a new one!"

Jake rolled over and shielded his eyes with his hand.

"Who is it?" he whispered.

Karen covered the receiver. "It's Annie Delaney. Some patient complained that one of our ER docs gave him a blow job last night!"

"And overcharged him for it?" asked Jake. He rolled away and scrunched a pillow over his head.

Anne continued. "Patient also claims he was drugged, that the doctor put something in his IV bag. We need to decide if we're going to suspend Dr. Weber immediately pending an investigation, and if we do, you have to direct the procedure."

"I don't know, Annie. Sounds pretty wild to me. Is this patient credible?"

"He had a pretty severe head injury, he may have been hallucinating. He's a bus driver, has a foreign accent. From the way he got hurt, I'd say he was a little cracked to begin with."

"What's Weber say?"

"He adamantly denies even being in the patient's room. His shift was over at 10:00 P.M., and he says he left the hospital before 10:30 P.M. The patient called the nurse a little past midnight. He says the assault took place approximately a half-hour before."

"Why'd he wait a half-hour to report it?"

"I don't know," Anne conceded. "That's all we have so far, except I did do a survey of the newspapers and magazines in the patient room and ER waiting area to see if the patient might have gotten the idea from something he read. Found a newspaper article on a study from Canada reporting that ten percent of Canadian doctors have sexually assaulted a patient."

"Nice work, Annie." Karen thought for a moment, her eyes roaming around the floor. She was reluctant to have a physician suspended from the medical staff based on the unsubstantiated allegation of a patient with a head injury, but she knew that if the patient was telling the truth and Shoreview took no action, it might happen again. She thought of a way to test the patient's story.

"Do we have a security camera in the doctor's section of the parking garage?" she asked.

"No, but there's a camera right at the guardhouse that video-tapes every car that leaves the garage."

"And the tape has a date and time display, doesn't it?"

Anne confirmed that.

"Call Max Schumacher in Security," Karen directed, "and get the tape from last night to check out Weber's story." She thought quickly. "And get the security cam tapes from the cameras at the front door to the hospital and the ER, too. Weber could have parked outside and sneaked back in. Look at the tapes and call me back."

"Aren't you coming in?" Anne asked.

"I'm not getting out of bed," said Karen, replacing the receiver and reaching for Jake under the covers.

Anne called Karen just before noon. The security cam tape from the parking garage clearly showed Carson Weber's silver Alpha Romeo leaving at 10:28 P.M. The tapes of the only two unlocked entrances to the hospital showed Dr. Weber had not reentered the building from 10:28 P.M. until after midnight. Karen concluded that a suspension of Dr. Weber was unlikely.

"May I ask one more question about hospital business?" Anne inquired cautiously.

"Fire away."

"Did you get the report from Gilbert Austin on Larry's catheter?"

"I did. Not good news, Annie. On Monday I want you to look into who might have resterilized that catheter. And, Annie . . ."

"What?"

"Don't work on it over the weekend. That's an order."

Friday afternoon in Baltimore, Maryland, Karen's college friend, Dr. Carl Gellhorn, reviewed the medical record and the angiogram from Larry Conkel's catheterization that Karen had shipped to him. He shook his head in disgust and disbelief.

Later that afternoon, Jake was at his drummer's house, rehearsing for the evening's performance at the Caledonia Club. The band was going to try out some new, ambitious chord changes on a couple of numbers that had become shopworn. Karen made herself a mug of herbal tea, wrapped a blanket around her shoulders, and sat by the bay window in her kitchen, looking out at the small, frozen backyard and the bleak western sky. Eight inches of snow had fallen Thanksgiving Day. Leaden, slate-gray clouds blanketed the city. As she contemplated Larry's death, the engineering report on the catheter used in Larry's procedure, Paula Conkel's lawsuit, and Larry's upcoming funeral, she tried to suppress her sense of foreboding. She shifted her thoughts, vacillating between concrete possibilities and fanciful intrigues, finding herself unable to draw a bright line between the two.

Concrete possibilities. Larry's investigation had been thorough and workmanlike. Karen was prepared to accept as reality that some of the Jefferson Clinic doctors were engaged in large-scale billing fraud. As for the engineering report, it was clear on one point: the catheter had been damaged. If the damage had occurred accidentally, then Larry's death was an accident. Accidental death in the hospital was normal reality. But the possibility that the damage to the catheter voided the warranty, and that a colossal uninsured liability would bankrupt Shoreview Memorial—that was hard to accept as real. Shoreview had been in Jefferson since long before Karen was born. She had put years of her life into it. Could it go out of existence? It seemed unlikely that any powerful force like the state would intervene to save it. Jefferson could get along with one hospital. No point in getting panicky about it, something would happen to divert the disaster. Wouldn't it?

Harder yet to accept was the idea that Larry's death was not accidental. No point in even thinking too much about that. Too awful, too . . . histrionic. Yes, but if it wasn't accidental, who was responsible? Dr. Bernard, who inserted the damaged catheter into Larry's heart and who happened to be one of the targets of Larry's investigation? Dr. Herwitz, who had performed the surgery during which Larry died? Herwitz was not targeted in Larry's investigation, but he was the president of the Jefferson Clinic. He had a lot to lose if Larry went public. Or, maybe, Bernard and Herwitz were in it together—a conspiracy. And what about Paula Conkel, looking to get rich on a lawsuit, retaining Ben McCormick before Larry was even embalmed?

Fanciful intrigues.

As she finished her second mug of tea, Karen identified the source of her sense of foreboding. It was a premonition that the responsibility for straightening out this imbroglio was about to land on her. All the ugliest problems at the hospital ended up on her desk, it seemed. Jake called it "the curse of the capable."

Karen considered a third cup of tea, but opted for a glass of wine instead. She moved from the kitchen to the living room, considered lighting a fire, and decided against it. Why wasn't Jake here to light it? Why wasn't Jake here to distract her so she could stop thinking about the mess at Shoreview Memorial?

At least it was better than thinking about her parents.

Friday night was a mixed bag for Jake and his band at the Caledonia Club. Musically, Jake thought they were *bad*, which is to say, very good. The rhythm section was uncommonly tight, the lead guitar was on fire, and the new chord changes had flowed like the River Jordan. But during the second break he overheard the club owner talking to one of the regulars at the bar about karaoke machines, how much people enjoyed them, and how much they cost.

Jake, like Karen, had a sense of foreboding.

On Saturday afternoon Karen and Jake entered the nave of Our Redeemer Lutheran Church and sat in a pew near the back. An amateurish organist played "Abide with Me," softly. Floral arrangements flanked the altar, with diagonal, Miss America–type sashes across them, reading, "Beloved Husband" and "Adored Father." One read "Valued Employee—Shoreview Memorial Hospital." Larry lay in an open casket in the middle of all this plant life, looking like an inexpertly rendered Madame Tussaud's model.

Anne Delaney, wearing her oft-employed black suit, sat down next to Karen. "Check out who's got the front row seats," she whispered.

Paula Conkel, the deceased's widow, sat nearest the aisle in the front pew to the right of the altar. Paula was short, just slightly overweight, and wearing her hair in the same heavily sprayed flip as in college. It had been out-of-date even then.

On her right were her two children, a seventeen-year-old boy and a fifteen-year-old girl. Karen remembered Larry confiding to her, "Paula and I haven't had sex since Jennifer was born." Fifteen grim years in the same house, married, without sex or emotional intimacy. Surely, someone as likable as Larry deserved better, she had thought. To the right of the children was Ben McCormick, the lawyer, looking as stern as a hawk. To Ben's right was a fair-haired woman who looked about forty years old.

"Who's the blonde?" asked Karen. "McCormick's wife?"

"Hardly," whispered Anne. "McCormick's wife is about twenty-two. That's Lisa Fuller, good friend of Paula's. She's also a nurse at Shoreview."

"Hmmm," said Karen. "Maybe it's time to troll for a little free information."

After the agonizingly long service, Jake slipped outside for a cigarette. After some obligatory small talk with Paula about how good Larry looked and how hard it must be for them all, Karen introduced herself to Lisa Fuller.

"I understand Larry and Paula were more or less estranged for the past few years," Karen said.

"I guess that's sort of true," Lisa conceded. "He kept an apartment, but he stayed at the house sometimes. Kind of strange. He had his own little separate room at the house. The weirdo even had a lock on it, but Paula used to go in through the window and snoop anyway. Some marriage. I guess they were trying to keep things going until the kids were out."

70

This is great, thought Karen. Push this a little.

"From what Larry said, they really had no physical relationship for a long time."

"True," allowed Lisa. "Paula said the same thing. I guess sometimes a man just loses interest in his wife."

What the hell, go for it, thought Karen. "Especially if the wife sleeps around."

Lisa stiffened and clenched her jaw. "Now, wait a minute. That's not fair. Paula tried to be a good wife to Larry."

Karen pressed. "Larry told me sometimes she was seeing more than one other man at the same time."

"Oh, yeah? Did Larry tell you about his own affair? It was a lot more serious than any of Paula's."

A large, pale hand clamped onto Lisa's shoulder. It belonged to Ben McCormick. "Lisa," he interrupted. "Why don't you go look after Paula. She needs a good friend right now." McCormick propelled Lisa away from Karen.

"So good to see you again, Karen," he said. "Sorry it has to be under such unfortunate circumstances."

"Gee, Ben," said Karen with a touch of sarcasm, "I didn't know you were so close to the Conkels."

Ben disregarded the comment. "Will you be in your office Monday?"

"Sure, Ben. Want to stop by for doughnuts?"

"My process-server will be stopping by with some documents. I assume you will accept service on behalf of Shoreview Memorial?"

"Serve whomever you like, Ben. Our lawyers, Winslow & Shaughnessy, will let you know if you blow it."

McCormick smiled and nodded. "Always a pleasure to do business with you, Karen. I'm looking forward to this."

As McCormick walked away, Karen said, "I'm not."

71

CHAPTER
10

Monday morning, Karen found herself waiting in Joe Grimes's office, and it made her uneasy. It made her uneasy because she was practical and Joe's office was impractical. She hated waste and Joe's office was wasteful. But mostly, she was uneasy because Joe's office was a legal problem for the hospital. The Internal Revenue Code, Karen knew, stated that none of a tax-exempt hospital's earnings could "inure to the benefit of a private individual." Shoreview enjoyed an exemption from income tax because it was engaged in charitable activities and was supposed to use its funds only for those charitable purposes, not to shower lavish perks on its executives. Karen had read just a few years ago about the head of the nation's largest charity using the charity's money to tour Europe with his girlfriend. It was a famous example of illegal private inurement.

When the IRS auditors came to Shoreview Memorial, the CEO's office would be locked. It was a shrine to private inurement. It was more lavish than the opulent offices of the senior partners at the large corporate law firm in Chicago where Karen had clerked during law school.

Karen understood the rationale for ostentatiously decorating corporate law offices. Besides creating an environment in which the most privileged and wealthy clientele felt comfortable, it sent a message. The message was: "What we do for our clients is uniquely valuable, and we protect and enhance their wealth so effectively that they gratefully pay us enough money to waste on Persian rugs, French writing tables, and paneling hewn from English walnut trees."

In the case of Joe Grimes's grandiose office, Karen saw no such rationale. Joe was the administrator of a struggling, tax-exempt hospital in a stagnant blue-collar town, but he had an office that looked like the boudoir of a decadent sheik. It was over 800 square feet, more than three times the size of any other office in the hospital. Its size amplified the economic impact of Joe's decision to install a parquet floor and subsequent decision to rip the floor out two months later in favor of hand-painted Spanish tile, which gave the place the acoustics of an airplane hangar. The desk, at which he rarely worked, was a monstrosity of ebony and black volcanic glass with gold inlay, on which he displayed his daily copy of the *Wall Street Journal*. The walls were covered with taupe grasscloth and framed tapestries. The custom titanium blinds could be opened and closed by remote control, but they were always kept closed to conceal the jarring view of a parking lot and a fast food restaurant. There was nothing in the room so functional as a bookcase or a file cabinet. Instead, there were polished stone casual tables holding up ceramic vases and exotic objets d'art from Mediterranean locales Joe could not have named. The most distinctive touch was a grouping of three enormous, waist-high terra-cotta urns from Morocco, one of which served as a pot for an unhealthy-looking palm tree with brown-tipped fronds.

The only message Joe's office sent, thought Karen, was: this man is a pretentious fool.

Joe Grimes walked briskly into his office, a black leather attaché case, which Karen guessed was empty, in his left hand and a pair of kid driving gloves in his right. Joe drove a leased BMW convertible, compliments of the hospital, ostensibly for use on hospital business. Karen called it the "private inurement mobile." When Joe arrived, she had been waiting for thirty-five minutes.

"Sorry I'm late, Karen," Joe said, casually tossing his Burberry trench coat over a Moroccan urn. On his slightly overweight body he wore a black cashmere double-breasted Italian pinstriped suit with pointed lapels and, in Karen's judgment, a bit too much cologne. Mousse slicked his dark brown hair straight back. "My meeting with the CEO of Connors Manufacturing ran over. I think we may be able to do a deal with Connors to use the hospital as their exclusive health care provider."

Connors Manufacturing was a company that assembled lamps, with a grand total of twelve employees.

"So, Karen, where do we stand on Jefferson's MRI deal?"

"No progress. There are significant legal problems with your whole concept."

"Karen, we need that MRI. We needed it yesterday."

Several years earlier, Shoreview Memorial's competitor, St. Peter's, had acquired a Magnetic Resonance Imager, or MRI, an expensive piece of diagnostic equipment that uses strong magnetic forces to produce high-resolution pictures of a patient's internal organs. With these pictures, doctors at St. Peter's were able to diagnose many conditions at a much earlier stage than Shoreview Memorial did using its older imaging devices.

"We're not just losing patients to St. Pete's because we don't have an MRI," said Joe. "We're losing prestige. It's a PR disaster."

"Easily solved," said Karen. "Just authorize the acquisition. The hospital can manage to lease or finance an MRI. We don't need the clinic in on it."

Joe moved around to the front of his desk and sat on a corner, dangling a leg. Karen recognized this as Joe's "let's talk turkey" pose.

"Karen, we need the clinic as our partner on the MRI. That's our edge on St. Pete's. If the docs get a cut of the action from the MRI, they'll send their patients here for an MRI when they need one, instead of to St. Pete's."

"Sure," said Karen. "If their cut is big enough, they'll send 'em here for an MRI even when they don't need one."

Joe leaned forward and grinned. Apparently, he had failed to note her sarcasm.

"Now you're getting it," he said. "I just read a study that showed physicians order four times more diagnostic tests when they own the equipment."

"Fancy that."

"Yeah. When the doc gets in on the profit from using the MRI, all of a sudden he decides a lot more of his patients need MRIs. Pretty cool."

"Maybe," Karen replied, "but the clinic won't put up any money to buy the MRI, and a joint purchase with a hospital where they refer patients is illegal."

"Oh, hell, so what?" Joe swung his foot. "Like you said, the hospital can get an MRI on its own. So why don't we just *give* the clinic fifty percent ownership? With the extra patients they'll put in here, we'll still come out ahead. It's a win-win deal."

Karen rubbed her temples. She had explained this to Joe at least three times already.

"Because it would be illegal. What credible explanation is there for giving away half of a multimillion-dollar piece of stuff?"

Joe failed to realize the question was rhetorical. "Because we'd get more patients in here! Come on, Karen!" His voice echoed in the cavernous office.

Karen was continually amazed that Joe's inability to grasp legal concepts was exceeded only by his brilliance at grasping duplicitous business schemes. "That's the point, Joe. It would be prohibited private inurement, because you'd be giving away something the hospital owns to private individuals. It's an obvious kickback for referrals, a clear violation of the Medicare Antikickback Law. And if the docs have an ownership interest in the equipment and then order tests for their patients, it's a violation of the Stark Ethics in Patient Referrals Law."

"Come on. Stop trying to make a federal case out of this."

"It *is* a federal case," said Karen. "You'd be violating three different federal laws."

Joe stood and moved back behind his desk. It seemed to Karen that his suit had somehow become rumpled during the conversation, maybe because his posture was sagging. Joe's cologne or hair mousse or whatever it was seemed to have acquired a sour nuance.

"Lawyers and their never-ending technicalities," he said, flipping his hand toward the ceiling. "If we want to do something nice for the physicians who support this hospital and its mission, why do the feds have to stick their noses in?"

"Because if they don't, the money the docs receive for sending patients for hospital or diagnostic services gets so rich, a lot of doctors just can't resist the temptation to put patients in the hospital or order tests or therapy when it isn't needed," said Karen.

"Doctors would never do something like that," Joe replied.

Karen tilted her head and cocked an eyebrow. "Show me your driver's license, Joe," she said.

"Why?"

"I want to see if you were born yesterday."

Joe gave her a half-smile. "Okay. Touché." He chuckled. "I remember a few years back, some physicians I knew made more money from the kickbacks than they made practicing medicine. Amazing how much hospitals are willing to pay for admissions, or how many more tests and services are ordered when the physician shares the profits from the equipment."

"Those are the simple facts of hospital economics, Joe." Karen and Joe both understood that hospitals and other health care providers wanted, like other businesses, to increase their revenues every year. It was a simple matter to sell more health care services by giving physicians, who control the process, incentives to order more tests and more therapy, and put more people in the hospital for longer periods. At least it had been a simple matter until the federal government, which pays a large portion of the tab for health care through its Medicare and Medicaid programs, passed laws to control health care costs by prohibiting certain financial incentives to encourage physicians to order more services.

"And the simple facts of hospital economics are what matter to me," said Joe, "not all those convoluted laws. We need to improve the bottom line, and the Board of Directors wants to see that improvement fast. What's the downside of violating these federal laws?"

"Fines big enough to bankrupt us. Exclusion from the Medicare program. There are even prison sentences attached to certain violations. But the good news is you'd be in a federal penitentiary, not a state prison."

Joe karate-chopped the air with the side of his hand. "Look, Karen, everybody knows there's almost no enforcement of these laws. Other hospitals violate them, and we're at a competitive disadvantage if we let ourselves be hamstrung. You're supposed to be the smart lawyer, figure out how to do what I want without getting us in trouble. Obfuscate the audit trail. Set up dummy corporations. Pay the docs for consulting services. Do what lawyers do. Just get the deal done!" He flopped down in his throne-sized desk chair, put the tips of his fingers together and rolled his head. "Was there something else, Karen?"

"I thought I was here to talk about Larry Conkel."

"Oh, yeah," Joe said, absently. "What's the deal on that one?"

Karen explained the cause of death and the warranty disclaimer. She reminded Joe of the notice from State Mutual Insurance threatening the hospital's malpractice coverage. She concluded with a description of Anne Delaney's interview with Paula Conkel and her attorney, Ben McCormick.

"So what do you plan to do?" Joe asked, leaning back in his chair. "This one's clearly in your area of accountability."

Thanks a lot, thought Karen. Joe seemed to be taking this with remarkable nonchalance.

"I had our attorney, Emerson Knowles at Winslow & Shaughnessy, fax a retainer letter to McCormick. We had the catheter tested; when we get it back, it will be placed in safekeeping. I'm researching the insurance issues myself. I'll be retaining a cardiologist from Johns Hopkins to review the chart and the angiogram."

Joe sat forward and frowned. As Karen expected, he didn't like the idea of getting outside doctors to critique the performance of his own medical staff. Outside opinions could not be controlled. "What's the point of that?"

"To get an independent opinion on the catheterization and the surgery," Karen explained. "Whether or not we can get at the manufacturer, it will help the hospital's position if the physicians are implicated. More pockets from which to get the settlement. Besides, before I authorize a settlement offer I need to know if Bernard or Herwitz mismanaged the case."

"What's wrong with an internal review by the doctors on our own medical staff?" asked Joe.

Karen paused. She pursed her lips to one side. "I'd prefer to have the truth."

"Enough cynicism," Joe declared. He extended an index finger toward Karen. "Get one thing straight. Shoreview Memorial is not going to denigrate its own medical staff, especially not two members of the Jefferson Clinic Board of Directors. It's not in anyone's best interests."

Joe straightened the knot in his red silk club tie, placed his fingertips on the top of his desk, and lifted his jaw. "I'm tired of people trying to blame everything on the doctors. These are fine physicians, dedicated men, respected by their colleagues." He reached out with his hands, palms up, fingers spread. "Invaluable to this community and this hospital."

"They're big admitters," Karen conceded.

Joe sat down and gazed at Karen. "You understand. Good." He jabbed the surface of his desk with his forefinger. "Karen, you are to handle this case with a minimum of ballyhoo. No publicity. No trial. No implicating the doctors. They deserve our protection. Nail the insurance company if you can. If you can't, get rid of this thing for $2 million or less and keep the doctors out of it."

Karen was stunned. Was Grimes really authorizing a settlement at nearly twenty percent of the hospital's liquid net worth, less than a week after the incident? Premature, she thought. Irrational. Fishy. Why was he in such a hurry?

Joe leaned back in his chair. "I spent the holiday in Vail," he said, suddenly affable, his way of signaling to Karen that the interview was over. "Did you stay in town?"

"Saw my parents."

"I hope they are well," said Joe. "Give my best to Jack."

Karen returned to her office and the blinking light on her telephone console.

"You have five new messages in your mailbox. Message one, received Monday at 7:15 A.M. To hear the message, press 2." Karen pressed 2.

"Hello, Karen, this is Carl." It was her former boyfriend, the Johns Hopkins cardiologist to whom she had sent the records of Larry's biopsy. "I guess it's an hour earlier out there. Anyway, I received the records and the angiogram from the Conkel biopsy and thought

I'd better give you a verbal opinion before I put anything in writing. In my view, this patient's care was grossly mismanaged by both physicians. For a myocardial biopsy, the cardiologist should have inserted the catheter in the femoral vein. The fact that he used the jugular vein tells me he isn't familiar with the procedure. Probably never did one before. It also means he probably used the wrong type of catheter. Given his obvious unfamiliarity with the procedure, I'm not surprised he damaged the catheter. After the catheter broke, the surgeon erred in putting the patient on heart-lung bypass. A patient with advanced cardiomyopathy cannot be weaned off of bypass. In my opinion, it would have been far better simply to wait and see. Plastic is inert. Depending on where the remnants of the catheter lodged, he may have had a chance of survival. Probably not, but when he was put on bypass, he was doomed. It's hard for me to believe the surgeon didn't know this. Maybe he had bad information from the cardiologist. Anyway, let me know if you want this in writing. Give Jake my regards. Good-bye."

"If you would like to hear the message again, press 2. To hear the next message, press 3."

"Hi. Annie here. Since Saturday afternoon I've talked to every tech and nurse who have anything to do with the cath lab, and nobody admits to having resterilized any catheters since we instituted the policy against it two years ago. Nobody. And nobody is aware of anybody else doing it, either. So I don't know where to go with that one. Found out one interesting thing, though. One of the cath lab nurses told me that when they did Larry last week, she noticed that there was only one catheter left on the cart. Normally the cath lab cart would be stocked with several. She said it was odd. Who knows if it means anything. If you want me to do anything else on this, give me a call."

"If you would like to hear the message again . . ." Karen pressed 3 to hear the next message.

"Hello, Mrs. Hayes. My name is Lou Chambers. I'm an attorney representing Dietrich Heiden. He's the young man who was assaulted in your hospital last Thursday. I'm going to . . . What? Shaddup, can't ya see I'm on the phone here? Sorry. I'm going to fax over a consent for release of the medical record. I also want copies of all the incident reports you got. I can subpeenee if necessary. My address is on the fax."

"*If you would like to hear the message . . .*" Karen pressed 4 to erase, then 3, then 2.

"Good morning. I'm Harold Wilson, an account executive with Midwestern Mutual Life Insurance . . ." 4 to erase, 3, 2.

"Mrs. Hayes, this is Maureen, Larry Conkel's secretary. I thought I should tell somebody, I wasn't sure who, I thought maybe Max Schumacher in Security. But you do all the stuff with confidentiality of records and stuff, so I called you. When I got to work this morning, Dr. Herwitz was in Larry's office, going through Larry's files." Karen sat up abruptly. She had just heard from Carl Gellhorn that Dr. Herwitz, the president of the Jefferson Clinic, may have committed an inexcusable and inexplicable error when he put Larry Conkel on heart-lung bypass, an error that had doomed him. Now Herwitz was shuffling through papers in Larry's office, where Larry kept the record of his investigation into the billing fraud at the Jefferson Clinic. She couldn't think of an innocent reason for Herwitz to be rummaging around in Larry's office.

"There's boxes and boxes of stuff in there," Larry's secretary continued. "I didn't see how Dr. Herwitz could find whatever he was looking for, so I asked if I could help him find something and he said, 'No, thank you.' I asked if it was okay for him to be looking at Larry's papers and he said it was. I just thought somebody should know. I hope I didn't do anything wrong. Bye."

Karen pressed the reset button and punched the phone number for the head of hospital security, Max Schumacher.

"Security. Schumacher."

"Max, this is Karen Hayes. What kind of authorization would you need to put a lock on Larry Conkel's office? I think it's best to secure his office until his family can collect his personal property. He has some valuable things in there."

"Yeah, that mug collection. I've seen it. Any executive could authorize that. Or Grimes."

"Put the lock on immediately. I'll sign whatever you need."

Karen's vague suspicions about Larry's death were growing stronger. Could Larry's death be connected to his fraud investigation?

Karen got out the report of the tests done on the catheter by Jefferson Engineering. She read again that sentence with the disturbing implication:

OUR CONCLUSION IS THAT THE SAMPLE MATERIAL HAS BEEN SUBJECTED TO HIGH TEMPERATURES RESULTING IN A BREAKDOWN OF POLYMERS.

She called the telephone number on the letterhead and asked for Gilbert Austin.

"My conclusions are quite definite, Mrs. Hayes."

"I mean, Mr. Austin, could the breakdown have been caused by somebody leaving the catheter near a radiator or in direct sunlight? Would it have to be from sterilization?"

"I see. Now that you mention it, I guess the report wasn't specific on that point. No, this wasn't just left in the sun, Mrs. Hayes. The type of changes that the spectroscopy and calorimetry showed, with that type of material, could only have resulted from extremely high temperatures, for a long duration."

"As would be used in sterilization?" Karen asked.

"Actually, much more extreme than would be necessary for sterilization. The catheter was really cooked."

Karen felt a chill. This was why the Jefferson Engineering report had given her the creeps. It was telling her in so many words that someone had intentionally damaged the catheter.

"Do you need any further tests performed, Mrs. Hayes?"

"I'll let you know. Thank you, Mr. Austin."

Her consternation and curiosity having moved up several notches, Karen dialed Anne Delaney's extension. The two women swapped stories about Larry's funeral, including Karen's exchange with Lisa Fuller, Paula Conkel's nurse friend.

"Annie, did you know Larry kept a separate apartment?"

"Yeah, I did. In fact, I know where it is. It's in that old brick apartment building right across the street from the hospital, called the Traymont. You can see it from your window. Wanted to save the commute, I guess."

Karen walked to the window and looked at the building Anne had described. It was four stories, flat-roofed, somewhat dilapidated. "Was Larry really having an affair? He never told me about it."

"Me neither, I have no idea," Anne professed.

"Annie, I need something else on this. I'd like you to find out who had access to the cath lab cart from the last time it was stocked before Larry's biopsy until they set up for his procedure on Monday morning. I need to know where the cart was kept, how it was secured, and who got near it. I mean anybody and everybody."

"I'll get right on it. But, Karen, if any hospital employee resterilized the catheter, we've blown the warranty and the hospital is on the hook. How does this help?"

"I'm not sure it does," Karen said. "I'm not sure it does."

Karen was not ready to tell Anne what she was just barely able to admit to herself: with what she had learned that morning, she was now investigating a possible murder.

CHAPTER

11

arly Monday afternoon Karen was at her computer terminal composing a memorandum to Joe Grimes, when a man in a dirty trench coat appeared at the door of her office with a Summons and Complaint from the offices of Benjamin H. McCormick. It was Paula Conkel's wrongful death lawsuit. "Sign the back of the copy, ma'am," the process server instructed Karen.

"Do an affidavit of service," replied Karen. "I'm not signing anything."

She continued to work until 3:00 P.M. on the memorandum to Grimes. Given the gravity of her suspicions, she needed to at least alert the hospital's Chief Executive Officer. In the memo, she reported the lab test results on the catheter and Anne's statement that no one admitted to resterilizing the catheter. She asserted that "serious consideration should be given to involving law enforcement authorities in the investigation of this matter, in light of the complex and suspicious circumstances." She sent the memorandum by electronic mail, through the hospital's computer system.

After sending the memorandum to Grimes, Karen tried to restore her sense of normalcy by working on some routine matters. She drafted a patient consent form for transfer of a patient with a spinal cord injury to a hospital in Chicago, after confirming with the discharge planner that Shoreview Memorial was not illegally dumping the patient because he had poor insurance. She said a silent prayer that the patient would not be jostled during the helicopter flight to Chicago and end up a paraplegic, recognizing that was all she could do about that potential risk.

Next, Karen reviewed a memo from the Director of Medical Records. The father of an eight-year-old girl, who had been a patient in the hospital's psychiatric unit when she was six, had requested a copy of his daughter's medical record. At the time of her therapy, the girl's parents were separated and she was living with her mother. During treatment, the girl had described in some detail how her father had sexually abused her when her parents still lived together. The state had never prosecuted the father, due to an absence of evidence corroborating the girl's description and the wishes of the girl's mother and psychiatrist that the girl not be subjected to testifying against her father in a criminal proceeding. The mother, who was Roman Catholic, never sought a divorce. Two years after the girl was discharged from the hospital, the father obtained a legal separation from his wife and joint custody of the child. Now he wanted to see what his daughter had told the psychiatrist about him. The psychiatrist said it would be a "calamity" for the child if the father were to be given the record. State law said a parent had a legal right to receive a copy of his child's medical record. Karen dictated a response to the Director of Medical Records: "No dice. If he wants the record, he can take us to court."

After forty-five minutes of such "normal" work, Karen returned to reviewing Larry Conkel's secret fraud investigation files. In the file numbered "2," she found a parenthetical reference that piqued her curiosity. Amid the records of clinic patients for whom services had been billed but not actually rendered was the hand-printed statement: "J.C. FRAUD. BILLED PATS.— HOSP. BILLING CONSP.—SEE FILE 3." Karen had already determined that "J.C." meant the Jefferson Clinic, and "FRAUD. BILLED PATS." meant fraudulently billed patient accounts. She supposed that "HOSP. BILLING CONSP." referred to a billing fraud conspiracy involving hospital charges.

But this supposition created a serious dilemma. She had assumed that she would eventually turn Larry's files over to the federal agency charged with enforcing the laws against fraudulent Medicare billing, the Office of the Inspector General. But now she needed to find out what was in the missing file, file number 3. Did it contain evidence that the hospital was involved in a billing fraud conspiracy with Jefferson Clinic? If it did, she would be ethically bound as the attorney for the hospital to maintain the confidentiality of the information and protect the hospital. It would be irresponsible, a violation of her ethical duty, as well as a catastrophic career move, for her to charge ahead and to turn files over to the feds that might be damaging to the hospital. Especially when she had no idea what those files showed.

On the other hand, if the file did not incriminate the hospital, Karen was free to obey the dictates of her conscience and report the crime. This was what she wanted to do. The Jefferson Clinic doctors who had bilked the system for millions while putting their patients through a lot of misery were monsters. Who would subject elderly people to unnecessary chemotherapy or cardiac catheterization just to inflate already huge incomes?

To sit idly by, watching the perpetrators enjoy their ill-gotten gains, keeping patients in the dark about how they had been used by their doctors, infuriated her. Her impulse was to blow the whistle. But what if the files *were* damaging to the hospital? Karen needed the contents of file number 3 to extricate her from her quandary. She had two guesses as to the location of file number 3: Larry's apartment at the Traymont and the locked room at his home.

She called Jake to tell him she would be a little late, that she had an errand to run.

The mailboxes in the lobby of the Traymont Apartments revealed that Larry Conkel had rented Unit 207. Karen's footsteps echoed in the long, terrazzo-tiled hallway of the second floor, which was lit dimly by deco wall sconces. The building had a musty smell, suggesting a wet basement and deferred maintenance.

Karen reached into her coat pocket and removed the steel key that she had found in the mug in Larry's office. She started to raise it to the lock on the heavy wooden door to Unit 207, when she was stopped by a soft female voice emanating from inside the apartment. Quiet laughter, then a male voice, then more laughter. A TV sitcom. Someone was in Larry's apartment, watching television. Someone was in Larry's apartment, apparently making himself or herself right at home, so soon after Larry's death. Karen immediately recalled Lisa Fuller's comment at the funeral that Larry was having a serious affair. She put her eye to the concave glass peephole. A faint, fuzzy glow flickered from within. She replaced the key in her pocket and rapped, unassertively, on the door. The sitcom was muted. The flickering glow at the peephole vanished, but the door remained closed and no one spoke. An eye had arrived on the other side of the peephole, and someone was looking out at her silently. She walked briskly away, keeping to the same side of the hall as Larry's apartment to avoid being watched through the peephole.

Karen got into her car and headed for the other likely location of file number 3, the Conkels' house, about a twenty-minute drive. Paula might be home and refuse to allow her in the house; the house might be empty; or one or both of the children might be home while their mother was out. If Paula *was* home and let

Karen in, Ben McCormick would have a fit, even though Karen had no intention of discussing the Conkels' claim against the hospital. She was merely attempting to recover a missing file on an unrelated matter. Could anybody connect the file missing from Larry's office with the Conkels' claim against the hospital? More to the point, could anybody prove that Karen suspected a connection?

When Karen's car was about one hundred and fifty feet from the Conkels' house, she hit the brakes hard enough to make the tires squeal. Here was a possibility that she had not considered: in the Conkel driveway was a black BMW convertible. Karen pulled forward slowly, and read the car's vanity license plate: "MEM CEO."

"The private inurement mobile!" Karen said, out loud. "What the hell is Grimes doing here?"

Karen stopped fifty feet past the Conkels' driveway and turned off the engine. The Conkels' house was decorated for the season with icicle lights along the gutters and a garish plastic wreath on the front door. As she watched the front door of the house in her outside wing mirror, the interior of her car got colder until she could see her breath and her fingers started to ache. Eventually, two bright floodlights illuminated the driveway, and the door opened.

Joe Grimes backed out through the door. Joe was hatless, wearing his Burberry coat. Paula was wearing a red knit dress, oddly formal for a weekday evening at home. Joe held the aluminum storm door open with his left hand, while briefly holding one of Paula's hands with his right. Karen couldn't see around Joe's broad back to tell whether he held Paula's right hand, as in a businesslike handshake, or her left, which would have suggested something more intimate. Paula was smiling. Not just smiling. Beaming. Joe closed the storm door, waved, and walked to his car. Karen slumped down in her seat. She heard the sound of Joe's engine, then slumped lower as his headlights lit up the interior of her car. When Joe's car was a block away, Karen sat up. She grabbed her cellular telephone and dialed her home number.

"Y-y-yello."

"Jake, it's me," whispered Karen.

"Why are you whispering?" asked Jake.

"I don't know," said Karen in her normal voice. "Jake, I'm going to be home later than expected. Hold dinner."

"Sacré bleu," said Jake, "ze soufflé will be ruined."

"What are we really having?"

"Soy burgers and canned vegetarian beans. Where are you? Sounds like the car phone."

"I'm in front of the Conkels' house. I drove over to look for a file missing from Larry's fraud investigation. When I got here, guess who I found visiting Paula?"

"Uh, the Chicago Bulls?" guessed Jake.

"No. Joe Grimes."

"Velly intelesting. He and Paula having a little assignation? A little tête-à-tête?"

"I don't know," said Karen, "but Jake, today I talked to the guy who tested the catheter that broke up in Larry. And I got an independent opinion on the performance of the docs. And Annie talked to the cath lab personnel. In a nutshell, it doesn't look like Larry's death was the result of negligence."

"Well," said Jake, "it wasn't the result of old age. You're saying Larry was murdered?"

"I'm trying to avoid saying it. I sent Grimes a memo this afternoon saying I think we need to bring in the police. Then I find a reference to a file that might implicate the hospital in the clinic billing fraud. Now I see Grimes huddling with Paula Conkel. I don't want him to get that memo."

"I dig," said Jake. "The hospital may be in bed with the clinic, and the hospital's CEO may be in bed with the victim's wife. If Grimes was involved in murdering Larry, telling him you're going to the cops could be hazardous to your health. You're going to get the memo you sent him back before he reads it."

"If I can," allowed Karen. "It won't be easy."

"Why not?"

"I sent it e-mail."

Karen felt self-conscious and furtive as she used her key to un-lock the door to the administrative offices in the old wing of the hospital. She glanced involuntarily at the security camera that peered at her obliquely from its perch at the end of the hall. There was no way anyone observing her could know she was not headed to her own office, but her awareness of what she was up to made her stop and look both ways before slip-ping through the doorway.

The administrative offices were dark and silent. Karen was relieved that nobody was working late, including Anne Delaney, who worked evenings with regularity. The rest of the adminis-trative staff usually went home for dinner at the end of the workday. Karen considered this a wholesome practice, a way in which the hospital, and businesses in Jefferson generally, com-pared favorably to the Chicago law firm where she had clerked. There, young lawyers routinely worked into the evening, scarf-ing down pizza or Chinese carryout. Also in stark contrast to the modus operandi in Chicago, Karen noted, was the minimal secu-rity in hospitals in places like Jefferson. Anne had described to her the stringent security measures necessary at Raasch Evangelical Medical Center in Chicago. At Shoreview Memorial, Karen knew, there would be only two or three security guards patrolling the entire hospital campus, and that most of their time would be spent in patient areas, where drugs and hypodermic supplies were stored and intoxicated or disturbed patients could cause problems. The administrative offices, including Joe Grimes's, were never locked, even though a lot of confidential records were kept there. Sometimes the hospital's casual security bothered Karen, but on this occasion she was glad for it. She took her shoes off before entering Joe's office, to avoid making noise on the tile floor, and left the lights off. She set her shoes down on the black glass of the desktop and turned on Joe's computer.

It seemed to take an hour to boot up. She needed to enter Joe's e-mail in order to delete the memorandum she had sent him that afternoon. When the program requested Joe's user name, Karen entered Joe's initials, J-P-G. Everyone at the hospital used his or her initials as their user names. The menu appeared on the computer monitor. One of the choices on the menu was "e-mail." Karen scrolled to e-mail and pressed "Enter." The program then demanded:

"ENTER PASSWORD."

Now for the hard part, thought Karen. She typed "J-P-G," held her breath and pressed "Enter." The program responded:

"PASSWORD INCORRECT. ENTER PASSWORD."

Karen sighed, "Oh, shit." She tried "J-O-E."

"PASSWORD INCORRECT. ENTER PASSWORD."

She tried "G-R-I-M-E-S." Incorrect. She tried "J-O-S-E-P-H," she tried his wife's name, her initials, his daughter's name, her initials, the name and initials of his beloved country club, the name of his college, his birthday, his telephone extension, the numbers in his street address, each time only to be reprimanded:

"PASSWORD INCORRECT. ENTER PASSWORD."

Karen heard voices echoing in the hall outside. She clenched her fists and closed her eyes. An idea was coming; then, there it was. She typed, "M-E-M C-E-O," and pressed "Enter." A list of Joe's e-mail messages scrolled up on the screen.

Her own message was listed third from the top. She only needed to scroll down to it, press "Enter," select "Read message" from a list of options, "Exit" the message, then "Delete" the message. Seven key strokes and she would be done.

The voices in the hall had grown louder. Karen recognized one of the voices. It was Joe. Grimes was about fifteen feet away, headed for his office, with a companion. She tried to think of an explanation for being in his office after hours, in the dark, with her shoes off and the computer on. She moved to push the power button on the computer, but realized the sudden darkening of the room would be noticeable from the hall. Joe and his guest were right outside the door, talking.

"You should quit the Jefferson Country Club, Len. Too much water on the back nine and the food isn't nearly as good as Westbrook's."

Karen looked around. She had no place to go. Under the desk? The desk had no modesty panel. That figures, she thought, its owner has no modesty. She grabbed her shoes and backed toward the corner, bumping into one of the large Moroccan urns.

"You'll get me to join Westbrook yet, Joe," said the other voice. It was Dr. Leonard Herwitz, the Chief of the Medical Staff. She could see part of his back through the door. Desperation flooded her. Out of alternatives, she lifted her left leg and set it down inside the urn, then did the same with her right. She shoved her shoes under the fronds of the palm tree planted in the adjacent urn, and bent her knees. Her hips jammed in the mouth of the urn.

"You could maintain both memberships for a while, then see which club you use more."

Karen's hips popped through the opening. She lowered herself into the urn. Her shoulders stuck. Dr. Herwitz stepped into the room.

"I might be able to swing that, if I wasn't being shaken down to invest in MRI equipment." The two men chuckled softly.

Karen folded her shoulders forward and squeezed them through the mouth of the urn. Her coccyx butted into the bottom of the urn, but her head still protruded from the top. She could see Joe entering the office. He switched on the lights. If he looked in her direction, he would see her. She realized the only reason she had not been spotted already was that Joe was not checking to see if any heads were sticking out of his urns.

Karen scrunched down as far as she could. Her knees were pressed against the inside of the lip of the urn. There was no room to pull her head in. She cocked her head sideways and tucked the left side of her head just under the lip of the urn's mouth. Her ear stuck on the edge. She pushed with her neck, and her head slid into the urn.

"Actually, Len," said Joe, "that's exactly what I wanted to talk to you about, the MRI. Take your coat off."

Abruptly, Karen was in darkness. Joe had tossed his coat over the urn.

"I have an idea about how we might get the clinic into the MRI profits."

"Something we couldn't talk about in the doctor's lounge, you said."

"Right," said Joe. "I think I've come up with a way for the doctors to get fifty percent of the action on the MRI without putting up any cash."

"I thought your lawyer lady said that was a no-no," said Dr. Herwitz.

"Uh-huh. Speaking of my lawyer lady, I see I've got an e-mail message from her. I guess my secretary left my computer on."

Karen's heart pounded like a jackhammer. She felt out of breath, but forced herself to breathe shallowly, quietly.

93

"One can always postpone a message from one's lawyer," postulated Dr. Herwitz.

"Ain't that the truth," concurred Joe. Karen heard the computer click off.

"Say," said Dr. Herwitz, "do you know why we're using lawyers in medical experiments now instead of rats?"

Joe played along. "Why?"

"Because there are certain things rats just won't do." Both men guffawed. "So what is this idea of yours?"

Karen heard Joe's desk chair squeak as he leaned back. Her neck ached, her feet began to get numb. "Well," Joe began, "say I've been in touch with a local, mmmm, philanthropist, a supporter of the hospital and its mission, whom I think I can persuade to make a large contribution, say, $1 million."

"Yes, say," rejoined Dr. Herwitz. Karen's curiosity took hold. Her claustrophobia backed off slightly.

"The money could be put into a newly created subsidiary of the hospital, which would purchase an MRI."

"Okay," said Dr. Herwitz. "Go on."

"I have a stockbroker who owes me. Not only has the hospital done all of its investing through him for years, I've sent him other business. He wants to keep it coming."

"Dean Williams at Jackson, DeSalle. I know him."

"Right," continued Joe. "Jefferson Clinic could open an account there, and the hospital subsidiary would also have an account. As the MRI throws off cash, fifty percent could be transferred to the clinic account from the hospital sub's account."

"Transferred?"

"After a fashion. The hospital sub could make a series of unlucky investments while the clinic makes a series of lucky ones."

"How could we be sure that happens?" Dr. Herwitz inquired.

"Twenty-twenty hindsight," responded Joe. "And backdated confirmation slips. Dean Williams can paper up a series of trades that eventually move half of the MRI profits from the hospital sub's account to the clinic's account. The Medicare auditors will never turn it up, and nobody's going to rifle Jackson, DeSalle's records, because the loser in the deal, the hospital sub, won't complain."

"Won't somebody on the Board of Directors of the hospital subsidiary kick up a fuss when half the profits evaporate?" asked Dr. Herwitz.

"The board of the hospital sub will be me, you, and Dean Williams."

The room was quiet for a moment. Inside the urn, Karen's breathing sounded like a typhoon. Her heart was thumping so loud she was afraid it would start the urn ringing like a bell. The scheme Grimes had laid out for Herwitz was a clear violation of federal law, since it was merely a ruse to transfer half of the hospital's profits on the MRI to the clinic. The payoff to the clinic was being made so that the clinic doctors would refer more patients for MRI diagnostics. It had been only a few hours since she had carefully explained to Joe Grimes why it would be illegal for the hospital to share MRI revenues with the clinic. Joe had wasted no time cooking up this elaborate subterfuge to hide the payoff.

Joe's proposition to Dr. Herwitz was criminal, but apparently Joe thought the scheme's gloss of financial sophistication made it okay somehow. How did a guy get this slimy? Was he born that way? And who was this mysterious, anonymous donor? Could it be Paula Conkel, about to become a wealthy woman due to Larry's untimely death? Was the million-dollar donation a payoff for arranging Larry's "accident"? Karen tried to quiet her breathing as Herwitz considered Joe's proposal.

"It's food for thought," Herwitz finally responded. "Can I talk this over with some of the other doctors?"

"I'd rather you didn't talk about it with anybody, not even your wife," asserted Joe. "Nobody except the Secretary-Treasurer of the clinic. That's Ed Bernard. You can let Ed in on it."

95

"How about the clinic's attorney?"

"Why do that? He'll just tell you it's illegal. But Len, it's a bigger risk for the hospital than the clinic, and I don't think it's much of a risk for us. Think it over, get back to me before Christmas if you can."

"Fine. Have to run now; Gina and I have tickets for the symphony."

Light flooded into the urn. Joe had picked up his coat. Karen heard shuffling and footsteps, and then it was dark again. The footsteps of the two men faded away.

In the best of circumstances Karen was not a devotee of business meetings, but she had never been so relieved and grateful to have a meeting end. She flexed the aching muscles in her neck slowly, so as not to scrape her left ear, pressed as it was against the inside of the urn.

Her head did not move. She pulled harder and pushed against the inside of the urn with her right elbow. Still no movement. She felt a rush of terror. Instantly, black circles appeared in the center of her field of vision, sweat emanated from her pores, and she felt herself begin to convulse. She pulled as hard as she could with her neck, pushed with her arms and legs. Nothing. No leeway to reposition her body.

Karen was trapped inside the urn.

CHAPTER
12

Panic ripped through Karen like the claws of a wild animal. She pushed out furiously in all directions without result. Abandoning all concern about her job or embarrassment, she cried out for help. "Get me out of here! Please, please, someone, get me out of here!" She screamed until her throat was raw. She fought back her panic and tried to think, tried to ignore her own violent trembling. She felt as if she might lose consciousness, which would be a relief, but then realized that with her neck folded over at a ninety-degree angle, if her muscles went slack she might crimp her trachea and suffocate. Top priority, she told herself, keep breathing.

Karen expected her life to flash before her eyes, but it didn't. One image from her past did impose itself, and she clung to it, drawing enough comfort to stop herself from blacking out.

The image was of Jake, smiling broadly, his face wreathed by enormous grape ivy leaves, in a place to which Karen returned, if only in her mind, whenever she felt overwhelmed. The image was linked with the feel of warm sun on her face and the fermentative smell of a forest in late September and was drawn from her memories of her wedding day.

On the morning of Karen and Jake's wedding, Gene Decker's house had been teeming with relatives preparing for the nuptials, but the atmosphere on what was supposed to be a festive occasion was as fractious and flammable as a border dispute in the Balkans. Gene and Elizabeth, having just recently separated, were barely civil to each other, and their respective siblings had sided along bloodlines and separated into hostile camps.

The only thing Karen's relatives agreed upon that day was their disdain for the groom's family, which consisted solely of Jake's brother Jason and a trio of Jason's uninvited, unwashed motorcycle buddies. They had roared up to the house on their Harleys, invaded the liquor cabinet, and made crude remarks to the female guests, even the elderly ones. When Karen's parents, aunts, and uncles carped at her about the antics of the Jason contingent, as if it were somehow her responsibility, she thought she would explode with disappointment, frustration and anger.

As she watched what was supposed to be the most joyful day of her life rapidly deteriorate, Jake had appeared at her side and took her by the hand. Together they had walked through sphagnum moss and golden tamaracks, up a steep hillside ablaze with scarlet sumacs to the base of a towering oak. The giant tree had branches that rotated around the trunk, and Jake and Karen climbed the branches until they emerged from the twilight of the forest floor to the bright sunshine above the canopy of the trees. The treetops were matted with a thick web of grape ivy, and Jake coaxed Karen into lying down with him in the nest of vines, which they could then rock gently, like a hammock.

Now, Karen concentrated on this mental image, deliberately slowing her breathing, and conjuring up the deep warmth she had felt when Jake, with nobody in attendance save birds, dragonflies and one noisy red squirrel, had reached into his pocket, produced her wedding band, and recited the vows they had planned for the church ceremony. Karen had recited her own vows, and they embraced, swinging in the grape ivy and gazing upon the spectacular view of the flowage, with its tawny waters whiffled into an intricate pattern of fan-shaped whitecaps. Afterward, they considered their marriage to have occurred at that moment, and the tense, trite ceremony later that afternoon to have been merely redundant.

Karen clung to the vivid memory of how, as she had looked into Jake's smiling face surrounded by the ivy leaves, all remnants of her earlier anger and frustration were swept away by a surge of joy at what seemed an impossible stroke of luck. In her entire life she had known only one person who could keep his head when all around him were losing theirs, only one person who hadn't cluttered his own radar screen with a lot of static, only one person to whom her feelings always seemed to matter, and she was marrying that person. Wasn't that enough, all by itself, to make a person happy?

Well, no, it wasn't. Not if that person was trapped in a giant urn, fighting for her life. The memory of Jake swinging to and fro in the vine hammock gave Karen an idea. If she could shift her body weight back and forth, she might get the urn rocking. If she could tip it over, it might break on the tile floor and she would be free. If it did not break, she could roll it, maybe get out the door and . . .

It was no use. Karen could not move enough to budge the broad base of the heavy clay pot. She had no alternative but to try to maintain consciousness until someone discovered her, hope that she did not slip into permanent psychosis in the meantime, and breathe, breathe.

CHAPTER
13

At 9:15 P.M. that Monday night, Steven Linder lay comfortably in his patient bed on the third floor of Shoreview Memorial Hospital, recuperating from carpal tunnel surgery he had undergone earlier that afternoon. The surgery already seemed like a distant memory. He felt remarkably good, beatific and serene as he chatted with a fellow patient from an adjacent room. The other patient, a thin man of medium height with short, graying hair, had a small port wine birthmark on his left temple and smooth, even features. He seemed quite interested in Steven's description of his surgery, his job, his life in general. The visitor smiled warmly as he listened, occasionally laughing sympathetically and putting his hand on Steven's knee. Steven began to feel euphoric and drowsy at the same time—a pleasant, floating feeling. His visitor reached one hand under the white sheet and pulled back Steven's hospital gown.

Inside the terra-cotta Moroccan urn in Joe Grimes's office, Karen Hayes shivered and whimpered softly. She had been trapped inside for less than three hours, but it had already been over an hour since she had given up anticipating morning, which seemed long overdue. Her cognition had shut down. Her consciousness spanned only the time frame from breath to breath. It took her several seconds to realize that a sound from outside the urn had reached her ears. The sound of footsteps on a tile floor.

The footsteps moved slowly across the large office. They paused, then moved again. Paused again. When the footsteps started moving again, they seemed to be getting farther away from Karen, moving toward the door. Whoever it was had apparently finished whatever he or she had come to do and was leaving. Whoever it was, whatever they were doing there, Karen did not want them to leave.

Karen tried to say, "Please, help me," but she was unable to engage her voice, and all that came out was a small, squeaky whimper. Except for her mouth and nose, she could no longer feel her own body. The footsteps grew louder, then stopped. Someone was standing by the urn. She heard a voice say, "If I laugh now, you'll probably divorce me."

It was Jake. Karen found her voice. "Get me out. Get me out now!"

Jake sounded startled by Karen's pathetic tone. "Don't worry, I'll get you out if I have to smash the thing. Everything's going to be all right. I promise you. Just hold on." Jake tried to push the heavy urn over, but quickly realized he could not control it. With Karen inside, the container seemed to weigh close to three hundred pounds.

Jake sat down on the floor and straddled the urn. He braced one foot against the desk and the other against a wall, grabbed the lip of the urn, and pulled. When the urn tipped onto him, he moved his hands underneath it and lowered it slowly. When it was almost resting on him, he slithered out from under it and repositioned his feet on the base of the urn.

Karen felt one of Jake's hands on her neck, the other sliding in over the top of her head. She heard her own voice, saying, "Oh, oh, oh, oh!" The hand on the top of her head slid in between the lip of the urn and her left ear and pushed downward, gently. Jake made a quick, twisting motion, like a chiropractor making an adjustment, and her head popped out.

Jake's eyes teared when he saw Karen's face, grayish-purple and blotchy. Her skin was cold and dilated blood vessels bloomed around her mouth and nose. She gasped hungrily for the fresh air outside the urn.

"Head's clear!" Jake called out. "Now, here come the shoulders." He put one hand on each of Karen's shoulders and folded them forward. "Push!" he yelled. "Push!"

Karen tried but couldn't move her numb legs. Jake gripped her shoulders and pulled them through the mouth of the urn. Her face landed on his belly.

"Shoulders are clear!" he exclaimed. "Come on now, just one more, here come the hips. One more. Push! Push!" Karen tried but her legs were completely asleep. Jake grabbed her waist and pulled and her hips squirted through.

Karen landed this time with her face on Jake's neck, weeping and gasping, her dread and stupor evaporating with astonishing quickness. Jake craned his head up, patted the urn with his hand, and said, "Congratulations, Mrs. Decker. You have a beautiful daughter."

Jake's attempt at levity penetrated, and Karen began, to her own surprise, to laugh. Fearing laughter would delay her recovery from the shakes, she caught her breath. "You're a miracle," she gasped. "However did you find me?"

"Ah," replied Jake, "a brilliant bit of ratiocination. On the phone you said you were going to Grimes's office. So when you didn't show up at home, I went to Grimes's office. When I got here, I heard someone whimpering inside this big clay pot. There you were."

Karen pushed herself up onto her elbows and said, "My hero."

While Jake returned the urn to its original position, Karen broke into Joe's e-mail and erased her memo. Joe was clumsy with his computer, so Karen knew it was unlikely that the disappearance of her message would be noticed. She retrieved her shoes from under the potted palm, and she and Jake escaped the office.

In the hall outside, Karen saw the silhouetted figure of a large, muscular man approaching. A huge key chain and a nightstick dangled from his belt. His right hand clutched a long, cylindrical object. When he was about twenty feet away, he stopped, raised his hand and pointed the object directly at Karen's face.

A bright light obliterated Karen's vision. The man was shining a flashlight at her.

"Mrs. Hayes!" said the man. "Are you all right?"

Karen recognized the voice of Max Schumacher, the head of Security.

"Turn off the flashlight, Max. You're blinding me."

Max lowered the flashlight and flicked the switch off. Karen's heart was pounding again. She was surprised her adrenal glands had anything left after her hours of terror. Her vision had started to clear, although everything appeared to be tinted red, and she could see Max standing in the dark hallway, walking toward her. She realized with dismay that she had no explanation to offer for her presence in Joe's office in the middle of the night.

Max had the thick neck of an ex-wrestler and could carry two hundred and fifty pounds and still appear to be in decent shape. Karen knew him to be friendly and good-natured, but she also knew he was an ex-cop and that little got by him.

He now studied Karen's face. "Are you sure you're okay? No offense, Mrs. Hayes, but you look like something the cat left outside."

"I'm okay, Max."

"Your skin is blotchy and your eyes look funny and your hair is all tangled. And why are you shaking?"

"Too much coffee."

"Why are you carrying your shoes?"

"Sore feet."

"Why is your skirt all wrinkled?"

"Bad dry cleaner."

"Why were you in Mr. Grimes's office?"

"Hi, Max," interjected Jake.

Max turned to Jake. "Oh, yeah, hi there, Mr. Hayes. Say, what gives? You guys are in Grimes's office after hours, Mrs. Hayes looks like hell—no offense, Mrs. Hayes—and I'm getting answers that sound like horse doodoo."

"Didn't you need something from your office?" Jake said to Karen.

Karen stared at him for a moment. "Oh, *that's* right."

Jake was buying time for her to think of an explanation. She walked slowly to her office. Every bone in her body ached. She was still trembling and dazed. Her mind was not working the way it usually did. Why *was* I in Grimes's office? Come on, think of something. Maybe I needed some documents from Joe's office. So where were they? I just went in to water Joe's palm tree. No good, Max could check the soil and it would be dry. How about, Joe left his computer on and I went in to turn it off. No! The worst thing to do would be to call attention to Joe's computer.

Exhausted and drained of ideas, she found her office. The light from a street lamp faintly illuminated the room. Shadows cast by the branches of the sugar maple outside her window fractured the walls and ceiling into jagged pieces. She shuddered. She was not ready to be alone right then.

"Jake!" He was just outside the door. Max was gone. Karen heard someone whistling beyond the stairwell door.

"Where's Max?" said Karen.

"He went back to his rounds," said Jake.

"How did you get rid of him?"

104

"I talked to him dude-to-dude."

"About what?"

"Stuff like, you know, how some couples might enjoy doing a certain thing in a lot of different places, and how that certain thing might get the woman's hair and skirt messed up, stuff like that."

"Jake, you didn't."

"Did."

"How embarrassing."

"I didn't say *we* did it. I said some couples. He may have jumped to a conclusion."

"Judas priest. Max will do a report on the incident. This will be all over the hospital within hours."

"I don't think Max will do a report."

"Why not?"

"Because he has too many other things to do. Like, he's going in to Chicago for a Bulls game. Oh yeah, remember to put those tickets Larry gave us in the interoffice mail tomorrow."

Karen put her hand on her face. "Jake, you didn't bribe the head of Security!"

"Did."

She moved her hand to his face. "Clever boy," she said.

Jake looked down and pointed at Karen's other hand. "Is that what you supposedly went back to your office for?"

Karen looked down. She was holding the crystal paperweight from her desktop.

Around midnight, Karen decided she would not need to be hospitalized after all. An extended hot bath, accompanied by two cold martinis and four ibuprofen tablets, followed by an hour-long full body massage accompanied by candlelight, incense and a tape of Japanese lute music selected by Jake, had restored her sense of physical and mental well-being to a remarkable degree.

As Jake put the finishing touches on the massage, kneading Karen's calves and ankles with scented oil, Karen told him about Carl Gellhorn's opinion that Bernard and Herwitz had mismanaged Larry's case. She speculated that Bernard or Herwitz might have known about Larry's investigation into the Jefferson Clinic billing fraud.

"If they did, Larry must not have known it or nothing anybody said could have made him change his mind and have his biopsy at Memorial," she said aloud. "Larry wasn't foolish enough to let Bernard operate on him if Larry was about to send Bernard to the slammer and he thought Bernard was on to him. Not even after I told him to think about the effect on his career of ticking off Grimes."

"Are you still feeling guilty about that?" asked Jake.

"No, not anymore," said Karen, sounding unconvinced. "Larry must have kept the investigation a total secret, or thought he had. Larry's secretary told me Herwitz was in Larry's office this morning looking for something. Maybe it was the fraud investigation file. Still, even with Carl's report there's no proof Bernard or Herwitz did anything intentional to cause Larry's death." She told Jake about Gilbert Austin's verbal report that the catheter that broke up inside Larry was heated far beyond sterilization.

Jake's massage moved down to Karen's feet. The candlelight flickered rhythmically; for a moment it strobed in time with the music. The fragrance of the massage oil blossomed in the room. The skin on the tops of Karen's feet looked opalescent in the candlelight.

"So someone who knew what would happen to the catheter cooked the hell out of it and somehow made sure it got into Larry?" asked Jake.

"Annie Delaney told me a cath lab nurse said there was only one catheter on the cart the morning they did Larry. Normally there would be several. Somebody rigged it so Larry would get the bad catheter."

"Who could've done that?"

"I'm having Annie check out who had access to the cart before Larry's procedure. I suppose it could have been any doctor in the hospital, any cath lab nurse or tech. Maybe someone walked in off the street."

Jake slid his hands up the length of Karen's legs, to redo her buttocks and lower back. "So then the question is, who would want to bump off Larry?"

"Oh, that feels good. Now Grimes had multiple reasons."

"Yeah, good old Joltin' Joe. You told me about the missing file implicating the hospital in the clinic's billing fraud. Plus maybe he's boffing the Conk's wife. Any other reasons?"

Karen explained Joe's premature urging of a $2 million settlement and his quick hatching of the MRI kickback scheme, with its mysterious million-dollar donor. She postulated, "Larry's death would have simultaneously ended the fraud investigation and created a source for the funds Joe needed to do his precious deal. If Joe killed Larry, he killed a whole flock of birds with one stone."

"And what about Paula?" asked Jake. "She's not coming out too badly. Big damage claim, life insurance, the house. Plus, she saves on divorce lawyer's fees."

"Her best friend, Lisa Fuller, is a nurse at Shoreview Memorial. Lisa might have boiled the catheter and planted it on the cart for Paula."

Jake sat up and extinguished the candle with his thumb and forefinger. "Not to step on your part, sweetheart, but is this really included in an in-house attorney's gig? Stewing about motive and opportunity?"

Karen closed her eyes and yawned. "It could affect the wrongful death case against the hospital if Larry was murdered. It's my job to defend the hospital. Besides, it looks like Shoreview Memorial has no insurance. If we lose that case, it could go broke; I'd be out of a job. Plus, I'm curious."

Jake lay down beside her and placed his hand gently on the nape of her tender neck. "Plus, you still feel responsible for Larry's decision to have his biopsy at Shoreview."

"Right," said Karen, drifting off to sleep.

CHAPTER
14

Anne Delaney popped an antacid tablet in her mouth and sat down across from Karen at the long polished fruitwood table in Conference Room I, which was located in the old section of the hospital. Slashes of sunlight through Venetian blinds illuminated a blizzard of dust motes, which Karen in her darker moods speculated might include asbestos fibers from ancient floor tiles and pipe wrap. Old steam radiators clanked like boxcars coupling.

"What happened to your neck?" asked Anne. "Rear-ender?"

"Must have slept on it funny," said Karen, touching the cervical collar she was wearing. A stiff neck was the only remnant of her incarceration in the urn. She gulped tepid coffee from a white Styrofoam cup.

"Apparently at the bottom of a pile of rocks," said Anne. "Why didn't you stay home?"

"Last Tuesday of the month," replied Karen. "Can't miss Ethics Committee."

The Ethics Committee of Shoreview Memorial Hospital consisted of nine persons: Karen, Anne, a social worker, an assistant minister from Our Redeemer Lutheran Church, and five doctors. This made it difficult for the committee to seat a quorum, since the physicians were frequently too busy to attend. But today when the chairman of the committee, Edward Bernard, the cardiologist who had done Larry Conkel's biopsy, arrived, the quorum was achieved.

"Meeting of the Ethics Committee will come to order," he announced, lighting up a panatella. With his head craned forward, he surveyed the room with bulging, bloodshot eyes. He wore the standard physician's white lab coat over a white shirt and a brown knit necktie in an overlarge Windsor knot. To his lapel was clipped an ID badge bearing a photo of himself as a much younger man, also wearing a brown necktie with a bad Windsor knot. "Do I have a motion to waive the reading of the minutes of the last meeting?"

"Sure, why not," Karen muttered. "All they say is 'there being no quorum, the meeting was adjourned'."

Bernard shot her a glance. "Reading of the minutes is waived," he said sternly. "New business. Miss Beauchamp, our social worker, has the floor."

The purpose of the Hospital Ethics Committee, according to its charter, was to "serve as a resource for the medical staff, other hospital committees, patients and their families in resolving issues with bioethical implications." This sometimes meant advising the Medical Research Committee on the ethics of medical experimentation using human subjects. It sometimes meant recommending policies on procreative matters, such as sterilization of low-IQ patients, or the use of advanced reproductive techniques like in-vitro fertilization or frozen embryos. Often, it meant helping settle disagreements over when to give up trying to keep a terminal patient alive who was either suffering or vegetative.

"We have a patient who needs heart-bypass surgery, but she lacks capacity to give consent," began the social worker. She was in her twenties, dressed in faded jeans, bulky sweater, chunky neck-lace, and hiking boots. "Her husband is deceased," she said. "She has two daughters who disagree. One wants her to have the sur-gery, one doesn't."

"I saw the case summary on this one," Anne interjected. "This patient is eighty-four years old. Besides the heart disease, she has chronic kidney disease. She's on dialysis."

"Why isn't she able to give consent for herself?" asked Karen.

"PVS," said the social worker. PVS was medical slang for "per-sistent vegetative state," where some functions such as blood circulation operated, but the cerebral cortex was totally and per-manently defunct.

The minister spoke. "What have we done to help the family reach a consensus?"

"I talked with both daughters," said the social worker, "as did both the attending physician and the cardiac surgeon. One daugh-ter is angry at the hospital for keeping her mother on dialysis. The other wants everything possible done to keep her mother alive. We've called a code to resuscitate this patient seven times."

Karen rubbed her eyes with her fists and opened them comically wide, surveying the room. "This is not a hard one, folks." She had read volumes on ethical health care decision-making. She believed it was part of her duty as a member of the Ethics Committee to know and apply the accepted principles of biomedical ethics. The principles had lofty-sounding names, such as nonmaleficence, beneficence, autonomy, and justice, but they could be boiled down to "do unto others" with a few twists and were the same princi-ples Karen used to make decisions in her life. Other members of the committee applied different principles.

"Who's the cardiac surgeon on the case?" asked Dr. Bernard.

"What difference does that make?" asked Karen.

Dr. Bernard's brow furrowed. "I just need to know who's exer-cising the medical judgment on the patient's need for surgery."

111

You just need to know if the Jefferson Clinic will get the fee, thought Karen. A radiator clanked. The clergyman spoke again.

"I think the important thing here is that we help restore harmony to the family. Perhaps we could offer some counseling."

Karen spoke. "There is no need to resolve the disagreement between the daughters to answer the bypass question. That question never should have come to this committee. It's not a question of ethics. It's a question of medical appropriateness. This patient is not a candidate for bypass surgery."

Dr. Bernard sat forward, projecting the smell of cigar smoke into Karen's space. "And when did you get your medical degree, Doctor Hayes?"

Karen plowed ahead. "The ethical question is whether the dialysis should be discontinued, and the patient no-coded." To "no-code" the patient meant that next time her heart stopped, she would not be resuscitated. "We have a permanently vegetative patient with chronic renal failure, two daughters who are suffering, and an unconscionable waste of resources. We're turning away children who need renal dialysis time. The consent of one daughter to make the patient a no-code would be adequate both legally and as a matter of hospital policy."

Anne spoke. "A disagreement in the family increases the risk of a lawsuit if the mother dies."

Dr. Bernard broke in. "Miss Hayes and Miss Delaney are both out of order. The committee has not been asked about discontinuation of life support. Miss Beauchamp, who's the surgeon?"

"Dr. Whitman." Dr. Whitman was a Jefferson Clinic physician.

"Miss Hayes did make one valid point," said Dr. Bernard. "The consent of one daughter is sufficient. The surgery is medically necessary, or Dr. Whitman would not have ordered it. We can't cut off necessary health care to someone just because of her age or the quality of her life." He wagged a long, bony index finger. "That's a slippery slope."

Karen's sore neck throbbed. Her worst suspicions seemed confirmed. Dr. Bernard was pushing the Ethics Committee toward putting a patient and her family through a pointless ordeal in order to bring a nice fee into the Jefferson Clinic. She decided to challenge Bernard.

"Dr. Bernard, we're not talking about exterminating the mentally challenged here. We're talking about an elderly patient who has lived a full life and at this point doesn't even know she's living. If you call that living. It's an easy distinction to make."

Dr. Bernard cleared his throat. "The Chair calls the question."

Karen felt her face flush with anger. Dr. Bernard was capable of railroading the committee. The social worker and the minister were likely to follow the lead of the only physician in the room. Karen decided to again risk raising a medical issue, although she knew what Bernard's reaction would be.

"The patient won't survive bypass surgery," Karen said.

"And how do you presume to know that?" said Dr. Bernard, cocking his head from side to side. "Dr. Whitman is a board-certified cardiothoracic surgeon with twenty-three years' experience."

"And a twenty-four percent mortality rate on bypasses," rejoined Karen, hoping she hadn't gone too far.

Bernard glared at her. "That is because he accepts so many high-risk patients."

"And *that*," said Karen, "is because he has three ex-wives and eight children to support. Otherwise, this case wouldn't even be under consideration."

After a moment of silence, the minister said, "Perhaps a little counseling . . ."

"We've wasted enough time on this," declared Dr. Bernard. "The Chair will duly note Miss Hayes's slander of Dr. Whitman and report it to President Grimes. Now, in case you've forgotten, the question has been called."

"You can't call the question," said Karen sardonically, "until a motion is made. There's been no motion."

"You lawyers!" blustered Dr. Bernard, his voice rising. "The motion is that this committee endorse the courageous effort of a qualified, respected surgeon to save the life of a patient!"

Karen's pulse fluttered, and her field of vision narrowed momentarily. She was losing it.

"I'll tell you what, Dr. Bernard," she said, "why don't you just have Dr. Whitman do up an operative report, put it in the medical record, and bill it out? No need to actually do the surgery. It would save everybody a lot of trouble."

Bernard's jaw dropped. Karen regretted her utterance instantly. By yielding to her anger, she had virtually announced to Bernard that she was wise to his billing fraud. Dr. Bernard picked up his agenda with shaking hands and slowly set it back down on the table. "Excuse me," he said, and strode quickly from the room.

Anne heaved an audible sigh. "Great. There goes our quorum. Mind telling me what that was all about?"

Karen slumped down in her chair and raised a fist to her forehead. She smacked herself and felt a jolt of pain in her stiff neck. "I don't know, Annie. Maybe it's PMS."

The minister smiled nervously. The social worker fiddled with her necklace. Karen closed her eyes. "What else was on the agenda?" she asked.

Anne picked up Dr. Bernard's discarded copy and read, "The Chairman of the Medical Research Committee asked two months ago for our advice on a research protocol proposed by our infectious disease specialist, Dr. Donaldson. It's an experimental treatment for AIDS."

The social worker spoke. "I hope it's not a double-blind study where standard treatments are withheld from one-half of the subjects, who get only an experimental drug. They must know by

114

now it's unethical to withhold treatment known to be efficacious from human subjects."

"No," said Anne, "that isn't the question. The question the Research Committee was asking is whether there's any ethical problem with allowing one of the physicians cosponsoring the protocol to serve as a subject."

Karen's eyes popped open. She grasped the implications of the Research Committee's question instantly. "One of our docs? Somebody on our medical staff has AIDS? Who is it?"

Anne looked Karen in the eye and shook her head, as if warning Karen to drop the subject. "Doesn't matter. It's moot. We didn't have a quorum last month. When we didn't get back to them, the Research Committee approved the protocol subject to our review today. If we don't get them an adverse recommendation today, the protocol goes ahead. With no quorum now, we're out of the loop. I move we adjourn. Karen, could you stay a while longer? I need to talk with you on another matter."

The minister and social worker left the room. Karen shook four ibuprofen tablets from a small plastic bottle and downed them with a gulp of lukewarm coffee. The heat came on, and the radiators clanked. Karen touched her cervical collar and groaned.

"You really should have stayed home today, Karen," said Anne. "Why kill yourself to make it to Ethics Committee?"

"Because," said Karen, "if I don't stop him, Bernard will have them carting respirators down to the morgue and hooking up corpses—after checking to make sure the corpses have adequate insurance coverage, of course. What was the other matter you wanted to talk about? Have you got the details on who had access to the cath lab cart before Larry's biopsy?"

"Not yet. I expect to have it tomorrow. What I wanted to talk about was another alleged sexual assault on a patient."

Anne described to Karen a complaint made the previous night by a surgical patient named Steven Linder. Mr. Linder claimed

115

that another patient he had met on the floor came into Mr. Linder's room, talked with him for over an hour, and then proceeded to fondle his genitals. Mr. Linder also claimed that he felt drugged at the time. The floor nurse confirmed that Mr. Linder was receiving a narcotic postoperatively for pain, but the patient said he felt a surge of drowsiness and a "buzz" right before the assault. Mr. Linder claimed to be familiar enough with the effects of drugs to know he was feeling something more than his post-op pain med.

"That's interesting," remarked Karen. "A similarity to the Dietrich Heiden complaint. Heiden said he was drugged, too, before the alleged assault by Carson Weber."

Anne chewed on the knuckle of her left index finger. "Uh, there's another similarity."

"And that would be . . . ?"

"Linder identified Dr. Weber as the assailant."

Karen blinked twice. The radiator groaned. "I thought he said he was attacked by another patient."

"He did. Dr. Weber was a patient on the same floor as Mr. Linder last night. They were next-door neighbors, in fact."

"Whoa!" Karen exclaimed. "Well, that about does it. No way this is a coincidence. Damn! We blew it on the Heiden complaint." Members of the medical staff were not employees of the hospital, so even if Dr. Weber *had* assaulted Dietrich Heiden, the hospital probably would not be liable. However, the hospital was much more likely to be responsible on a second assault, if it failed to deal effectively with the first assault.

"Not your fault, Annie. It was a good investigation. The parking garage videotapes just made it seem more likely that Heiden was confused, or lying. The only thing we've got going for the defense of this Linder complaint is that Weber was a patient at the time of the assault. He wasn't on duty as a physician. By the way, what *was* he in the hospital for?"

116

Anne's gaze dropped to her lap. "He's the physician who's one of the subjects in Dr. Donaldson's research protocol. He signed himself in to start the tests."

Karen pulled off her cervical collar and threw it across the conference table. She rubbed her painful neck with both hands. "So the doctor who's been sexually assaulting our patients has AIDS. Isn't that *special?*"

Upon returning to her office, Karen called Joe Grimes and reported the second allegation of sexual assault against Dr. Weber. She requested that Grimes contact Leonard Herwitz, Chief of the Medical Staff, to convene a special meeting of the Medical Executive Committee, for the purpose of suspending Dr. Weber's medical staff privileges. Karen felt remorseful that she had reached the wrong conclusion about the first complaint against Weber, but she had little doubt that the Medical Executive Committee, which was charged with the responsibility for disciplining wayward medical staff members, would suspend Dr. Weber. From her experience with the committee she had gleaned a general principle: if the members of the committee could imagine themselves committing the same infraction as the errant physician, they would go easy on the culprit; if not, they'd throw the book at him. This general principle, combined with the overt homophobia that prevailed in the culture of the medical staff, boded ill for Carson Weber.

Grimes said he would try to get the meeting scheduled at the end of the day. Then he said he had something else to discuss with Karen.

"Good news on the MRI," he said exuberantly. "You can stop worrying about private inurement and illegal kickbacks and all that stuff. I think I've found a donor who will make a large gift to a new hospital subsidiary to acquire the MRI, and the clinic doctors have agreed to voluntarily send their patients here to support the program. I've been using my legendary powers of persuasion on Dr. Herwitz."

Joe's mention of the MRI deal brought back a memory of the interior of the clay urn, and Karen's stomach jumped. Her sore neck ached. Joe was moving forward with his plan to sneak the hospital's money to the clinic by corrupting the stockbroker into phonying up confirmation slips showing stock transfers that never took place. Using a "donation" Joe may have gotten his hands on by arranging Larry's death. She gritted her teeth.

"Gee, Joe, how do you do it? All taken care of, just like that. And a week ago, we were stymied."

"I still need some help from you, Karen. Think about how much we can pay the clinic for consulting on selection of the MRI equipment and so forth. Estimate on the high side."

Great, she thought and stuck out her tongue at the telephone. It's not enough the clinic is getting half the MRI profits from the hospital. Now they're squeezing consulting fees out of it, too. What might they cook up next?

CHAPTER 15

eonard Herwitz, accompanied by the sound of the ever-present clanking of the radiators, called the special meeting of the Medical Executive Committee to order at 6:00 P.M. Tuesday in sweltering old Conference Room I. Dr. Herwitz's svelte figure and erect posture looked as straight and sharp as one of his scalpels.

The committee ate fried chicken and french-fried potatoes from plastic plates on cafeteria trays. The hospital dietician had made prior attempts to serve low-fat fare at committee meetings, but the healthier food had received bad reviews from the doctors.

Karen helped herself to a serving of soggy green beans, a dry dinner roll, and skim milk. At the long fruitwood table across from her, Dr. Bernard avoided eye contact. The smell of his cigar smoke, suspended in the air of the stuffy conference room like cobwebs, did little to enhance the cafeteria meal. She nodded at Dr. Herwitz, who nodded back, smiling. He was almost her father's age, but Karen had to admit that Herwitz was a good-looking man. He always seemed to show more interest in her than most of the other doctors did.

Dr. Caswell, the oncologist who figured prominently in Larry Conkel's fraud investigation files and who Karen thought looked like an undertaker, was present. Two other committee members attended—an anesthesiologist named Futterlieb, whom Karen had heard referred to by other doctors as a "frat boy," a euphemism that meant he had a drinking problem, and an internist who was young, clean-cut, and new to the committee. Joe Grimes was there as a guest.

"Why don't we start the meeting while people eat," suggested Dr. Herwitz. "That way we can get out of here at a reasonable hour." He paused for a bite of fried chicken. "Joe, why don't you tell the committee what you told me earlier."

Joe described the complaints against Carson Weber: one allegation of assault involving nonconsensual oral sex and a subsequent allegation involving fondling. Joe explained the similarity of the allegations, the dates and times, and why Weber was a patient in the hospital at the time of the second sexual assault.

"That would put the first incident on the night of Thanksgiving," Dr. Herwitz observed.

"Correct," said Joe.

"I guess," said Dr. Caswell, "Carson has his own idea of Thanksgiving dinner." A couple of the doctors chuckled.

"Maybe he thinks that's what the term 'drumstick' means," said the anesthesiologist. The committee members laughed.

"Do you suppose," the internist interjected, "he prefers light meat or dark?" More laughter.

"I bet," said Joe, "what he really goes for is stuffing!"

Dr. Herwitz interrupted the subsequent chortling after several seconds. "Now, gentlemen, let's not forget we have a lady present."

Joe, seeming a little intoxicated at having gotten a laugh from the doctors, said, "That's no lady, that's my shyster!" He was rewarded with another laugh. Smiling pleasantly, Karen thought to herself, What a bunch of assholes, and interrupted the laughter.

"We need a committee member to make a motion to summarily suspend Dr. Weber's medical staff privileges."

"So moved," said the internist.

"Seconded," said Futterlieb, the anesthesiologist.

"Hold your horses," said Dr. Bernard. "Let's not rush to judgment. All we have is stories from patients who by their own admission were on drugs."

Leave it to Bernard to try to use the fact that Weber's victims claimed they were drugged to discredit them, thought Karen. Was there no limit to this man's disregard for patients?

"That's not quite all we have," she said. "Dr. Weber admitted the second assault to the floor nurse. Anne Delaney got a written statement from her. In addition, we did a drug screen on the patient. Somehow, this patient received a drug other than the one ordered by the attending physician."

"You're jumping to conclusions," said Dr. Bernard, wagging his index finger. "Maybe the nurse screwed up the medication, then fabricated Dr. Weber's confession to cover her own ass."

Karen cast her eyes to the ceiling. God, how he rankled her.

"That's ridiculous," she said. "The nurse didn't even know about the first assault, and she didn't know we would do a drug screen. The drug screen came *after* Weber's confession."

Dr. Bernard furrowed his brow and leaned forward. "I don't know what's going on here. Isn't a man innocent until proven guilty in a court of law? That's what the Constitution says!"

Karen felt fatigued and frustrated at the same time. "No, Dr. Bernard, the presumption of innocence is not in the Constitution. More to the point, this isn't a criminal prosecution. We're not going to put Dr. Weber in jail, we're just deciding whether he can exercise his medical staff privileges in this hospital."

"No," asserted Dr. Herwitz, "we are not. Mrs. Hayes, the standard for summary suspension is that the physician poses an immediate danger to patients. That standard is not met. No suggestion has been made that Dr. Weber is not practicing competent medicine. We cannot discriminate against a physician based on

121

sexual preference. Now, I know Dr. Weber has AIDS, but as long as he uses universal precautions there is no significant danger to patients."

"Dr. Herwitz," Karen asked, "don't you yourself refuse to perform surgery on AIDS patients?"

"That's an entirely different matter. The risk of transmission from patient to physician is well established. There is no established risk of transmission from physician to patient if universal precautions are followed. The Chair will entertain a motion that Dr. Weber be required to enter an impaired professionals program under the auspices of the County Medical Society." If the physician adhered to the program, he could continue to practice while he received treatment.

"Let me get this straight," interjected Karen. "A physician with AIDS who is sexually assaulting patients does not pose an immediate danger to patients?"

"So moved," said Dr. Bernard, ignoring Karen.

"Seconded," said Dr. Caswell.

The motion passed by a vote of three to two. Karen was astonished that Herwitz would want to keep Weber on the medical staff, and that Bernard and Caswell would go along with him. It was the first time in years that she had been wrong in her prediction of a Medical Executive Committee vote. Was she losing her touch? Why were the Jefferson Clinic doctors protecting Weber? What was happening in this hospital?

After Dr. Herwitz adjourned the meeting, Dr. Caswell regaled the committee with a story he had heard about Dr. Weber. Occasionally emergency room physicians saw male patients, especially late at night, who came to the ER with foreign objects lodged in their rectums.

"A few weeks ago," said Dr. Caswell, "Weber sees a patient who's got a cucumber stuck in his ass. It takes Weber fifteen minutes to remove the thing. When he gets it out, he says to the patient,

'You know, you really should chew your food more thoroughly'." The doctors filed from the room doubled over. Joe Grimes asked Karen to stay for a minute.

"Dr. Bernard was in my office this afternoon, Karen," he said. "Your behavior at the Ethics Committee meeting this morning was way out of line. And you were contradicting him just now. It's not your job to alienate the medical staff. I know you're a good lawyer, Karen, but if I hear any more about you harassing Dr. Bernard . . ."

"Harassing? I was disagreeing, I wasn't harassing."

"Don't split hairs, Karen. Just remember what your job is. If you want to keep it." Joe turned and walked away quickly.

In the gray concrete parking structure, Karen tried to hold her briefcase and two file folders in one hand as she unlocked her car door with the other. An overweight man with black, greasy hair and a full beard on his way to an adjacent stall brushed up against her, causing the file folders to slip and drop to the cold, dirty concrete. A sheet of paper from one folder fell out, and the breeze from the folder hitting the concrete blew it under the car. Karen was afraid that if she backed the car out, the document would blow away. Restricted by her stiff neck, there was only one spot where Karen could reach the paper under the car, so she moved to it, got down on one knee, reached under the car, and grabbed the document. As she did so, the engine of a pickup truck in the adjacent stall started up. The engine sounded unmuffled and rough, and an acrid, white cloud of exhaust surrounded her. She got up hurriedly and clumsily, shredding the knees of her pantyhose. She waved her hand in front of her face and coughed. The engine revved, and the cloud of exhaust grew denser. The stench seemed to coat the inside of Karen's mouth and throat. Her eyes burned. She ran to her car door, opened it, threw in the file folders and her briefcase, and got in. The adjacent vehicle revved its engine again and a visible white cloud entered Karen's car before she slammed the door. Coughing and choking on the noxious vapor, which hung inside her car like a little patch of fog, she backed out.

When she stopped her car to shift into forward gear, the rusted-out pickup truck with the unmuffled engine pulled out of its space, backing toward her. When she realized the pickup truck was not slowing down as it approached, she hit the horn. The other driver, the bearded man who had knocked her file folders from her hands, braked, and their bumpers made contact. It was only a slight jolt, but it sent a sharp pang through Karen's neck. The other driver revved his engine twice, rolled down his window, gave her the finger, and drove away.

CHAPTER
16

Wednesday morning the city of Jefferson plunged into subzero temperatures, the kind of midwestern morning that sapped car batteries and California expatriates of all energy. When Karen arrived at her office, red-cheeked and breathless, she had five voice mail messages waiting for her. Her outside attorney, Emerson Knowles, had called to discuss the complaint in the Conkel lawsuit filed by Ben McCormick. Anne Delaney had called to discuss the results of her investigation into the cath lab cart and who had access to it prior to Larry Conkel's biopsy. Two salesmen had called, one offering office copiers and the other pushing life insurance. Her mother had called, inviting Karen to lunch.

Before returning any of the calls, Karen stared out the window of her office for five minutes and tried to sort her priorities. She felt beleaguered. Getting to the bottom of Larry's death seemed her most urgent piece of business, emotionally, at least. Defending Ben McCormick's lawsuit was at the top of the list, job-wise. She got mildly panicky thinking about the dilemma of whether to report the clinic billing fraud to the federal authorities without knowing what was in Larry's missing file. And what to do about Joe's illegal MRI scam? It all seemed too much at once. She was still rattled by her encounter with the threatening man in the pickup truck the previous evening. She had tried to brush it off, not even bothering to complain about it to Jake. But now it was eating at her. Was the episode somehow connected to one or more of the other matters?

Karen returned her mother's call first. The two agreed to meet at the Casa del Sol Restaurant at noon.

Karen returned Anne's call next. As usual, Anne wasted no time before getting down to business.

"I have a complete scenario from the time the cath lab cart was restocked until the cardiologist and the cath lab team arrived to set up for Larry's biopsy. The head cath lab nurse set up the cart after the last procedure on Saturday. The nurse insists the cart was fully stocked the last time she saw it. She called Security from the floor when she finished, and Max Schumacher came and locked up ten minutes later. The cart was locked in the cath lab until Security unlocked it just after 5:00 A.M. Monday morning."

This meant that if anyone other than the head cath lab nurse planted the defective catheter, he or she either did it Monday morning before Larry's procedure or entered the lab while it was locked.

"Who has keys to the cath lab?" asked Karen.

"Only Security. Max has one key and the only other key is in safe deposit."

"What about master keys?"

"There's one master for external door locks and one for internal locks on offices, storage rooms and maintenance supply closets. The masters don't open the cath lab."

"Who has keys to the safe deposit box where the other key was kept?" asked Karen.

"Max Schumacher and Joe Grimes." Anne described the steel door and sophisticated lock on the cath lab and the lack of a window or other means of entrance to the lab. "Nobody entered the lab until Dr. Bernard arrived just before 7:00 A.M. to set up for

126

Larry's biopsy. The head cath lab nurse arrived at 7:00 A.M., and the other nurses and the techs within a few minutes after."

Karen scribbled notes furiously. "How do we know nobody entered the lab between 5:00 and 7:00?"

"Hey," Anne gloated, "for once I'm a step ahead of you. Fortunately, the cath lab is at the end of the main hall on the first floor of the new wing. That hall is covered by one of the security cameras. It's about one hundred and fifty feet away, but anybody coming or going from the cath lab would be picked up. I was up late last night viewing the tape. Max unlocks the cath lab door at 5:05 A.M. Bernard enters at 6:55 A.M. A lot of people walk by in the interim, but nobody goes in the cath lab. I've made a chronological list of everyone who walked past the lab during that time period."

Karen commended her. "You're a virtuoso, Annie." So no one had entered the cath lab after it was unlocked until Dr. Bernard showed up to do Larry's biopsy. Karen paused from her note-taking and felt the tip of her nose with the back of her hand. Her nose was like ice. The day before it had been so hot in her office she had been sweating. "God," she said, "we can afford computer upgrades every six months, but the heating system in this place is from the Pleistocene Era."

Karen paused again. "Annie, doesn't it seem odd to you that Bernard was the first to arrive at the cath lab? Usually the nurses and techs get everything ready, then the patient arrives and is kept waiting until he's ready to give up and go home, and then the cardiologist breezes in and zips through the procedure."

"Yeah, it's unusual, but irrelevant. Couldn't affect the hospital's liability."

Karen thought for a moment. Anne was intelligent and excellent with details. She would be doing most of the fact-gathering. Most important, she was trustworthy. Karen needed an ally; she decided it was time to share her suspicions. "Anne, I want you to promise not to repeat what I'm about to say."

"Oh, I love secrets. Cross my heart. Let's have it."

Karen filled Anne in on the follow-up verbal report from Gilbert Austin, the engineer who had tested the catheter used in Larry's biopsy, including the fact that the condition of the catheter made it look as if the catheter had been intentionally sabotaged. She told Anne about Carl Gellhorn's opinion on the mismanagement of the case by the doctors. "So, Annie," Karen concluded, "I'm considering the possibility that Larry's death was not accidental."

With her free hand, Anne pulled a lock of hair into her mouth and bit down on it so hard a few ends broke off in her mouth. She scraped her tongue with her teeth and spit. "Oh geez, Karen. Why would anybody want to do that to Larry?"

"I have some theories on that, too." Karen gave Anne a brief synopsis of Larry's fraud investigation files. "Just wanted you to be open to the possibility that Larry was mur . . . that this was intentional, as you do your investigation."

"Thanks, Karen. Thanks a bunch."

"For sharing my secret?"

"No. For scaring the shit out of me."

After Anne hung up, Karen returned the call from her outside counsel, Emerson Knowles. Together they went through Ben McCormick's complaint in Paula Conkel's lawsuit line by line. Except for the allegation that Shoreview Memorial Hospital was a hospital, Emerson wanted to deny everything. Typical litigator, thought Karen. It came as no surprise to her that outside counsel like Emerson were happy to spend lots of time and their clients' money contesting every allegation in a complaint. After all, they got paid by the hour. But

Karen, as an in-house attorney who was responsible for the legal budget, was willing to concede that the sky was blue and the grass was green and limit the dispute to the points that really mattered. She persuaded Emerson to admit a few allegations, such as the address of the hospital and the fact that Larry Conkel was a patient there "on or about" November 21. They discussed McCormick's claim that the hospital was negligent in granting Dr. Bernard privileges to perform the biopsy. Karen jokingly suggested arguing as a defense that if the hospital should have known Dr. Bernard was unqualified, Larry, as the hospital's Chief Financial Officer, should also have known and therefore was negligent in selecting Dr. Bernard as his cardiologist. Emerson thought the idea had some merit, and Karen had to explain she was only joking. She then made a more seriously intended suggestion that Emerson send requests for Larry's medical records to St. Peter's Hospital and the other cardiologist who had seen Larry. She knew it was important to have as much information as possible about the health of anyone claiming malpractice, to determine whether other health reasons contributed to the injury. Then she and Knowles discussed the relief requested in the complaint.

"He's asking for $5 million for Larry's estate, another $5 million for Larry's wife, and $2 million apiece for each of the children. Twelve million dollars total. Plus $12 million in punitive damages."

Karen snorted. "If he wins it all, he'll have fun collecting. That far exceeds the entire liquid net worth of the hospital."

Emerson reminded her that State Mutual Insurance Company would pay any damages over $50,000. Karen told him about the notice from State Mutual voiding the hospital's malpractice insurance because its quality control program did not meet state requirements.

"Well, if worse comes to worst," Emerson said unctuously, "remember that Winslow & Shaughnessy has an excellent bankruptcy department."

"Emerson," replied Karen, "you're such a scream. I think I'll sit on your next bill for a few months before we pay it."

As soon as she put the receiver down, Karen groaned to herself. "Nice going," she muttered. "Alienate your lawyer at the outset of the most important case of your career."

Karen spent two hours doing legal research on the grounds for voiding malpractice insurance policies, but she made little progress. She was having trouble concentrating. She picked up the phone and dialed her home number.

"Y-y-yello," said Jake. Karen could hear Muddy Waters playing in the background.

"I need to talk about something."

"Spill."

Karen told Jake about the large, bearded man who had knocked the folders out of her hands the night before, then bumped her car with his pickup truck, and given her the finger. Jake used some of his comprehensive vocabulary of street argot to characterize the culprit, and Karen confessed her fears.

"Do you think he might have been deliberately trying to intimidate me? That somebody at the clinic knows I've seen Larry's files and is trying to send me a message?"

"Do you?"

"It definitely spooked me. Yes. I had the distinct feeling the guy was trying to scare me."

"Did he?"

"Yes."

Jake raised the issue of reporting the incident to the police.

"But what would I report?" Karen asked. "That someone was rude? Hard to make a police matter out of bumping the car and obscene gestures."

"Yeah, I suppose the boys in blue wouldn't consider it to be anything out of the ordinary," Jake replied, "but make sure you tell Schumacher in Security all about it. And Karen . . ."

"Hmm?"

"Be careful."

PART II

"You better watch yo'self."

—WALTER JACOBS, AKA LITTLE WALTER

CHAPTER
17

Karen drove cautiously over the slick city streets to meet her mother for lunch. The bridge over the Weyawega Flowage was particularly icy and treacherous, as the icicles hanging from the teeth of the concrete lions forewarned. She had to park three blocks away from the Casa del Sol, a formidable walking distance in a subzero windchill. She got to the table at precisely 12:00 noon, her nose running and cheeks bright red. Her mother was waiting at the table, a nearly finished Bloody Mary in front of her.

Elizabeth Decker was shorter than Karen, more round-shouldered. Her gray hair was dyed auburn and she wore more makeup than Karen, but it failed to conceal the deep creases around her mouth, the sagging skin around her gentle eyes, the crepe-paper wrinkles in her neck and forehead. Karen looked at her mother and saw her own cosmetic destiny.

The restaurant pickings in Jefferson were slim. The Casa del Sol was a franchise that served mostly American food, with a few Tex-Mex selections and Margaritas on the menu, and serapes and sombreros hanging on the beige stucco walls. Karen ordered refried beans and a taco. Elizabeth Decker ordered a club sandwich and another Bloody Mary.

Since it was the middle of a workday, Karen drank carbonated water with a twist of lemon, but she would have gladly downed a stiff drink. She felt agitated having lunch at a restaurant with her mother. It was a rare event, even rarer because it was not a birthday or Mother's Day. The painful conversation on Thanksgiving about Karen's failure to conceive was still a fresh injury.

Karen reassured her mother at length that the cervical collar was nothing serious. She was also required to explain that she did not have a cold; her nose was running from the frigid air outside. The two women complained about the weather for a while. Karen endured an update on her sister's children, including a detailed account of their respective Christmas lists. Pamela and the children were staying with Mrs. Decker for the holiday week.

"Pammy told me about your big argument with your father on Thanksgiving," said Mrs. Decker, sipping her second Bloody Mary. "I don't think children should be exposed to that sort of thing, do you?"

Karen let the hypocrisy pass. "No, Mom," she sighed. "I'm sorry, but Dad just puts me right up the wall. His chauvinistic remarks. And the way he's always putting down Jake."

"Karen, your father is neither stupid nor chauvinistic. He respects your career, and he has a lot of regard for Jake, too. He just doesn't understand the business with the music. And he's frustrated because you and Jake haven't had a child."

"Yeah, and he uses that against me every chance he gets," rejoined Karen, gripping her water glass tensely. "Just another item on the long list of ways I've disappointed him. Starting with the fact that I wasn't a boy, and you already had a girl. Now there's no one to carry on the Decker name."

"Oh, for heaven's sake, don't be ridiculous. You never disappointed your father. He doesn't care about the Decker name." Elizabeth finished the Bloody Mary and stared wistfully across the room. "Actually, I was the one who wanted a boy." She looked back at Karen. "Daddy was always proud of you. Remember when you won that Science Award in college? That big piece of crystal? He acted like it was the Nobel Prize."

"Yeah," said Karen, "and now it's holding down a pile of papers on my desk. Has all the value of a brick. Let's face it, Mom, Pammy was tall and beautiful, the All-American cheerleader, and I was the runt of the litter. Then Pammy comes up with the grandchildren. I don't blame Dad for favoring her, but that's no reason to hate me."

The waiter arrived with their entrees and poured a glass of white wine for Mrs. Decker. When the waiter left, she dabbed her lips with a white napkin and smeared lipstick onto her chin, a sure sign the drinks had kicked in. It seemed to Karen that her mother showed intoxication more obviously and more frequently than she used to.

"I cannot believe a smart girl like you would say such a stupid thing," proclaimed Karen's mother. "Now I'm going to end up telling you something no mother should ever tell her child." She reached a shaky hand toward Karen, then pulled it back. "Sweetie, don't you know Daddy always loved you more than Pammy? It wasn't intentional. He couldn't help it. That's the way it is with parents sometimes. Pammy was a lovely child, but it was obvious from infancy that you had what Daddy valued."

Karen held a forkful of refried beans poised in front of her mouth. "And that would be . . . ?"

Her mother took a gulp of wine. "The Decker *brain*," she announced, rolling the "r" in "brain" theatrically. "Remember how he used to pontificate about evolution and the primacy of the cerebral cortex, how he said that the hegemony of the human species on the planet proves the advantage of quality of offspring over quantity as a Darwinian strategy? At heart, the old windbag fancies himself a scientist. And you, my dear, are his legacy. That's why he's heartbroken about you not having a child." She took another gulp of wine. "Pammy's brood, bless their hearts, don't count. Except maybe to ten."

Karen chewed her beans quietly. She was astonished by her mother's revelation. Was Karen's interpretation of her family dynamics, the understanding that she had held for years, completely topsy-turvy? It certainly was by her mother's reckoning.

"Pammy sure doesn't see it that way, Mom. I always get the feeling she's lording it over me because she got the looks."

"She's not that shallow, Karen. Pammy may be a little defensive because she's jealous of your career. Remember how your dad stepped on her Hollywood dreams? She gets a part at the community playhouse now and then, but I don't think it gives her much satisfaction."

"She doesn't seem jealous. The way she's always bragging about her kids to me."

"Naturally. What's she supposed to brag about? You're the one with a good marriage—while she has Brett." She said "Brett" with undisguised disdain. "Of course she has to focus on the kids."

Elizabeth sipped her wine, while Karen used her fork to sort through the contents of her taco. Eventually, Karen asked her mother why she had suggested lunch.

"Your father has been diagnosed with prostate cancer," she said bluntly. "He needs your help, Karen. He would value your advice."

Karen was concerned. She agreed to call her father, but displayed skepticism that her father would listen to her advice.

"Dad doesn't think much of my ideas, Mom. He even blames me for your divorce."

"Ha!" blurted Elizabeth. "Pammy told me about that one. The idea that your feminist politics caused me to rebel. That's a hot one! Well, you can put it out of your head. Boredom and

menopause were better guesses. Just so you don't blame yourself, I'll tell you something else I shouldn't. And don't you ever
repeat it to anyone. Not your father, not your sister, not even
Jake. I left Daddy because I got interested in another man. You
girls were all grown up, and I took a gamble on something that
seemed promising. He was handsome and very successful. It
didn't work out, but there was no going back. As you know,
Gene is not the best forgiver in the world. But I don't cry over
spilt milk. That's just the way it is." Karen's mother finished
her wine and looked Karen in the eye. "When you gamble,
sometimes you lose."

Karen slowly lowered a forkful of refried beans to her plate.
Her appetite was gone. Whether this was caused by the dark
ring of grease congealing around the beans on her plate or by
something her mother had said, she was not certain.

When she returned to the office, Karen called the Office of
the Inspector General in Washington, D.C. She got the
name and telephone number of a deputy prosecutor who
handled Medicare billing fraud. Then, she sat and thought.
She could not turn Larry's files over to the feds until she
found file number 3, the file Larry's note said contained information about a hospital billing conspiracy related to the
clinic's fraud. She needed to know what was in that file. She
could not risk betraying her client to federal prosecutors.
But the hospital's possible involvement in the fraud was not
the only thing that held Karen back. She had no independent confirmation of the matters described in Larry's files.
She then realized that her indiscreet comment to Dr.
Bernard at the Ethics Committee meeting, in which she had

revealed her suspicions about the clinic's fraudulent billing practices, was actually liberating. There was no longer any reason to conceal her suspicions from the clinic doctors. Bernard had talked to Grimes about Karen's outburst at the Ethics Committee meeting. Bernard had undoubtedly also alerted the doctors involved. Karen rifled through Larry's files, selected a couple of claim forms and a newspaper clipping, picked up her telephone receiver and dialed. A receptionist answered.

"Jefferson Clinic."

"Dr. Norman Caswell, please." Dr. Caswell was the oncologist whose outlandishly excessive income had triggered Larry's investigation, the cancer specialist who billed for chemotherapy he never gave, and overprescribed chemotherapy to boost his earnings. And a dead ringer for Bela Lugosi. The receptionist informed Karen that the doctor was "with patients." She took Karen's name and extension. Dr. Caswell called back almost immediately.

"Karen," he said warmly. Karen started. Dr. Caswell had never called her by her first name before. Word must have gotten around that Karen was to be appeased. "How are you? I saw your father in the Oncology Center last week. How's he doing?"

Karen started again. God, she thought, keep this guy away from my father.

"Dr. Caswell, you really shouldn't discuss patients out of their presence. For all you know, my father hasn't even told me about his prostate cancer."

"Oh, you lawyers. What can I do for you?"

"Doctor, we have a payment dispute with an insurance company," Karen lied. "Could you tell me what your records show as the last two dates of treatment for William S. Dragos, patient number 176605?"

"Hold on a minute, I'll have my gal punch it up on the computer." Karen waited. "Here it is," said Dr. Caswell. "August 18 and September 5 of this year."

"And you remember Mr. Dragos coming for treatment on those dates?"

"Absolutely. Melanoma patient. Pleasant fellow."

"Thank you, Dr. Caswell."

Karen sat back and looked at the newspaper clipping she had removed from Larry's file number 4. It was an obituary for William S. Dragos, dated July 29.

CHAPTER
18

It was 5:00 P.M. Karen felt weary as she donned her down coat and wool hat, grabbed her briefcase with a mittened hand, and headed for the door of her office. The phone rang, and she hesitated before returning to her desk to answer. It was Anne Delaney.

"Got another medical staff problem for you, Karen."

"I don't need another one, Annie. My plate is full. I'm going home *right now*."

"It's another anesthesiologist imbibing his own anesthesia. You like those."

"Not tonight. I'm going home *right now*."

"It's Dr. Futterlieb."

A member of the Medical Executive Committee was in trouble. Futterlieb was the affable "frat boy" Karen suspected of having a drinking problem. She had to deal with it and silently cursed herself for answering the phone. She sat down, pulled off one mitten, and took notes.

"I just saw him yesterday," said Karen. "He's on the Medical Executive Committee. Who reported him?"

Anne relayed the report she had received from the head nurse in surgery. Late that morning a nurse had walked into an operating room and found Dr. Futterlieb passed out on the floor with an anesthesia mask strapped to his face. She removed the

142

mask and called the emergency room. Futterlieb recovered, but when interviewed by the Chief of Surgery, the anesthesiologist admitted he used anesthetic agents habitually. Dr. Futterlieb had developed the knack of self-administering the precise amount of gas necessary to keep himself suspended just this side of unconsciousness, an effect he found pleasurable and addictive. Over time, he needed to increase the dosage to achieve the same result. That day, he had given himself a bit too much gas and had gone under. He was lucky the nurse walked in. In another ten minutes he would have sustained permanent brain damage. In twenty minutes he would have been dead.

"I thought you'd better be involved right away," said Anne. "This is obviously a matter for the Medical Executive Committee, but I don't know what we do when the doctor in question is a member of the committee. If Futterlieb doesn't participate, which obviously he oughtn't, how do we determine what's a quorum, what's a majority? Do we count him or not?"

Karen said it did not make much difference. She was sure that all the committee would do was put him in an impaired professionals program.

"They can't do that," said Anne.

Karen, who assumed Anne was merely expressing surprise and disbelief, rhetorically asked, "Why not?"

"He's already in one," said Anne.

After waiting out a brief tirade from Karen, Anne added, "You're going to like this next part even better. The Chief of Surgery said we had to understand Dr. Futterlieb was not himself today. He had a very upsetting experience early this morning, in obstetrics."

"Judas priest, Annie! What the hell is an impaired anesthesiologist doing in obstetrics? Why would we allow that?"

Anne explained that Dr. Futterlieb had lobbied hard and successfully to stay on the "On Call" schedule for obstetrics.

Deliveries of babies were lucrative for anesthesiologists, because the hospital paid them a stipend to ensure round-the-clock availability of anesthesia services to women in labor. Consequently, all of the anesthesiologists fought for slots on the O.B. "On Call" schedule.

"So what was Futterlieb upset about?"

Anne explained that Dr. Futterlieb had made a serious mistake during a labor and delivery, one that was inexcusable. He had placed an epidural—a type of anesthesia injected between the mother's vertebrae to relieve labor pain—too high. As a result, the mother had convulsed, but had been successfully resuscitated.

"What about the baby?" asked Karen.

"The baby died," Anne replied quietly.

"I'm going home *right now*," said Karen.

Karen did not go home right then. Her car would not start. The same was not true of the rusted-out, unmuffled pickup truck driven by the overweight, bearded man who had given Karen the finger the night before. It roared past as Karen stood shivering in the dark parking garage, waiting for Jake to arrive with the jumper cables, again assailing her eyes and throat with noxious fumes. By the time Jake showed up and determined that jump-starting the Volvo would be ineffective since the battery had been stolen, Karen was fuming.

"I can't stand this place anymore! This hospital is an abomination, a hellhole, a . . ."

"A *bête noire*?" proffered Jake as he started the Mustang.

Karen laughed involuntarily. "Don't interrupt my dudgeon. I mean it, Jake. It's beyond the *pale*. It's not enough that the cabal at the Jefferson Clinic is treating people who aren't sick and billing Medicare for treating people who are dead, while Joe Grimes cooks up ever more Byzantine ways of dispensing payola. No. Now we have murderers sneaking around and rapists assaulting patients in their beds. What kind of a place is this?"

"Pretty normal place, I'd say," said Jake, lighting his first cigarette of the day. Karen waved the smoke away, scowling. Jake opened his window a crack and continued. "You've got about a hundred doctors on your medical staff. If a dozen of them are real miscreants, that's still only twelve percent. Not so bad. Half of the musicians I know are felons of some sort. Folks are flawed."

"Yeah," said Karen, "some even smoke cigarettes when they're supposed to be quitting. But rotten musicians don't hurt anybody."

"I've listened to some vocalists damn near killed me," retorted Jake.

Karen fished her parking card out of her purse and handed it to Jake. Jake inserted it into the automatic card reader and the wooden arm rose to permit their exodus from the garage. Karen glanced resentfully at the prime parking spaces reserved for the physicians.

The two rode in silence for several minutes through the neighborhood surrounding the hospital. It was composed mostly of older residential buildings—frame duplexes, dirty brick apartments such as the Traymont, where Larry had kept an apartment, and frumpy bungalows. One newer fast food restaurant served refugees from the hospital cafeteria and the employees of the small, grimy factory planted in the middle of the neighborhood before the city adopted a decent zoning ordinance. Other than the new wing of the hospital and the hamburger franchise, the only contemporary building Karen

145

and Jake passed on the way home was the gleaming postmodern edifice of the Jefferson Clinic. Just past the clinic, they drove through an old industrial area, where a dozen haphazard smokestacks sprouted cloudlike plumes that glowed red and purple from the remnants of the sunset. Sandwiched between the timeworn factories were rows of narrow, clapboard Victorian-style houses, their open front porches bespeaking a more congenial era, before decks and patios were concealed in the rear. Nearly every other street corner maintained a tavern, the kind that offered shots and tap beers. Karen had heard Jake perform in at least half of these bars and had learned never to order a martini in one.

Looking at the sooty, rusting factories where they made machine parts, tools, paper goods, and farm implements, it occurred to Karen that the only thriving businesses in Jefferson were hooch, hamburgers, and health care. No high-tech startups in Jefferson, no entertainment industry, no home offices for multinational conglomerates. Still, Karen realized that although they had little glamour and got little media attention, places like Jefferson were where most of the work of the country got done.

As they neared home, she spoke. "You know, Jake, it's not just the miscreants, as you call them, that drive me nuts. Granted, those are a small minority. It's the incompetents."

"Out of a hundred docs," observed Jake, "forty-nine are going to be below average."

"But they all have years of medical school, years of residency training."

"Sure," replied Jake, "and I know guys who've had twenty years of instrumental lessons who can't blow a line to save their asses. Not everything can be taught. Does four years of college and three years of law school guarantee you a lawyer knows his torts from his tuchas?"

146

Karen conceded the point, but she still sulked. "People trust hospitals. They expect us to take care of them."

Jake extinguished his cigarette. "Maybe they expect too much. They don't want to think that the doctors are just imperfect human beings out to score some jack like everybody else. The thought that a doctor might be crooked or incompetent is too scary. Same way people don't want to think cops are subject to the usual human frailties. It makes people feel too helpless."

"And the doctors make it worse," Karen declared, "by using jargon that laypeople can't understand."

"Yeah, like lawyers don't do that," quipped Jake. "If your doctor or lawyer says something you don't dig, you should make them explain it until you do. It's your nickel, and it's your neck."

"I know. You're saying the patient is responsible for his own care. I agree. But it still infuriates me that the good physicians don't do anything about the quacks."

Jake pulled his rusted-out Mustang into their driveway. "Understandable, though. It's like a fraternity. Makes them all more secure if they stick together. It's another way they're like the cops."

Jake turned off the engine. He touched the tips of his missing fingers. Karen knew he was remembering terror and blood, his father carrying him on foot to the doctor's house. "Another way doctors are like cops. If you ever really need one, you never forget it if one comes through for you. Speaking of cops, do you want to report the ripped-off battery?"

"No. They'll just make out a report and tell us to file a claim with our insurer. I'll talk to Max about it."

"Did you tell Max about the guy who rammed your car and gave you the finger?"

Karen squirmed in her seat. "I forgot."

147

Jake gave her a skeptical look.

"I'm embarrassed to talk to Max," said Karen, "since you had your dude-to-dude talk with him."

"You're gonna have to get over that," said Jake.

"I know," said Karen. "I'll tell him tomorrow."

"Are you sure you're okay?" said Jake.

Karen nodded, but her face still was troubled. Jake studied her expression, and picked up her left hand. "What is it? Spill."

"We killed a baby today," she said. Tears rolled down her cheeks. Her infertility seemed to have intensified her response to such misfortunes.

"I'm sorry, sweetheart," Jake said gently. "I really am."

The phone was ringing when Karen and Jake opened the front door. Karen tracked slush across the beige carpeting and dropped her briefcase to the floor. She picked up the receiver with her mittened hand.

"Hello? Hello? . . ." She listened briefly and then banged the receiver down.

"Who was that?" asked Jake.

"Just some Good Samaritan calling to tell me not to do anything stupid."

CHAPTER
19

Her neck accented with pearls since she had discarded the cervical collar, Karen sat at her computer terminal Thursday morning composing a letter to Charles Packard, Deputy Attorney, Office of the Inspector General. She intended to summarize the contents of Larry's files and her own conclusions. Karen was a slow, hunt-and-peck typist, but the alternative would have been to have Margaret type the letter, which would have been the equivalent of reading it over the hospital PA system. Karen was not yet sure if she would ever send the letter.

The previous night, she and Jake had talked at length about personal responsibility. Karen had described the snarl of conflicting duties in which her job had ensnared her. Her ethical duty as an attorney, her duty as a hospital employee and Joe's subordinate, her duty as the friend to whom Larry had entrusted his secret, and her duty as a health care professional appeared irreconcilable. Viewed from one perspective, she had no choice but to report the clinic to the Inspector General. From another, she was absolutely prohibited from reporting. Jake, who was usually helpful, failed to come up with any answers. Instead, he exhorted Karen to remember that it was "just a gig." He also referred to an element of the "Eightfold Path of Buddhism" which pertained to occupational duties: "Right Livelihood."

"It means you have to try to make a living without hurting anybody or anything," Jake had explained. "It's harder than it sounds."

Karen had awakened too early Thursday morning, feeling annoyed with her husband.

She decided to keep her options open for the time being. She would draft the letter to the Inspector General, keep looking for file number 3, and continue to investigate Larry's death. At 9:00 A.M. Joe Grimes called. He asked Karen to meet with him at 10:00 A.M. about the MRI project.

As soon as Karen hung up, her telephone chirped again. It was sleazy Lou Chambers, the attorney for Dietrich Heiden, the patient who said Carson Weber assaulted him on Thanksgiving night. Chambers reminded Karen of his demand for medical records and incident reports. "You can pick up the medical records during regular business hours," she told Chambers. He could try to subpoena the incident reports, but Karen advised him that the hospital would bring a motion to have the subpoena quashed.

"We'll see about that one, Ms. Hayes. Also, I wish to notify you of another matter."

Karen heard Chambers belch. "My services have been retained by one Steven Linder to bring an action for damages resulting from an assault upon his person whilst he was a patient in your facilities."

Damn, thought Karen. There goes any chance of keeping the second sexual assault victim from finding out about the first one and using it against the hospital.

"How did Mr. Linder happen to select you as his attorney?"

"That would be privileged, Ms. Hayes."

"You know the hospital has no involvement in Mr. Linder's claim, Mr. Chambers. The alleged assailant was another patient whom Mr. Linder invited into his room."

"We'll see about that one, too, Ms. Hayes."

Karen tried to put Lou Chambers and his lawsuits out of her mind so she could make some headway on her report to the Inspector General. Before she had typed a single sentence, she received another call, this one from the hospital's outside attorney, Emerson Knowles. As Karen had instructed, he had delivered requests for Larry Conkel's medical records to St. Peter's Hospital and Larry's first cardiologist. He would call Karen Friday to let her know if those records provided any new information.

Within a minute after Emerson hung up, Karen's work on the letter to the Inspector General was again interrupted, this time by her secretary. Margaret stood nervously in the doorway clutching a long document covered with tiny print.

"Mrs. Hayes," she said meekly, "I need your help on a legal matter. A personal legal matter."

"What is it?" asked Karen, cutting herself off before she added "this time." Over the years, Margaret had come to her for help on small legal matters so many times Karen felt like she had two clients, the hospital and Margaret.

"My lease," said Margaret, stepping quickly to Karen's desk and handing her the document. Margaret settled her emaciated frame into a guest chair without waiting for an invitation. "I just renewed it for a year, but now my boyfriend wants me to move in with him. I don't think I should have to pay rent if I'm not going to be living in my apartment anymore, but the landlord says I'm obligated for the whole year even if I move out. Is that right?"

Karen did not relish helping someone break a lease for no good reason, another of the distasteful legal favors Margaret often requested. Once, Karen had persuaded a department store owner not to press shoplifting charges against her secretary, even though the storeowner had Margaret on videotape shoving a handful of string bikinis into her sweatpants. On another occasion, Karen settled a dispute between Margaret and a college student who

151

was upset to learn that the odometer of the secondhand Plymouth he had bought from Margaret had been tampered with. Karen had helped Margaret beat several traffic tickets, including one for drunk driving. Karen always had misgivings about helping, but it was hard to say no to someone who could make Karen's job a lot harder. Margaret was not above using the subtle art of secretarial blackmail. If Karen resisted Margaret's requests, Karen's correspondence would be typed more slowly and less accurately and Karen's guests would be received even less politely. "I should have fired her long ago," Karen thought.

When she had first encountered Margaret's passive-aggressiveness, she dealt with it head-on, reporting instances of poor performance on Margaret's evaluation form. The Director of Human Resources discussed the evaluation with Margaret, and Margaret retaliated by misfiling several important documents. Karen was up all night finding the papers needed for a 7:00 A.M. closing. Unless she was prepared to fire her secretary, and it seemed too late now, Karen realized she would have to continue to accommodate Margaret.

Karen always made something of an attempt to avoid giving Margaret free legal services by instead giving her advice on how to live her life so she wouldn't need the legal help. Pay the shoplifting fine and stop shoplifting. Give the college kid his money back and sell the Plymouth with an accurate mileage statement. But her advice fell on deaf ears. Margaret apparently suffered from some congenital, systemic condition that disabled her from dealing off the top of the deck. Telling Margaret to play it straight did no more good than telling her to eat better or change her eye color. Her deviousness seemed to be hardwired.

Karen gave it another try, anyway. "Are you sure you want to give up your apartment?"

"Sure, I'm sure. I can save a lot of money splitting rent with Marty."

"How long have you been seeing Marty?" Margaret went through boyfriends like pantyhose.

"Long enough."

"Then why did you renew your lease?"

"The opportunity to move in with Marty just came up, right after I signed my renewal."

"How?"

Margaret narrowed her eyes and looked at Karen as if she was about to say "none of your goddamn business," but stopped herself. Instead she said, "His . . . brother was living with him, but he suddenly moved out."

"So why the rush? Why not wait a couple of months before making such a big change?"

Margaret tossed her waist-length hair and repositioned her bony hips in the chair. "Marty can't swing the rent by himself," she said. "I'll miss the opportunity if his . . . brother wants to move back in."

Karen could tell Margaret was lying. Probably met this Marty about a week ago. But nothing could be accomplished by continuing the cross-examination, except inducing Margaret to go on one of her impromptu strikes. And she knew the files more accurately than Karen ever would.

Karen scanned the lease. It took her less than a minute to find a way to break it.

"This lease is unenforceable," she said. "It contains a *cognovit* provision." This provision was not only unenforceable, but its use prevented the landlord from enforcing the entire lease. Karen was amazed that some landlords continued to use it, apparently out of habitual nastiness.

She handed Margaret a ballpoint pen and a pad of lined paper. "Take a letter," she instructed and proceeded to dictate a letter to the landlord that told him where to mail the security deposit and, in polite legal language, where to put his lease. "You can kiss your security deposit goodbye, Margaret," she said, "but you can stop paying rent. The landlord won't take you to court. Just get your stuff out before he gets this letter, or he'll probably lock you out. Good luck with the move."

Margaret thanked Karen a bit offhandedly and darted from the room. Karen felt the same prickly remorse she always felt after helping her secretary.

At 10:00 A.M., Karen brushed out her hair, touched up her makeup, grabbed a pad of paper and a pen, and walked the length of the hall to Joe Grimes's office. When she was ten feet from the door, she detected the putrid odor of cigar smoke. Ed Bernard was there.

"C'mon in, Karen," announced Joe, "we're just getting started."

Joe was behind his desk, wearing a black suit, a gray dress shirt, and a solid black necktie. The monochrome look, very trendy, very Joe. Ed Bernard and Leonard Herwitz were seated in the two upholstered guest chairs in front of Joe's desk, Bernard in wrinkled blue surgical scrubs and Herwitz in a crisp white lab coat. Karen was relegated to an odd little Frank Lloyd Wright–type teak chair that appeared to be designed to be occupied by a rhesus monkey. As she arranged the skirt of her gray dress and awkwardly sat down, a glimpse of the clay urns sent a shudder through her.

The three men appeared to be in good spirits. Karen noticed three empty, plastic champagne flutes on Joe's desk.

"Getting an early start on New Year's Eve?" asked Karen.

Joe chuckled. "I thought a little celebration was in order. Karen, I want you to start drawing up contracts for the three radiologists from the clinic, and Drs. Bernard and Herwitz, to provide consulting services to the hospital on the selection of the MRI equipment, for $10,000 each."

Karen's face flushed and her left foot started to tap involuntarily on the tile floor. Joe was going full speed ahead with the

154

illegal plan that Karen had overheard him describe to Dr. Herwitz while she was hiding in the urn. Joe wanted her to phony up some consulting contracts for the clinic to provide funds to seed its account with Dean Williams at Jackson, DeSalle. Then the clinic would receive fifty percent of the profits from the MRI acquired by a new hospital subsidiary, which would make a series of "unlucky" investments using Dean Williams as its broker. The investments in the clinic's account, on the other hand, would be stellar performers, and the whole scheme would be papered over with backdated confirmation slips.

The amazing thing was that giving the doctors a financial incentive to refer patients to the MRI would make the MRI so profitable that the hospital would come out way ahead, even though it was giving away half its profits up front. The only losers would be the patients who got MRIs they didn't need, and the people who would foot the bill—taxpayers and those paying health insurance premiums.

It wasn't just that Joe's plan was legally risky for the hospital. The deception and corruption involved, and the doctors' apparently gleeful acceptance of it, disgusted Karen, reminded her of a butcher surreptitiously adding sawdust to ground beef.

The three men smiled smugly and glanced at one another conspiratorially. Karen willed her nervous toe to stop tapping.

"So, Joe," she said, "that would be an even $50,000 going to the clinic, more or less simultaneously with the acquisition of the MRI. That about it?"

Joe confirmed. Dr. Herwitz asked, "Is there a problem with that, counselor?"

Karen explained that an IRS audit or Medicare investigation of the MRI program would undoubtedly sweep together all contemporaneous transactions between the hospital and clinic. Overpayment for consulting services would be easily exposed.

Dr. Bernard chewed on his cigar. "Don't you lawyers have anything better to do than make trouble for people who are trying to save lives? For Christsake! If it gets an MRI into this hospital, that should be enough."

"Well, it's not enough," responded Karen. "I'm not trying to make trouble, I'm trying to avoid it. I'm just telling you what the law is."

Dr. Bernard uncrossed his legs and recrossed them. "The law, which is created by a bunch of other lawyers! Why do we have lawyers telling us what we can and can't do? It's ruining the practice of medicine. Why don't you pass some laws that make it harder for lawyers to make a living for a change?"

"Dr. Bernard, I'm not in the legislature. I don't make the laws."

Joe intervened. He said it was nothing to get excited about. The doctors would each document forty hours of consulting services, and a rate of $250 an hour could easily be defended.

"You've told us the law, Karen," said Joe. "That's your job. We can make the business decision to accept the risk. It's not much of a risk, if you ask me. So just do the documents. We'd like drafts before Christmas."

Karen clenched her jaw. She had explained the legal problems, Joe understood them, and he was plunging ahead. She was out of ammunition.

Dr. Bernard regarded her through narrowed eyes and cigar smoke. "I'd like to know if she's found any time between her attacks on the medical staff to do anything about this bullshit Conkel lawsuit. I thought the hospital was going to keep the doctors out of the case. That so?"

"So far, only the hospital has been served," said Karen. "I'd be surprised if it stayed that way. Ben McCormick usually sues everybody who is within a hundred yards of the plaintiff at the time of the injury."

"But in this case," insisted Dr. Bernard, "there's no way anybody can fault the doctors. How can we be responsible if the hospital furnishes us with defective catheters?"

Joe played with his vertical-blind remote control while Dr. Herwitz pretended to read the label on the champagne bottle. It was in French. Karen knew Bernard's question was rhetorical, but she elected to answer it anyway.

"For starters, you might be responsible if you mishandled the catheter, or if you mismanaged the care of the patient after the catheter broke."

Dr. Bernard wrinkled his brow. Veins stood out on his neck. "No one could possibly suggest any such thing."

"Sorry," Karen corrected him. "A cardiologist from Johns Hopkins reviewed the record and said exactly that."

Bernard and Herwitz sat bolt upright in unison and looked at Grimes. Joe fumbled the remote control for a moment. He rotated his desk chair to face Karen.

"I expressly instructed you not to bring in an outside expert on this case. This is insubordination."

Karen felt her momentum building. She relished rattling the conspirators a little.

"Relax, Joe," she said. "It was just a college friend of mine. There's nothing in writing. One thing he said, Dr. Bernard, is that he suspected you had never done a myocardial biopsy before. Is that true?"

Bernard dropped his cigar in a huge onyx ashtray on Joe's desk. His upper lip dewed. "I've done thousands of catheterizations," he muttered, his eyes darting about.

"I'm sure you have, doctor," said Karen, "but was Larry your first myocardial biopsy?"

Dr. Bernard looked back and forth from Grimes to Herwitz. There was a tremor in his hands. "What is this, a cross-examination? Why am I being subjected to this?"

Joe admonished Karen to drop the discussion, but Dr. Herwitz continued it.

"Did your friend say anything about the surgery?"

"Yes," Karen acknowledged, "he said the patient never should have been put on heart-lung bypass. He said that was a death sentence for a patient with Larry's condition."

Dr. Herwitz leaned toward Karen, his forearms on his knees, a woeful expression on his face. "You know, Mrs. Hayes, this is a medium-sized hospital in a small city. We're clinicians here, the physicians in the trenches. Don't assume we've been negligent because some ivory-tower pedant from Johns Hopkins is able to find fault with a snap judgment made in the heat of battle. It isn't fair."

Karen was unprepared for frankness, and it caused her to adjust her attitude slightly. Herwitz was *better* than Bernard. He seemed to care, and there was some merit to his argument.

"I'm not assuming anything, doctor," she said. "I just want us to be prepared for what Ben McCormick is going to make out of it if this was Dr. Bernard's first biopsy. He's going to argue that the procedure should not even have been performed here, that we should have sent Larry to a facility that does myocardial biopsies routinely. He's going to tell the jury that we willfully put Larry's life in jeopardy because of greed, because we try to hold on to every patient whether he or she belongs here or not. McCormick has used that type of argument before to get punitive damages."

Bernard exploded. "You see what I'm talking about? *That's* why malpractice premiums are sky-high! *That's* why we have to practice defensive medicine. You want to know why health care costs are out of control? It's you goddamn lawyers!" He jabbed at Karen with the butt of his cigar. She could feel the bile pouring into her bloodstream.

"You goddamn vultures," Bernard continued, "will say anything. You cast the foulest aspersions you can think of, the worst possible accusations . . ."

"Oh, no, Dr. Bernard," interjected Karen, "that's not the worst possible accusation. The worst possible accusation would be . . ."

"It's outrageous," Dr Bernard continued. "Joe, the hospital better get in front of me on this or . . ."

"The worst possible accusation would be that Larry's death was not an accident," Karen finished.

Dr. Bernard stared straight ahead, his mouth agape. "She's out of her mind. Grimes, your lawyer is a paranoid schizophrenic."

Joe clapped his hands together. "All right, enough already. We're not here to debate the merits of the American legal system. We're here to do a deal. Let's get back to business."

"Yes, let's," concurred Dr. Herwitz.

"Karen, any problem getting the consulting contracts for the doctors prepared by Christmas?"

Karen simmered. She dropped her chin and peered at Joe from under lowered, linear eyebrows. "I've got a pretty full plate right now. What's the rush?"

"There's a big price increase in the works for the MRI equipment. If we don't get the deal done soon, we'll have to pay more. That will screw up the pro formas and business plan for the program, and we don't have a replacement Chief Financial Officer yet who could redo them. So you can have until the end of the year, but no longer."

Sieg heil, mein Führer, Karen said to herself. "Will that be all?"

"Not quite," said Joe. "I'd also like you to do up a simple set of Articles of Incorporation and Corporate Bylaws for a new subsidiary of the hospital. Call it 'Shoreview Millennium Corporation.' Keep it simple, just a three-member Board of Directors. I'll be on the initial board, along with Dr. Herwitz."

Karen examined the three men, their self-satisfied smiles restored. Dr. Bernard took a few puffs on his cigar. Dr. Herwitz ran his thumb and index finger along the crease in his pants. Joe tipped back in his swivel chair, clasped his hands behind his head, and propped his feet up on his desk, crossed at the ankles.

"For the third director," said Joe, "we should consider someone from outside the hospital."

Temptation overtook Karen. A sly smile appeared on her lips. "How about," she suggested cheerfully, "Dean Williams from Jackson, DeSalle?"

Joe lost his balance momentarily and struggled to sit up. Dr. Bernard started coughing on his cigar smoke. Dr. Herwitz stared at her.

Enjoying their discomfiture, Karen couldn't resist. "Did I read your minds? We paranoid schizophrenics have psychic powers!" Now they knew that at least part of their secret was out, but they would never be able to figure out how she knew.

Joe blushed and, locking eyes with Dr. Herwitz, shrugged his shoulders. Dr. Bernard stubbed out his cigar. "Excuse me," he said, "I have to get back to patients."

He paused in the doorway, his upper lip sweating profusely. He pointed his index finger at Karen. "You've been prying into a lot of things that are none of your concern. One way or another, it's going to stop." He turned and strode down the hall.

Dr. Herwitz rose. "Joe, I'll be running along now, too. I think we'd better give this MRI thing a little more thought. I'll get back to you. Good day, Mrs. Hayes."

Karen headed for the door just behind Dr. Herwitz, intent on beating a quiet retreat now that she had undercut the physicians' confidence in Joe's MRI scheme.

"Karen!" Joe shouted. "We're not done. Close the door and take a seat."

Karen stopped and reluctantly returned. Joe stood up, walked around to the front of his desk, and sat on the corner, one foot on the floor and the other dangling, in his usual manner. He looked at her silently for several seconds.

"You realize, Karen, you may have just demolished the most important deal I've put together all year. Now, I don't believe in psychic powers, so I'll have to deal with Dean Williams and his big mouth in due time. He's seen his last piece of business from this hospital. But honest to God, I don't know what's gotten into you lately. You're obviously under a lot of stress. Is it Larry's death?"

Karen's feelings of triumph were fading quickly. She began to feel weary again. Joe was right. She *was* stressed.

"It's a lot of things," she conceded, "but Larry's death is the main thing."

"It was a real loss to the hospital," said Joe. "He was an able CFO. He'll be hard to replace."

Karen studied Joe's face. He seemed sincere; he was a good actor. She looked into his eyes, hoping to learn something from them when she ambushed him with her suspicions.

"Joe, I've been investigating Larry's death, as you know, in connection with the defense of Ben McCormick's lawsuit. The evidence I've collected thus far leads me to the conclusion that Larry was murdered."

Joe's face remained impassive, but as he moved to push himself up from his perch on the desk corner, he jabbed himself in the hand with his desk pen. Whether he was rattled because he was involved and afraid of being unmasked, or was merely reacting to the idea that one of his executives had been murdered, Karen couldn't tell. The ambush was a bust. Joe rubbed the sore spot on his palm and tilted his head slightly to one side. "You say you have theories for your ridiculous assertion?"

"Several. Someone who works at the hospital was almost certainly involved. Either someone who worked in the cath lab the Saturday before Larry died, someone who was involved in Larry's biopsy, or someone who had access to a key to the cath lab."

Karen continued to watch Joe's face carefully. He looked unbelieving but concerned. Karen went on. "Someone who had some technical knowledge about catheters, what the effect of heat on one would be. A doctor, or someone familiar with medical supplies." She paused, and looked Joe directly in the eye. "Or someone in administration."

Joe flushed, walked back around his desk, and sat down in his swivel chair. He pressed the tips of his fingers together and looked at his hands. He took a deep breath.

"Karen, you apparently have no idea how bizarre this accusation sounds. The stress is taking more of a toll on you than I thought. I really think you're coming unhinged. We can't have that right now when there are so many important deals in the works. For the sake of the hospital and your own sake, you need to take some time off."

"I've used all my vacation time for this year, Joe, but Jake and I have a week planned in March."

"No, Karen," said Joe with a bit more force. "I mean right away. You're going to take some time off immediately."

Karen felt a sharp pang in her stomach as her adrenal glands discharged. It hadn't occurred to her that Joe might freeze her out. She felt unprepared. "Like I said, Joe, I don't have any vacation time accrued. Maybe after the first of the year I could take a few days off."

"No," he blared. "Not after the first of the year. Now. Forget about accruing vacation time. You're taking a leave of absence until the end of the month. Frankly, right now I can't afford to have you running around blowing up important deals and pissing off the doctors. And now you're going to start getting everybody stirred up about an imaginary murder plot? Go home and enjoy the holidays, and forget about us down here. Have Margaret box up any files you're working on and send them over to me. I'll have Emerson Knowles pick up anything that can't wait until you get back."

Karen's mind scrambled for something to bargain with. She was surprised to discover how important it was not to be shut out before she finished her investigation into Larry's death.

"Margaret isn't familiar with the files I'm working on right now. I'll need some time to straighten a few things up." She sounded desperate to herself.

Joe waved his hand. "Okay, you can finish out the week, but that's all."

"It's Thursday, Joe," she pleaded. "I need more than one day."

Joe stood and walked the forty-foot length of his office. He held the door open, dismissing her.

CHAPTER
20

" S ecurity. Schumacher."

Karen could hear Max munching on something. She had worked into the lunch hour on her letter to the Deputy Inspector General about the clinic fraud. Time was running out simultaneously on her investigation into Larry's murder and her search for file number 3, the file she hoped would tell her whether she could ever send her letter. She fought the impulse to rush her work. If she hurried, she might miss something.

"Max. Karen Hayes. I need a favor."

"Sure, Mrs. Hayes," said Max. "You name it."

Karen listened for any hint of snideness in Max's voice, but failed to detect any. Apparently, he was going to let the episode in Joe's office pass without comment. Amazing what a couple of tickets to a basketball game could accomplish.

Karen explained that she wanted Max to check the safe deposit to make sure the extra key to the cath lab was there. If it was, she wanted him to take the key out of the safe and call her back. He called back in ten minutes.

"It was there all right. Got it with me. What next?"

Verifying that Max now had both copies of the cath lab key on him, she asked the security chief to meet her at the cath lab. They arrived at the door to the lab simultaneously.

"What's this about, Mrs. Hayes?" Karen observed that Max's gray crew-cut maintained perfect verticality on top. Although the hairstyle was enjoying a resurgence, she guessed Max's crew-cut dated back to the days of Southern Rose pomade. The dark circles under his eyes made his large, bulbous nose look like it was carrying saddlebags.

"Just a little experiment, Max." Karen had checked earlier to make sure the cath lab would not be in use from noon to 1:00 P.M. Now she asked Max to lock the door to the cath lab and try both keys on it. Both worked. Then Karen tried the large steel key she had found in Larry's "Little Walter" mug. It didn't work. Karen thanked Max for his help.

"What did the experiment prove, Mrs. Hayes?"

"Nothing, Max," Karen allowed. "But it eliminated a few possibilities." The possibility that someone had stolen the cath lab key from safe deposit and replaced it with a dummy had been eliminated, but not the possibility that someone had borrowed the key from safe deposit and returned it. Karen had also eliminated one possible answer to the question of where Larry's second key fit, admittedly a long shot. Mostly, Karen figured, the experiment was just a failure. A waste of time she couldn't afford.

She took a few minutes to report the theft of her car battery to Max, who said he would write it up. She then returned to her office to brown-bag her lunch.

Twenty minutes later, Karen called Anne Delaney. She asked Anne to get the manifest from the medical waste disposal company for the waste collection immediately following Larry's biopsy. Medical waste disposal was expensive, and one of the reasons was that all the used junk had to be catalogued before it was carted away. Anne was to check how many catheters of the type used in Larry's biopsy were listed on the manifest; then, compare the manifest to the number of those catheters used in the cath lab that day, according to the schedule and the patient operative reports. Karen asked Anne to report on the results within twenty-four hours.

Anne was her usual cooperative self. "Be glad to, Karen, but why am I doing this?"

"I'm trying to determine whether good catheters were removed from the cart before Larry's biopsy, and then disposed of inside the hospital. It would narrow the field." Karen spoke rapidly. "I doubt that anyone would have planted the bum catheter on the cart, then put the good catheters in a waste disposal container right there in the cath lab. They would just have walked out with the good ones. Except perhaps Dr. Bernard, who could not have risked smuggling the good catheters out of the cath lab, not with the nurses and techs showing up five minutes after he got there. He would just have dumped them in the waste container. If either Grimes or Paula's friend Lisa Fuller planted the bad catheter, they could have disposed of the good catheters either inside or outside the hospital."

"Whoa, Seabiscuit!" ordered Anne. "You're way ahead of me. You're taking this murder thing seriously, aren't you?"

"I sure as hell am."

"Okay. I understand the reason Bernard is on your list of suspects. Paula, too, I guess. The estranged spouse has to be on the list. But Grimes?"

"It's a little complicated, Annie, so bear with me. I'm certain that Larry believed he had kept his fraud investigation into the Jefferson Clinic a secret. Otherwise he never would have allowed Bernard to do his biopsy. But somehow Herwitz found out about it, and I think Bernard knows, too. If two doctors at the clinic know about Larry's investigation, there's no telling how many people know. Grimes, almost certainly."

Anne brushed some dandruff from her dark wool skirt. "All right," she said, "I'll get the disposal manifest and the cath lab schedule and compare numbers. But what's the big hurry?"

166

"Grimes is kicking me out," explained Karen. "After tomorrow, I'm on an involuntary leave of absence for the rest of the year. I won't have access to my office, to you, to Max, to anybody here. I won't be able to work on Larry's case, the report to the Inspector General on the clinic billing fraud or any other hospital business."

"I can't believe Joe would do this. We can't get along without you for a month."

"You'll survive, Annie. But I have the feeling a month from now any evidence bearing upon Larry's murder will be buried, or fouled up beyond all recognition. I hate to ask this of you, Annie, but I need you to do one more thing on this."

"Shoot."

"Review the main hall security camera tape for the entire time from when Max locked up the cath lab the Saturday afternoon before Larry's biopsy until Dr. Bernard arrived Monday morning. See if anybody goes in the lab at all. You can view it on fast forward, but even that way it will take hours."

With characteristic unselfishness, Anne agreed to perform the tedious task. She asked, "Have you thought about going to the police?" Karen had, but sidestepped the question by insisting that she had too little to go on, and that it would be irresponsible to bring a lot of bad publicity down on the hospital on the basis of mere speculation.

Karen didn't tell Anne that she was afraid—afraid of what she did not know and how it might hurt her or someone else. She did not tell Anne that an hour earlier, she had tried a key she had found in Larry's office in the door of the cath lab, because she thought that Larry could have committed suicide in a manner that would leave his life insurance benefits intact for his family. She did not tell Anne that she had by no means completely eliminated the possibility that some nurse or tech had resterilized the catheter and lied about it afterward. Karen didn't want to sic the police on someone who had merely made a mistake. Nor did she tell Anne that inviting in the authorities might start a chain reaction that would end in the demise of the hospital.

She didn't want to be the bull in a china shop. She wanted to do her job so as not to hurt anybody. Right Livelihood. Jake and his damn Eightfold Path. He was right; it was harder than it sounded.

CHAPTER
21

In early December darkness cloaked the city of Jefferson before the end of the business day. Karen turned off the lights in her office and looked out into the cold night. A lone streetlamp glistened from hundreds of tiny icicles clinging to the branches of the sugar maple outside her window. The evening was frigid, but still. The smoke from a nearby factory rose straight up, while a light snow fell straight down, as if in reply. Hospital employees who could not afford spaces in the parking garage filed out the front door, bundled in coats and scarves and parkas, cursing the long walk to their street-parked cars and praying that their door locks and gas lines would not be as frozen as their toes.

Since her aborted visit to Larry's apartment in the Traymont across the street, Karen had figured out which window belonged to Unit 207, and she had checked it for light each evening. The apartment had been dark since she left it on Monday. Apparently, whoever was in Larry's apartment had been as surprised as she was and had not returned. She still had to take her best shot at locating file number 3, and Larry's apartment was the most likely location. She removed from the center drawer of her desk the large steel key she had found in Larry's office and put it in her coat pocket. Then she picked up the receiver of her telephone and dialed.

"Y-y-yello."

Karen could hear John Coltrane riffing in the background, playing a song she loved, but couldn't remember the name of. "Hi, honey, it's me. I've got an errand to run, I'll be a little late. Can supper wait?"

"Sure, no problema," said Jake. "We're just having leftover bean soup and fresh-baked bread."

"You baked bread?"

"No. Bartlein's Bakery baked it. What time do you want me to come and rescue you? And where—Grimes's office or the parking garage?"

"That's hilarious, sweetheart," Karen retorted. "I'll only be a half hour late. And after tomorrow, you'll have me home twenty-four hours a day for a month. Grimes gave me the hook. I'm on an involuntary leave of absence for the rest of the year."

"Paid?"

"Fat chance. I've got no union here, and no contract. Joe wasn't in a charitable mood."

"Bummer. But what the hey, it'll be a gas to have the break. We're getting good snow this year, we can get in some skiing."

"Sure. By the way, Jake, have you noticed that absolutely no one with an intact brain says 'bummer' anymore?"

"Yeah, I have. Bummer."

The click of Karen's heels on the terrazzo floor echoed down the dark, high-ceilinged hallway of the Traymont's second floor. The musty odor of the hallway was partially masked by the smell of Italian cooking emanating from one of the units. Karen checked the peephole of Unit 207 and put her ear to the door. Seeing no light and hearing no sound, she put the steel key from Larry's office in the lock and turned.

It opened.

Feeling furtive, Karen entered and flipped a light switch. She closed the door behind her quietly.

The apartment was a small efficiency unit, just one room about fifteen by twenty. It had thick, dark oak moldings, dull hardwood floors without rugs, and outdated white appliances. The furniture looked like it came with the place. Although the room was less cluttered than Larry's office, in front of the mullioned window was a folding table holding an elaborate assemblage of computer components. One area of the folding table, which was cleared of computer components, had a solitaire hand laid out on it. Someone had left in too much of a hurry to finish the game. Karen noticed a red Queen that could be moved to an open black King heading one of the columns of cards. She resisted the urge to intervene.

There were no file cabinets in the room. Karen hurriedly checked the chest of drawers, the kitchen cabinets, and the pull-out drawers of the end tables. No file folders. She checked the closet, which was half-empty. No folders.

"I'm going too far," she said aloud as she pulled the cushions off the convertible sofa.

After fifteen minutes of searching the small room, she concluded that file number 3 was not there. On her way out, she noticed a key chain with two identical brass keys hanging from a hook in the kitchen area, directly below a wall-mounted shelf holding coffee mugs. The mugs were adorned with the logos of various prescription medicines—the sort of thing pharmaceutical companies gave away to doctors to promote brand-name drugs. The keys were the type used for interior door lock sets, the kind people had on their bathrooms.

Remembering what Lisa Fuller had said about Larry having a locked room at his house—a possible location of file number 3—Karen removed the keys from the hook and put them in her coat pocket. As she did so, she observed a curled bank check standing up in one of the coffee mugs on the wall shelf above the hook. She took the check out of the mug. It was drawn on an account of the Jefferson Clinic and made payable to Emergency Medical Services Corporation. She returned the check to the coffee mug, turned out the light and left.

Returning to the hospital parking garage, Karen could see from thirty feet away that the driver's side window of her Volvo had been smashed. She started to run toward the car, then stopped as a jolt of apprehension passed through her. She looked around and listened. She saw no one, heard nothing. She skulked toward the car, glancing from side to side. When she got to the Volvo, she could see that the front seats were covered with broken glass. The driver's door was unlocked. She opened it. On the driver's seat was a frozen lump of what appeared to be human excrement.

"Oh, jeez," exclaimed Karen, making a face of revulsion. "What kind of sick bastard . . ." She walked around the car and unlocked the front passenger's door. Wrinkling up her nose, she reached inside for her cellular phone. It was gone. "Son of a bitch," she commented, and trotted out of the garage.

"Y-y-yello."

Jake was still listening to Coltrane. "Hi, sweetheart. I need you to come and rescue me after all. My car got vandalized again."

"Parking garage again? Good. That urn bit was a real *bummer*."

172

Karen was shivering and her teeth chattering when Jake arrived in the Mustang. She didn't wait for Jake to get out of the car; she barely waited for the vehicle to come to a stop before she leapt into the passenger side, hungrily seeking heat. Jake kissed her perfunctorily and got out to examine the Volvo. His eyes were full of concern when he got back in.

"You downplayed this one a bit, Alto," he said. "This isn't just vandalism. Somebody is threatening you."

"You think?"

As Jake looked at her, Karen thought the concern in his eyes had acquired a hint of reproach.

"Denial isn't your shtick," he said. "Yeah, I think the Good Samaritan who called to tell you not to do anything stupid is developing the theme. And I think you think so, too."

"Could be," said Karen.

Jake reached over and clasped her left hand. She could feel the warmth of his hand through the glove.

"You're shaking," he said.

"I'm cold."

"It's not that cold. You're scared."

She bit her lip. "I have to go to Paula Conkel's house. Let's go."

"You don't want to report this to the police?"

Karen sighed. "I thought about that while I was waiting for you. The police will view this like the other incidents, as property damage and minor theft. An insurance claim. I can't tell the police why someone might be threatening me. It's all confidential, and more significantly it's just conjecture at this point. I'm not in a position to bring the cops in on this, and besides, I'd lose control of it."

"I dig. But at least report it to Max."

"I will, tomorrow. Now, Paula's. Go."

CHAPTER
22

"You can't just sit in the car, Jake. Paula might see you out here and think it's strange."

Jake sucked in a deep inhalation of menthol-laced smoke and let it out slowly. "Let me get this straight. We're going to go in unannounced, and I'm supposed to rap with Paula while you go into Larry's locked room and rummage around for a file."

"Right."

"And she won't think that's strange."

"Get out of the car."

Jake shifted his feet nervously on the slate-blue carpeting in the Conkels' living room. The room smelled of potpourri. Jake hated potpourri. Karen had brandished Larry's room keys like a badge and blown past Paula with a display of feigned confidence. "Larry borrowed some computer software from me. He told me he took it home. I need it right away. Won't take a minute."

Paula stood with her arms crossed, her mouth in an irritated pout. She was wearing a red sweater with a sequined Christmas tree on it and green stirrup pants, looking quite festive for a grieving widow.

Jake made an attempt at conversation. "So, Paula, you following the Bulls?"

"I don't watch football," she replied coldly.

Jake put his hands in his pockets and rocked back and forth on his heels. He noticed that Paula had already moved Larry's beer mug collection from his office to a large armoire in the living room. "Say, Paula, this might not be a good time to bring this up, but there's a beer mug in Larry's collection I'd like to buy from you. It's the one with the picture of Little Walter on it."

"Little who?" snapped Paula. "Excuse me, I have to make a phone call."

"Sure," Jake said quietly. "Go right ahead."

A few minutes later, Karen stood in Paula's kitchen, a cordless phone in one hand and a leather briefcase in the other, being lectured by McCormick. She had not bothered to remove her coat. Her face was flushed, more from emotion than from being overheated.

"I strongly suggest—no, I demand—that you leave my client's premises immediately," bellowed Ben McCormick. "Your direct communication with her is a blatant violation of the canons of ethics. I won't hesitate for a moment to report you to the State Bar. Your license will be suspended before you're out of the driveway."

"Cool your jets, Ben. I haven't said one word to her about the lawsuit, which is the subject of your representation. I just stopped by to pick up some of the hospital's property, which as the hospital's attorney I have every right to do. Your client admitted me to the premises voluntarily."

"Fine. Now, as Mrs. Conkel's attorney, I am instructing you to leave the premises at once. In ten seconds you will be reported to the police for criminal trespass. One, two . . ."

Karen tried to remain cool. "You want to talk reports to the police? I'm giving serious consideration to reporting your client."

McCormick paused. "For what, pray tell?"

"How about criminal conspiracy and murder one?" said Karen. "I have some pretty good evidence that Larry's death was a homicide. A lot of it points to your client. Which not only puts Paula on the hot seat, it's a dandy defense to your lawsuit."

"This is preposterous!" McCormick exploded. "Threatening criminal charges to extort settlement in a civil action is another violation of the canons of ethics. You're getting in deeper all the time, Hayes. Just how do you imagine Mrs. Conkel carried off this dastardly deed?"

"She has two possible accomplices inside the hospital who had the opportunity to do it. Your client also has a perfect motive, in the form of a multimillion-dollar lawsuit, Larry's estate and life insurance."

McCormick chortled derisively. "You're out in left field, Hayes. While I agree the lawsuit against the hospital is worth millions, the notion that a spouse would set up a medical accident on speculation of a jury verdict is absurd."

"Then how come," asked Karen, "Paula showed up with you in tow the day after Larry's death? I know how long it takes to get an appointment with Ben McCormick."

Jake peered at Karen through the hallway and made slashing gestures with his index finger across his throat, cueing his wife to cut the conversation short. Karen waved him off.

"My office was already representing her before her husband's death, on a fraudulent conveyance claim. And that's the problem with the rest of your so-called motive. Mr. Conkel had advised his wife that he had cut her out of his estate plan months ago. He told her his life insurance benefits and estate all go into a trust, of which she is not a beneficiary."

176

Karen felt a hollow feeling in her stomach. This she had not anticipated. It certainly altered the landscape surrounding Larry's death. "Who are the beneficiaries?" she asked, failing to completely conceal a note of embarrassment in her voice.

McCormick cleared his throat. He seemed embarrassed, too. "We don't know yet. His records are a mess. But my associates are going through everything, page by page. We won't be surprised in probate court." McCormick recovered his tone of arrogant bluster. "And now, Ms. Hayes, I'm going to continue counting. Three, four . . ."

Karen smiled as Jake pulled the Mustang out of the Conkels' driveway. Finally, something in one of her investigations had gone her way. She popped open her briefcase. "I took a little abuse, but I got what I came for," she said. She held a reddish-brown folder aloft. "File number 3!" she exulted.

Jake shifted the Mustang into first and put his hand in his coat pocket. "I did okay, too," he said. He pulled his hand out and raised it. "The Little Walter mug!" he exclaimed.

CHAPTER
23

Karen woke up feeling contented Friday morning, in spite of her impending layoff. By the time she and Jake had arrived home the night before, enough snow had fallen for Jake to suggest doing something they had not done in years. They filled a wineskin with Chianti, a knapsack with bread and cheese, put on their cross-country skis, and went skiing in the city streets. It was one of many things Jake liked to do that Karen thought was insane before she tried it, but thought was delightful after. Late at night, with a snowstorm in progress, there were almost no vehicles moving about, and the streets made excellent trails. The blanket of fresh snow made the city eerily quiet. Karen and Jake skied through the center of town and over the high, arching bridge with its pretentious pillars and ridiculous lions. Then they broke a trail through the state forest, and picnicked beneath their favorite oak tree on the bluff overlooking the Weyawega Flowage. Afterward, they had showered together, unplugged the phone, and enjoyed long, slow coitus.

By midmorning, the sun was shining for the first time in two weeks, and the temperature rose into the fifties. Like the snow covering the hospital grounds, Karen's good mood melted away rapidly after she got to work. First, she had a disturbing conversation with Carl Gellhorn. When she called to ask the Johns Hopkins doctor to put his medical opinion about Larry Conkel's biopsy in writing, Carl was resistant and sounded uncommunicative. Karen wondered if she had accepted too readily the remarks Carl had left on her voice mail. She pressed him on what he had said.

"One of the doctors here suggested that it wasn't fair to apply the standards of a Johns Hopkins academic specialist to a spur-of-the-moment decision made by a small-town practitioner."

"There might be something in that," replied Carl coolly. "I don't know what standards might apply in the bucolic midwest." There was a slightly derisive tone in the way he said "midwest." "Plus, I had the benefit of knowing the outcome. And, after all, I wasn't there personally to observe what happened."

Karen was furious. Now Carl was hedging his opinion, an opinion on which she had relied. She had quoted his impressions to the Chief of the Medical Staff, at some risk to herself. Karen wondered if the "fraternity" phenomenon Jake had described was taking over, and Carl was protecting his fellow physicians. Or, had Carl just been hypercritical and perfunctory in his initial opinion?

"Carl, what are you saying? Your voice mail message said the case was grossly mismanaged. Was it or wasn't it?"

"It's not that simple, Karen. And don't get petulant with me. There is no upside for me in criticizing these doctors. Frankly, I thought it took a lot of nerve to involve me in this. All things considered."

Karen withered. So that was Carl's problem. She remembered him as having been so civil when, the night after her first date with Jake, she had broken off their relationship in the middle of a regular Saturday night date. He had remained polite and even friendly right through graduation. All these years later, she realized that she had misinterpreted their relationship. He was not truly a friend after the breakup. He was just waiting in the wings in case she became available again. Not a friend, but an indignant

179

jilted boyfriend nursing a grudge. It *was* presumptuous of her to ask him a favor. She felt mortified and betrayed at the same time. Carl had spouted off about the case to impress her with how much better he was than the doctors with whom she was associating. But when faced with the prospect of breaking ranks and actually providing evidence against his brethren, he headed for the hills.

"Okay, Carl. I won't need anything in writing. Send me a bill for your time."

"I will. Give my regards to Jake. Is he still playing the harmonica?"

Karen considered correcting Carl and explaining that what Jake played was properly called "blues harp," but she decided it did not matter if Carl thought he had scored a point in some meaningless competition. She ended the conversation quickly and got to work on Larry's files.

The remaining vestiges of her earlier good mood disappeared in a flood of frustration when she began to examine file number 3. It contained no memoranda, no letters, no reports, no text at all. Nothing to help explain its cryptic contents, which consisted of several sheets of white paper containing columns of numbers, dates, and dollar amounts. She was right back where she started, not knowing whether the file contained evidence of a conspiracy involving the hospital. If it did not, Karen had planned to promptly send off her report to the Deputy Inspector General. If it did contain such evidence, at least she would know the truth. But the contents of the file were indecipherable. Now she would have to confront Joe Grimes about it. The odds she could get anything out of him were remote, especially in view of the way he had maintained an inscrutable facade when she had ambushed him with her suspicions about Larry's death. And he had ordered her off the job.

By midmorning, Karen's frustration had reached fever pitch. She had not heard back from Anne. She had not heard back from Emerson Knowles. She thought about Grimes and his out-ofbounds business schemes, about Bernard, Caswell, and Herwitz and their flouting of the Medicare laws and the Hippocratic oath, about Futterlieb and his taste for self-anesthetization, about the Medical Executive Committee's tolerance of patient rape. She thought about the Medical Licensing Board in Illinois, which rarely in its history had taken away a physician's license for incompetence. She thought about Lou Chambers and Ben McCormick, members of her own profession who would do anything, say anything, to squeeze a fat fee out of someone else's tragedy. She thought about the medical suppliers who had figured out how to take advantage of a health care system so bloated and slack that they could charge $260 for a piece of plastic that cost $8 to make. She thought about the drug companies that gave away millions of dollars in free merchandise to physicians every year to promote sales, and medical equipment manufacturers that offered doctors everything from Caribbean vacations to prepaid prostitutes as rewards for pushing their products.

The worst of it was, Karen realized, that what she was seeing at Shoreview Memorial was commonplace, which was why the federal government estimated that the nation's health care system lost over $100 billion annually to criminal fraud, more than the entire health care budget of most countries. Health care providers collected over $30 billion a year by charging for services they did not even render, more than the booty purloined by all of the burglars, armed robbers, and auto thieves in the country put together. She pondered the American health care system that cost more than twice as much per citizen as those of most other countries. Yet the system managed to rank near the bottom among industrialized nations in such indices of effectiveness as life expectancy and infant mortality.

Corruption, waste, incompetence, apathy. Unbridled greed. Karen wondered whether it was time to call a Code Blue on the whole system.

181

At 11:00 A.M., Anne reported to Karen that the security camera tape showed no one entering or leaving the cath lab from the Saturday afternoon before Larry's biopsy until the following Monday morning. As usual, Anne had gone beyond the requirements of her assignment. Anne had checked the records of the Materials Management Department, the delivery forms from St. Francis Medical Supply, the disposal manifests and the cath lab schedule. Karen felt warmed and calmed to find someone else in the hospital doing her job and doing it well. Listening to Anne reminded Karen that there were actually a lot of people there who did their jobs well, like Max and Larry, and many of the nurses and doctors. They just weren't necessarily the ones who got the most attention.

According to the records Anne collected, the hospital had five dozen catheters on hand the Saturday before Larry died. A dozen were stocked in the cath lab that afternoon. Larry's catheterization was the only procedure performed in the lab Monday morning. But another dozen catheters were moved to the cath lab on Monday after Larry's operation.

"If I remember correctly," said Karen, "the cath lab nurse said there was only one catheter on the cart Monday morning. Apparently, she was right. That's why they had to restock Monday afternoon."

"Apparently," said Anne. "But wait, there's more."

Anne went on. Two catheterizations had been performed in the lab Monday afternoon and six on Tuesday. On Tuesday night, two events occurred: the medical waste disposal company picked up eight discarded catheters from the waste container, and twelve

182

catheters were returned to Materials Management by the emergency room staff.

"How did the catheters end up in the ER?" asked Karen.

"Nobody seems to know," said Anne. "They were just stuffed into a supply cupboard. Who knows how long they were there? I noticed the addition to stock in Materials Management, and when I asked they told me about how they had been found and returned to stock."

Since then, twenty procedures had been performed in the cath lab, twenty catheters had been collected by the waste disposal company, and another two dozen had been delivered to the hospital by St. Francis Medical Supply. Currently, fifty-six were on hand.

As Anne spoke, Karen quickly penciled a chart showing the number of catheterizations performed, how many catheters were in stock, how many were used, how many were discarded, and how many were left.

"It looks to me like the dozen stocked in the cath lab on Saturday afternoon walked out and ended up in another department's supply cupboard."

"Looks like," said Anne.

"But think about this, Annie. If I add the number of catheters we started out with, sixty, to the number delivered, twenty-four, I get eighty-four. Subtract the number the waste disposal company picked up, twenty-eight, I get fifty-six. That's the exact number we have on hand."

"Sure," said Anne. "It adds up perfectly. That's what you'd expect."

"No, it isn't," said Karen. "I'd expect one to be missing."

"Which one?"

"The one they used on Larry. Part of which is in safekeeping, part of which is at Jefferson Engineering, and the rest of which is still in Larry. Where did *it* come from?"

Before lunch, Karen called Max Schumacher to ask if there had been any reports of vandalism in the parking garage recently, other than the thefts of her battery and car phone. Max said no. Karen then asked Max to view the parking garage security camera tapes for the two afternoons when her car had been vandalized. If a rusted Chevrolet pickup truck left the garage before 5:30 P.M. on both days, Max was to take down the license plate number.

"Will do, Mrs. Hayes," said Max. "I'm surprised you're still using the garage at all, with the problems you've had."

"I'm not using it. I've got my husband's car today, parked on the street. Thanks for getting that service in to clean up the Volvo."

"Glad to help. If the pickup truck is on the security cam tape, do you want me to get the name of the owner?"

"You can do that?"

"I'm an ex-cop, Mrs. Hayes. I can get it tomorrow."

Max said he would be at the hospital Saturday afternoon. Karen asked him to call her at home.

Karen spent her lunch hour writing a letter to State Mutual Insurance Company disputing the contention that the hospital's malpractice insurance was void. She could feel herself rushing. Too many balls in the air this time. Drop one and they all hit the floor.

At 1:00 P.M., her telephone chirped. She answered.

"Legal Department. Karen Hayes."

"Mrs. Hayes, this is Leonard Herwitz calling." Karen felt a painful surge of adrenaline spurt into her bloodstream.

"How are you today?" asked the surgeon.

"I'm fine, Dr. Herwitz. What can I do for you?"

"Call me Len. I was just calling to see if I might be of any assistance to you on a matter you're handling."

"And that would be . . . ?"

Dr. Herwitz hesitated. "Karen, I understand you've been working on one of Larry Conkel's files. One having to do with the clinic."

Karen silently cursed herself for her rash remark to Bernard at the Ethics Committee meeting. As she had feared, Bernard and Herwitz had figured out she had Larry's files.

"I just want you to know," said Dr. Herwitz cordially, "that if I can answer any questions, be of any help to you, I would be happy to make time to discuss it with you."

Karen wasn't much good at dissembling, but she gave it a try.

"Dr. Herwitz," she said, "I really don't know what you're talking about."

Dr. Herwitz laughed nervously. "You are an intelligent young woman, Karen, and I admire your zeal. I'm talking about the report to the Inspector General you're working on."

Karen's neck suddenly began to ache again. Bernard and Herwitz could not possibly have deduced from her remark at Ethics Committee that she was preparing a report to the Inspector General. The only people she had told about it were Jake and Anne. She had worked on the report at her computer terminal, but, unlike Grimes's, Karen's computer password was a string of eight random letters, impossible to guess. She suddenly felt weary and slouched in her desk chair. There was only one possible explanation for Herwitz's knowledge of the report she was preparing, and it was depressing.

"Um, Doctor, assuming I am working on a report to the Inspector General, what assistance could you offer?"

"I might be able to help you understand some of the past practices of a couple of our clinic physicians, practices that I assure you have been discontinued."

"I think I understand those practices pretty well. And it's more than a couple of physicians, Dr. Herwitz."

"Len. The important thing now, Karen, is that we do what's in everybody's best interests. There's no need to destroy the careers of good men who made a few mistakes in the past, mistakes that can be corrected."

"That I don't understand," said Karen. "How can you correct having put over a hundred people through the misery of chemotherapy when it had no chance of doing them good?"

"A report to the government won't help those people now. It won't do the hospital any good." He paused for emphasis. "And it won't do you any good, either."

"Are you threatening me?"

"Heavens, no. Just the opposite. I'm suggesting it could also be in your personal best interest to work with the clinic on this problem, instead of against it. I mean your personal . . . financial best interests."

"You're offering me a bribe."

Dr. Herwitz sighed. "I was thinking more of a consulting fee, to help us with our legal compliance efforts. I must say, Karen, you have your mother's bluntness."

My mother? thought Karen.

Herwitz continued. "Don't reject the idea without thinking about it, Karen. I know how you and Jake have had to do without some of the things you've wanted, places you'd like to travel to that you haven't been able to afford. It can't be easy being the wife of a struggling musician."

Karen slumped further in her chair and put her hand on her forehead. "How do you know about my family finances, Dr. Herwitz? Or for that matter, my mother's bluntness?"

"Karen," he said warmly, "your mother and I were very close for a long time. We're still good friends. I'm sure if you would talk to her about your concerns regarding the clinic, she could give you some guidance. Please talk to her before you do anything that can't be undone."

Karen's jaw dropped. She remembered her mother's description of "the other man" as handsome, sophisticated and very successful. There weren't many men in a town like Jefferson who fit that description. Leonard Herwitz was one. So Herwitz was the heel who took Elizabeth Decker away from her father. What next?

Karen raised her voice. "Let's review the record. You rake in obscene amounts of money practicing mediocre medicine. A bunch of your boys get caught doing things worthy of Joseph Mengele, and instead of canning them on the spot, you cover it up. You try to bribe me, and then you try to hide behind my mother."

"One call to Joe Grimes," blurted Dr. Herwitz, "and you're out of Shoreview Memorial permanently." He lowered his voice. "Don't push me. I don't want to hurt you. It would break Elizabeth's heart."

Karen exploded. "*That's* something you would know about, wouldn't you? So you want me to help out the man who wrecked my mother's marriage and then dumped her?" She slammed the phone down.

Karen paced the length of her office several times, feeling slightly nauseated. Instinctively, she knew how Herwitz learned of her report to the Inspector General. But, as she turned the matter over and over in her mind, looking for explanations, none came to her. She composed herself and walked to the door.

"Margaret," said Karen, "I'll be making a very important call to Anne Delaney. Highly confidential. I don't want to be disturbed."

She closed her office door, leaving it ajar just a crack, as she called Anne.

"Annie, big news here," she whispered, walking quietly to the door and peering through the crack at the back of Margaret's head. Margaret held her telephone receiver to her right ear, her left hand covering the mouthpiece.

That's right, Margaret, thought Karen. Loyalty, gratitude and decency be damned. Suck up to authority. You had already betrayed me when you asked me to help you break that lease! No matter how cynical I get, she stewed, it's never cynical enough.

"What is it?" asked Anne.

"My secretary is being fired this afternoon. 'Bye, Annie. 'Bye, Margaret."

CHAPTER
24

At 2:00 P.M., Karen called Joe Grimes. Three hours left to clean up as much as she could before being banished.

"Joe, what are we doing about Dr. Futterlieb?" Futterlieb, the anesthesiologist who had been found passed out from an overdose of recreational anesthesia, had completed the detox portion of his impaired professionals program. "He's still on the call schedule for obstetrics. Have you called a Medical Executive Committee meeting?" Joe said that a meeting was scheduled, but that Karen need not concern herself with it. She was not invited. The legal aspects of the matter would be handled by outside counsel, Emerson Knowles.

"Anything else?" asked Joe curtly.

Karen explicated the clinic billing fraud investigation. Joe took the position that it was not hospital business and that Karen should not be spending hospital time on it. Karen countered that the doctors involved were all members of the hospital medical staff and that Shoreview had a duty to allow only qualified, ethical physicians on staff.

"We're not responsible for what they do in their private practices," said Joe. "Besides, billing practices have nothing to do with a physician's qualifications or medical ethics."

Karen sighed. Joe had more blind spots than the worst seat at Wrigley Field. Discussing ethics with him was like discussing astrophysics with Barney the Dinosaur. She changed her approach. She pointed out that some of the unnecessary treatment the guilty physicians had rendered had taken place at the hospital, as outpatient procedures.

"So what? The physician orders the treatment, we just provide the facility. We can't be questioning the physician's orders. I'm telling you, this is none of our business."

Karen had run out of alternatives, except to blurt out that Larry's files referred to a conspiracy involving hospital billing of the same patients the clinic had billed fraudulently.

"Not likely," said Joe. "If we had been involved in anything like that I would have found out about it. More likely, Larry was mistaken."

Karen pointed out that Larry was competent and exceptionally careful.

"Larry was a geek," said Joe. "I'm surprised Paula didn't divorce him years ago. She's a sharp woman."

"You been hanging out with Paula lately, Joe?"

"No."

"I saw you leaving her house on Monday."

"What, you tailing me? I was delivering a gift from the hospital, on account of what happened to Larry. You understand, it's what Anne Delaney calls 'plying the plaintiff.' It's good risk management."

"So is *poking* the plaintiff," mumbled Karen under her breath.

"Enough," said Joe. "Have Margaret pack up those files of Larry's and deliver them to my office before the end of the day. And I'll see *you* in January."

Karen spent most of the rest of the afternoon copying Larry's files and loading the copies in the trunk of the Mustang so the originals could be sent to Joe as ordered. As 5:00 P.M. approached, she stood staring out the window of her office, feeling sad and discouraged. She was out of time and out of ideas. The warmth of the sun and the day's traffic had turned last night's snow into dirty gray slush. By the time she got home, Jake would be setting up at the Caledonia Club.

She was relieved that Jake's Mustang had survived the day undamaged on the street. Her Volvo was in the shop. Jake was getting a ride to the gig in a fellow band member's van.

The drive home was miserable, the road a slushy mess. Passing pickup trucks and SUVs sprayed layers of salty, muddy slop onto her windshield. The wipers of the vintage car were not up to the task, and Karen had to stop frequently to clear a spot on the windshield, first with facial tissue and then, when that gave out, her gloves.

Karen's range of emotions, wide as it was, rarely ran to feeling sorry for herself. But on the way home that night, she allowed herself a few self-pitying thoughts. She had always done what she thought she should. Worked hard, applied her considerable ability, tried to make herself useful, tried to be honest and fair. Played by the rules. The result was that she found herself frustrated, underpaid, and now, out of a job. Worst of all, it seemed to her that she was *disrespected*. Why did it seem to her that too many people abused their positions, took what they wanted, explained their actions with transparent lies, and got away with it? Didn't it bother them that other people knew what they were up to? Knew that they were dishonorable, opportunistic, and crooked? Well, why should it bother them; everybody still seemed to treat *them* with respect. And although she resisted the thought, it was there, putting a hard, mortifying edge on her self-pity: *they* were all reproducing.

191

When she stopped for gas, her stomach was growling. The service station mini-mart had no real food, so Karen, knowing better, wolfed down a sugary chocolate cupcake wrapped in oily cellophane and laden with preservatives. By the time she pulled into her driveway she felt drained, defeated, and dyspeptic.

CHAPTER
25

Standing on the front porch of her house, keys in hand, Karen could hear music coming from inside. Jake was not due home from the Caledonia Club for hours. The house was dark. A saxophone was playing, a capella. Karen did not recognize the song—a slow, bluesy number—but she recognized the style. It was Jake.

Karen entered quietly and listened while Jake finished the song. The living room of their old Victorian house was sparsely furnished, its decor combining Karen's unpretentious conventionality with Jake's eccentricity. In front of the fireplace, which was too large for the room, a brown twill convertible sofa and a matching loveseat faced each other across a mahogany butler's table. The only other furniture in the long, narrow room was a tan overstuffed easy chair in the corner with a brass floor lamp next to it. The white plaster walls were bare save for one enormous unframed Rothko-esque abstract oil, painted by a former member of Jake's band. A seated Buddha carved from jade surveyed the room placidly from the mantelpiece.

Jake sat on the arm of the easy chair, a battered saxophone case, a full ashtray, and a half-empty bottle of Gordon's gin at his feet. The room smelled of cigarette smoke and lime incense. Karen decided she just didn't have it in her at the moment to scold him about smoking. When Jake finished playing, he slid off the arm of the chair into the seat. He pulled a cigarette from the front pocket of his black silk shirt, lit it, took one puff, and crushed it out. Karen threw her coat on the sofa, sat on the arm of the easy chair and stroked his hair. His head dropped into her lap.

"We lost our gig," he said. The owner of the Caledonia Club had informed him during setup that tomorrow's Saturday performance would be the last night for the band. When Jake told the other members of Code Blue that their long-term engagement was being precipitously terminated, they had rebelliously packed up and left rather than finish out the last two nights.

"How could that happen?" asked Karen. "You guys are the best draw in Jefferson. Who could they get to replace you?"

"Not who," said Jake despondently. "What. They're putting in a sound system and a karaoke machine."

Karen expressed sympathetic outrage. A sound system could never compare to live music. Amateur vocalists could be amusing for about ten minutes, then they became tiresome, and eventually intensely annoying. "That club owner is a Philistine," she concluded.

"Maybe," allowed Jake. "But he's also a businessman. He knows the simple facts of nightclub economics. The club owner adds up the profit margin on the booze he sells to the customers who wouldn't be there but for the band. If it doesn't exceed the cost of the band, it's history. The karaoke machine costs what he pays us for two nights, and he has the thing forever."

"Or until the fad dies," corrected Karen. "How can people prefer that garbage to real music?" Jake countered that it was lucky for the two of them that their personal tastes were out of step with the masses. If everyone liked the things they did, they would never have been able to afford to see some of the greatest jazz and blues geniuses of the century perform live. Over the years they had, on a modest budget, seen Mingus, Sonny Rollins, Bill

Evans, Frank Morgan, Horace Silver, Muddy Waters, Jimmy Rodgers . . .

"Remember the night we paid a two-dollar cover charge to sit ten feet away from Otis Spann? Greatest piano player I've ever seen. The same night, we could've stood in line for five hours and paid a hundred bucks to sit in an auditorium with bad acoustics for Barry Manilow." Karen opined that for Barry Manilow, bad acoustics would be a plus. They laughed, and Karen slid into the seat next to Jake.

"Aren't you going to ask how my last day at work went?" asked Karen.

Jake obliged. "How'd your last day at work go?"

"Don't ask," said Karen. She told Jake about her unsettling conversation with Carl Gellhorn, the opacity of file number 3, and Anne's catheter count. She related Dr. Herwitz's attempt to buy her off and, when that failed, to drag her mother into it.

"I can't see Mom with Leonard Herwitz," she said. "Mom's so straightforward and he's so slippery."

"There was the door to which I found no key," said Jake, "there was the veil . . ."

Karen nudged him in the ribs with her elbow. "Yeah, yeah, I know. Omar Khayyam. Then I had another disappointment. My secretary, Margaret, ratted me out." She told Jake about catching Margaret eavesdropping and about Herwitz's knowledge of the letter Karen was writing to the Office of the Inspector General. Then she described her failure to get any helpful information from Joe, her exclusion from the meeting regarding Dr. Futterlieb, and the slushy, miserable drive home.

"All in all, another red-letter day for Karen Hayes, attorney-at-law."

Jake went to the kitchen and got two glasses filled with ice cubes and a bottle of dry vermouth. He came back into the living room and filled the glasses with gin and added a splash of vermouth to Karen's. Karen moved to the sofa and wrapped her coat around her shoulders.

"Why is it so cold in here?" she asked.

"Because the furnace is out," announced Jake. "Furnace guy can't come until tomorrow morning. I'll make a fire in the fireplace."

"Good place for it," said Karen testily. "And make my next martini up. It's too cold for rocks."

Jake saluted comically and went out to the front porch for firewood while Karen hauled out sleeping bags and blankets, moved the butler's table out of the way, and opened the convertible sofa. When Jake had the fire roaring, they moved the mattress onto the floor in front of the fireplace. Karen downed her martini in record time and handed Jake the empty glass.

"Could you freshen this up?" she requested. Jake returned promptly with a full glass and a shaker.

Karen sat cross-legged on the mattress and drained half of her glass, staring blankly into the fire. Jake sat down next to her, brushed her hair aside gently, and kissed her neck.

"Got my period today," said Karen.

Jake let her hair fall back in place. The two clinked glasses and bottoms-upped. Jake refilled the stemmed glasses from the shaker. "You know," he said, "they say you should never drink when you're under stress."

"Shtresh?" said Karen, rolling her head and hiccupping. "What shtresh?"

They laughed a little, and Jake put his arm around Karen. "Do you suppose," said Karen, "anybody in their forties has a life anything like they thought they'd have when they were eighteen?"

"Sure," said Jake, "people in totalitarian countries."

Karen and Jake talked for an hour about the ambitions of their youth and the realities of their approaching middle age. Karen had dreamed of a career in government until she became disillusioned with politics. Somewhere along the line she had concluded that there were a lot more bad guys than good guys in public life, a phenomenon that Jake attributed to the fact that bad guys were by nature more attracted to power. Jake said he had hoped someday to work with "really heavy" musicians, making original, nongeneric music. "But if that doesn't happen by the time you're forty, it probably ain't in the cards."

Karen sighed. "Neither one of us ever set out to make a lot of money."

"Yeah," said Jake, "and that part of the plan's goin' great. You had anything to eat?"

He heated up a can of tomato soup while Karen tossed a salad. They ate in front of the fire, saying little. When they finished eating, they put the dishes in the sink, took off their clothes, and donned matching white cotton yoga pajamas. They crawled into two sleeping bags that Karen had zipped together into one and piled a mountain of blankets on top. They lay on their left sides, facing the fire, Jake caressing Karen from behind.

"I feel like I've failed everybody," said Karen.

"You haven't failed anybody, sweetheart. You're just a little down tonight."

"Aren't you going to feel like you missed out if we never have a child?" asked Karen.

"How can I miss something I never had?" replied Jake.

"Don't you want someone to carry on the family name?"

"I don't know my family name. My ancestors came from Eastern Europe and somebody changed it somewhere along the line. It probably started out Haysoporitchsky or something like that."

"But what about perpetuating your genes? Don't men have a thing about that? My dad does."

"Well," said Jake, "I'm not that crazy about my genes. My dad had a stroke before he was fifty, my mom had arthritis and liver disease, and my brother did eight years for aggravated assault. Hardly worth perpetuating."

197

"But all that talent . . ."

"Nothing but a cheap trick," said Jake, grabbing a log from next to the mattress and shot-putting it into the fireplace.

Karen got up onto her left elbow and felt the heat from the fire with the palm of her right hand. The shadows of her fingers danced on Jake's face. "They say people need to have children to be truly fulfilled."

Jake snorted. "Who says that? The editors of *Parents* magazine?" He reached around to Karen's left shoulder and rolled her toward him. He held her face in his hands. "Listen to me. If you want to keep trying to get pregnant, that's fine with me. If you don't, that's fine, too. I don't need anybody but you, Alto. Never have, never will. If I'm sad about anything, it's the thought that some kid is missing out on having a great mom. But what the hell, that's the kid's loss."

Karen pushed Jake over on his back, nestled her head just below his collarbone, and draped her left leg over his. She pulled his left arm around her like a blanket.

"Hold me like this all night," she said.

"You still feel bad about Larry, don't you? You still feel responsible."

"I missed something," said Karen. "There's something I haven't thought of."

"You'll think of it."

"It's too late. I've blown it."

Jake closed his eyes. As he drifted off, he could feel Karen's warm tears puddling on his chest.

PART III

"*Nobody can hurt you but your so-called friends.*"

—JOHNNY LITTLEJOHN

CHAPTER
26

In her dream, Karen was in a dark, cavernous parking garage, searching for her car. The garage floor was covered with broken glass. She was in a hurry to get somewhere, but she couldn't remember where. Every time she saw what she thought was her car, it changed into something else. Finally, she found her Volvo, but she couldn't get the key into the door lock. It got very dark in the garage, and she had the feeling she was being watched. She turned around. A man with one eye was standing behind her, staring. She was terrified. The eye blinked, and she woke up. She had a distinct feeling the dream was trying to tell her something, but any chance she had of interpreting it vanished when she opened her eyes.

Jake sat in front of the fire, in lotus position, still wearing his yoga pajamas. Karen sniffed; no coffee was being made. Good. Jake's coffee was the worst.

"Hey, Swami, you want your nonworking wife to brew up some java?"

"Om," said Jake.

"'At's where the 'art is," said Karen in a Cockney accent. She popped up and shuffled into the kitchen. The kitchen felt much colder than the living room. But for some reason, Karen enjoyed the familiarity of the little kitchen more than usual, in spite of the chill. The cupboard contained instant coffee, ground decaf, and a small foil bag of fresh, whole gourmet coffee beans, acquired for special occasions. "I'm in no hurry to go anywhere," she said out loud, and grabbed the foil bag. As the water heated up, she sat in the window seat and contemplated the sky. It was a bright, clear day, but apparently frigid. The slush from the previous day was frozen solid. Frost crystals embellished the window.

When the water was near boiling, Karen turned on the electric grinder and poured in the coffee beans. The kitchen was filled with a mellow, extravagant fragrance. Karen made the coffee using a French press, mixing the freshly ground beans with the boiling water, letting it brew, and then removing the grounds from the coffee by pushing a straining device attached to a plunger through it. As the coffee brewed, she warmed her hands on the burner of the electric stove and looked around at her kitchen. The floral pattern of the linoleum floor had footpaths worn into it. The countertops were nicked, the wallpaper was passé. Yesterday, she and Jake had been "DINKS"—Double Income, No Kids. Now, they were NINKS. Remodeling would have to wait.

Karen hollered, "When's the bozo coming to fix the furnace?"

"Om," said Jake. "Om manni padmeh um."

Karen poured the steaming coffee into two white ceramic mugs and padded back into the living room. She set a mug directly in front of Jake. His visual focus remained on the embers in the fireplace, but she saw his nostrils flare. Karen sat on the edge of the mattress and slurped the hot coffee.

"Reach Nirvana yet, Gunga Din?" she inquired.

Jake smiled and let out a deep breath. He picked up the mug, held it under his nose, closed his eyes and inhaled. "Ah, *that's* Nirvana. What's on the agenda?"

Karen told him she had promised her mother that she would call her father to discuss his prostate cancer, a prospect she viewed with the same eager anticipation she had for major dental work.

The house needed big-time cleaning. She needed to buy a few magazines, maybe some Chinese food for dinner. No gig tonight, they could rent a movie.

Jake put his coffee mug down, held his hands in "air guitar" playing position, tossed his head back, and sang, "Born to be wiiild!" Karen laughed and gulped the coffee. Jake often expressed amazement that Karen could gulp down beverages that scalded his tongue if he sipped them.

As they finished their second mug of coffee, the furnace repairman, who turned out to be a woman, arrived. Dealing with repair people, male or female, was Jake's job. Karen disappeared upstairs. The furnace repairwoman quickly determined that the cause of the problem was a burned-out fuse, something Jake could have, and but for his funk of the previous evening would have, figured out. Fifty bucks for a service call, down the drain. He paid with cash and went upstairs to check on Karen.

"What are you doing?" he demanded as he entered the bedroom.

"What does it look like I'm doing? I'm obsessing." Karen was sitting cross-legged in the middle of their king-sized bed, with the photocopies of Larry's files spread out around her. "This reference to the hospital billing conspiracy, it's driving me nuts. File number 3," she said, grabbing the file with both hands and shaking it, "it's nothing but dates and numbers and dollar amounts. It couldn't just be a mistake. Larry was too careful. It can't mean nothing. Maybe Larry was playing one last stupid practical joke before, as he used to put it, his number went onto that big balance sheet in the sky. It makes me want to scream. It's lucky he's dead or I'd kill him."

Jake grabbed the folder firmly and yanked it out of her hands. "Go call your dad," he said. "You're not obsessing. You're stalling. Call your dad now, and I'll get your Volvo back from the shop."

Karen stuck her lower lip out in a pout. "Sometimes you can be so wack," she said.

"So wack?" said Jake. "What's that mean?"

"Such a *bummer*." She stomped out of the bedroom, down the stairs and into the kitchen.

Gene Decker was dressed in pajamas and a terry-cloth bathrobe at 11:00 in the morning when the telephone rang.

"Oh, hi, Tootsie Roll."

Karen ground her teeth at the sound of the hated pet name. She asked her father how he was doing, how was work, what was the weather going to be like for the Bears' Sunday game. It seemed impossible to find a comfortable way to segue into a discussion of his prostate cancer.

"You didn't call me to discuss football, did you?"

"No, Dad. I called to discuss the . . ." She paused. "The medical situation."

"You're pregnant!" he exclaimed.

Karen rolled her eyes. "No, Dad, I'm not pregnant. I meant *your* medical situation."

"What do you mean?"

When Karen told him she knew about his prostate cancer, he seemed upset and embarrassed that she had found out about it. Maybe, thought Karen, at some level he did not like the idea of his daughter thinking about her father's possible incontinence or impotence. She decided to fudge on how she had found out, since the idea of his ex-wife and his daughter chatting about his problems over lunch would probably make him even more uncomfortable.

"One of the doctors who saw you at the Jefferson Clinic told me. It's nothing to be ashamed of, Dad. You know, every man gets it eventually, if he lives long enough. Practically all men in their eighties have it, but very few die of it."

Mr. Decker allowed that he did not know those things, which made Karen annoyed at the doctors who had seen him. Couldn't the doctors have educated her father a little about the disease?

"What are they recommending, Dad?"

Mr. Decker had already been to see four physicians. His internist had detected the tumor during a routine physical exam. The internist had referred Mr. Decker to a urologist, who had done a blood test for prostate specific antigen and performed a biopsy of the tumor. The malignancy confirmed, the urologist had recommended an immediate prostatectomy, complete removal of the prostate gland.

Her father cleared his throat nervously. His internist had also referred him to an oncologist, a cancer specialist, at the Jefferson Clinic. The oncologist had recommended hormonal treatments, but had also had him seen by a radiation oncologist, a type of cancer specialist who used radiation to treat tumors, at the clinic. The radiation oncologist had recommended radiation therapy, which Karen knew carried a risk of damaging the bowel and leaving her dad with diarrhea for the rest of his life.

"I didn't know I had to make a choice. None of the doctors said that their treatment was in lieu of the others. The surgery is scheduled for the week after Christmas. The radiotherapy starts in January and goes for three months. I have an appointment with Dr. Caswell next week to find out when I start the hormonal treatments."

"Stay away from Caswell," warned Karen.

"Why? What's wrong with him?"

Karen struggled with the question for a moment. It presented her with another ethical dilemma. Had she learned about Dr. Caswell's nefarious activities in the course of her job, so that she was bound to keep the information confidential? Had Larry passed the information to her in her capacity as the hospital's attorney or merely as a friend? She still did not know whether the files implicated her client, the hospital. Oh, the hell with it, she thought. This is my father.

"Dr. Caswell will sell you whatever makes him the most money. He doesn't care about anything else." She proceeded to tell her father the history of Dr. Caswell's lucrative practice, how Dr. Caswell made treatment decisions solely on the basis of maximizing his own reimbursement. She also told the story of learning about Caswell from Larry Conkel's secret files.

"That's quite a shocking story, Tootsie Roll," said Gene. Karen winced. Her father said, "Dr. Caswell seems like a decent fellow."

Karen considered for a moment what she could say to persuade her father. "Dad," she said, "you seemed to be quite uncomfortable with the risks of surgery. Are you worried about impotence?"

"I don't want to talk about it."

"Did Dr. Caswell tell you impotence was an automatic consequence of the hormonal therapy?"

He paused. "No."

"Did your urologist tell you whether the tumor has developed beyond the capsule of the prostate gland itself?"

"No."

"Do you know if it has metastasized?"

"No, I don't know."

Karen had heard enough. "Dad, I'm going to send you some things in the mail. Pamphlets and copies of articles about prostate cancer. Did you know that the vast majority of men who get it die of something else?"

"Yes, I knew that," said Gene. Karen suspected he was lying, so as not to appear completely uninformed.

"I'll also send you the name and phone number of a urologist in Evanston I know personally. He has a superb reputation, and he doesn't do any surgery himself. He'll give you an objective opinion. You can trust him."

206

"What do I do about my appointment with Dr. Caswell?"

"Stay away from Caswell!" commanded Karen.

"Okay, Tootsie Roll. And thanks, I really appreciate this. Is there anything I can do for you?"

Karen did not hesitate. "Yes, as a matter of fact there is, Dad. Please stop calling me Tootsie Roll. I've hated that name ever since I was thirteen."

"What am I supposed to call you?"

"Try 'Karen'."

"Okay . . . Karen. That sounds funny."

Karen swallowed hard. This conversation was going much better than expected. She decided to gamble a little, try for some actual intimacy.

"Dad, I also wanted to tell you I'm sorry I was such a bitch on Thanksgiving."

Mr. Decker chuckled. "You were, weren't you? Well, that's okay, I'm sorry too, Toots . . . Karen. I know Mom didn't leave me because of anything you said to her. That was an asinine thing for me to say."

Karen responded that it was unfair for her to have said he ignored the family, and that they would probably never know exactly why her mother left.

"Not true," said her father. "I know." It appeared that he had known his wife was involved with another man months before she moved out. He even knew who the man was, and named him: Leonard Herwitz. Karen did not disclose her own prior knowledge.

"You never told Mom you knew?" she asked.

"No, and she'll not hear it from you!"

Karen swore to secrecy. Her father asked her how her job was going. Ordinarily she would have said fine and let it go at that, but on this occasion she opened up. She told her father about her forced leave of absence and about her failure to either resolve her suspicions about Larry's case or do anything about the clinic's abuses.

"So Larry's file says the hospital was in a conspiracy with the Jefferson Clinic?"

"Well, not exactly," said Karen. "What it says is, 'Clinic fraud billed pats, hosp billing consp—see file 3.' Then file 3 just has a lot of numbers and dates."

"And you think 'consp' means conspiracy?" he asked.

"Sure. What else could it mean?"

"Conspectus," said Gene Decker. "Probably, file 3 contains a billing conspectus."

Karen felt her stomach bounce like a plane that had just hit an air pocket. "What the hell is a conspectus?"

"It's a digest—a summary," her father explained, obviously pleased with the opportunity to instruct his daughter. "I would say that file 3 is most likely a digest of the main information from the hospital billing records on the patients who were billed fraudulently by the clinic."

Karen closed her eyes as a light went on—a light that, to her chagrin, illuminated her own misstep. A wave of intense discomfiture passed through her. Of course. There it was.

"Dad, I, uh, gotta go."

"Oh? Okay. And for what it's worth, tell Jake I'm sorry about Thanksgiving. I know I'm out of sorts a lot. Sometimes I don't know what's the matter with me."

Karen considered whether she should venture deeper. Seize the moment, she decided.

"Sometimes *do* you know?"

"Sure," he said. "My problem is, I'm still . . ." He cut himself off. Karen listened to five seconds of silence.

"You're still what?"

Gene cleared his throat. "I'm still too damned busy at work. In fact, I've got some work to do right now."

"Okay. 'Bye, Dad."

"'Bye, Tootsie Roll."

Karen put the phone down, nearly certain that what her father had almost let slip, what he had choked back, was, "I'm still in love with your mother."

She ran up the stairs into the bedroom and pulled several sheets from file 3 and a few memoranda out of file 1. The clinic and the hospital used different patient numbers, but it took only a few minutes to determine that the dates of service on some of the outpatient services performed at Shoreview matched up with the clinic bills for physician services. Larry had merely been confirming on which dates an actual service was rendered at the hospital versus those dates for which the physician service was completely fictitious.

Just like Larry to be so thorough.

She checked the bedroom alarm clock. It was after 1:30 P.M. She gathered up the file folders, crammed them in her briefcase, and ran downstairs. Jake was in the living room with stereo headphones clamped on his ears and a cigarette going in a glass ashtray.

"Jake," she yelled. "Jake!"

"What?" he yelled back, lifting one earphone. Ornette Coleman emanated from the headset.

"*You* don't have to yell," Karen pointed out. "Put out the cigarette. I'm going into the office."

"I thought you were done with that gig for the month."

"I just figured out there *is* no evidence of hospital involvement in the clinic billing fraud. I'm going in to finish my letter to the Office of the Inspector General."

"Weren't you bounced as of yesterday?"

"Actually, Joe said, 'the end of the week.' I figure I have until midnight tonight. I need some stuff on my computer."

Jake removed his headphones and turned off the stereo. "How'd you figure out the hospital isn't incriminated by Larry's files?"

Karen frowned and dropped her briefcase on the floor. She lowered her chin. "I jumped to a conclusion. Larry's abbreviation, 'consp,' doesn't mean conspiracy. It means conspectus. It's just a billing summary."

Jake laughed. "Man, Larry was kind of a nerd, wasn't he? Who uses a word like 'conspectus'?"

"My dad knew it."

"I rest my case." Jake helped Karen on with her jacket as she scooped up the briefcase. "You wearing your yoga togs to the office? Cool."

"No time to change. Besides, nobody'll be in the administration offices on Saturday afternoon, except maybe Annie. And I'm not worried about offending Annie's fashion sense."

"Go get 'em. Your chariot awaits."

Karen ran out the front door, her jacket open and flapping in the cold wind. She slipped on the glare ice at the top of the concrete steps leading to the driveway, but caught herself with the handrail and kept right on moving down the steps. Jake followed her out onto the front porch. He called after her.

"A woman of valor who can find?" he said. "Her value is far above rubies."

Karen turned. "Omar Khayyam?" she inquired.

"I think it's from the Torah." Toy Proverbs.

Karen waved. "Shalom. Gotta go."

Karen backed the Volvo, now intact, down the driveway, squealing the tires when she braked to shift the car into first gear. She took liberties with the speed limit and stop signs on the way to Shoreview Memorial, and wasted twenty minutes getting nabbed at a speed trap. As she arrived in front of the hospital parking garage, a group of robed Christmas carolers from Our Redeemer Lutheran Church, visiting the nursing home next to the hospital, filed slowly across the driveway, chatting and smiling. Karen gave them a blast with her horn. They parted, and she went hurtling into the garage.

It was late afternoon by the time Karen swept into her office, plopped her briefcase on her desk, and threw her jacket onto a guest chair. With determination and without wasted motion she sat down at her desk, rotated her briefcase to face her, and popped open the latches. She lifted the selected portions of Larry's files from her briefcase and placed them in neat piles in front of her. When she ran out of space on the desktop, she moved a stack of papers, the one held down by the softball-sized crystal paperweight, from her desk to a space on her credenza next to her telephone console. That was when she noticed that the red "Message Waiting" button was blinking on the console.

No time for that, she thought, as she punched the "on" button of her computer. As the computer booted up, she rotated her chair back around to her desk, pulled a pen out of her drawer, and began making notes. She had not acquired the knack of writing at the keyboard. She preferred to make at least a rudimentary sketch of each paragraph in handwriting, then type from her notes. But she found she could not concentrate on the letter. The blinking message light kept nagging at her. She rotated her desk chair back around to the telephone, lifted the receiver, and pushed the button to hear the message.

"*Enter your code number now.*" Karen did so. "*You have one message in your mailbox. Message one, received Friday at 5:15 P.M. To hear the message, press 2.*" The message had come in after she had left the office on Friday afternoon. She pressed 2.

"Karen, it's Emerson Knowles. Hoo boy, have I got some news for you on the Conkel case!"

CHAPTER
27

In the fall of her senior year in college, Karen had received an award for attaining the highest academic average in her class in natural science courses. The honor was something of an embarrassment, inasmuch as she was a history major who had no intention of going on to graduate school in science. As a science student, she did not consider herself in the same league with the wonks who practically lived in the lab. She hated lab and could never get the cookbook experiments to come out right. But because she had a knack for scoring high on the multiple-choice exams favored by Hartford College science professors, she had taken as many science courses as her schedule would allow, her sole purpose being to up her grade point average, to help her gain admission to law school or a graduate program in history. Receiving the science award seemed to her like getting a prize for gaming the system.

The prize also presented her with a dilemma. Along with a gaudy, cut-crystal paperweight, the recipient of the award received a scholarship for a graduate science program at a university in England. It was unthinkable to turn the award down. No one ever had. Her parents and everyone else who knew her assumed she would accept a prestigious fellowship worth thousands of dollars in free tuition. Everyone, that is, except Jake, who understood that she might want to avoid two years in an educational cul-de-sac of five-hundred-year-old buildings, four thousand miles away from him. But he offered little guidance on the decision, other than spouting Buddhist aphorisms and a seemingly useless pop psychology cliché in vogue at the time: "Trust your feelings."

Karen was not one to trust her feelings. She did the rational thing, the expected thing, and took the fellowship. Her term in England was the loneliest, dreariest, most wretched time of her life. It was not, however, a complete loss. Her fellowship research project took her into the university hospital, which set in motion her interest in health care. Plus, the experience was so lamentable that it did teach her to trust her feelings. Over the years she had gotten better at interpreting them. As she listened to Emerson Knowles's voice mail message, she stared into the crystal paperweight and waited for the feelings to come.

"My hat's off to you, Karen. Great idea to get Conkel's medical records from St. Peter's Hospital. I think it's safe to say we've got the damages part of this lawsuit under control. You ready for a little quiz? Question one. Name a recently deceased hospital Chief Financial Officer who not only had an enlarged heart, but also was HIV positive. Good guess. Question two. Name an egotistical, overrated personal injury attorney whose damage case just went down the crapper. Right again. Imagine what the HIV positivity together with the heart disease does to Conkel's life expectancy. Ho, ho. Before this, we had a forty-year-old victim who might work another twenty-five years, might live another thirty or thirty-five. But with this, Ben McCormick can kiss his claim for lost income to age sixty-five goodbye. What's even better, he can kiss jury sympathy goodbye. Hell, by the time I'm done putting on expert witnesses the jury'll think the hospital did the guy a favor. And the jury won't like the victim for putting our doctors and nurses at risk by not disclosing his HIV status. That's if the case ever gets to a jury. Hey, I bet Conkel never told his

213

kids or his friends about this. His wife isn't going to want publicity either, so we can use this to pressure her into a cheap
settlement. The more I think about this, the better it gets. So
congratulations, the hospital got lucky on this one. Stop worrying about your malpractice insurance, you won't need it. Have
a nice weekend, celebrate a little, call me Monday."

"If you would like to hear the message again, press 2."

Karen hung up. The last thing she felt was celebratory; she felt
strange. Was it fear? No, fear was familiar, she would recognize it
immediately. This was more like a combination of anticipation and
frustration. But anticipation of what? And why frustration? She got
out of her chair and walked to the window. A light snow flurry had
just started. Ideas swirled in Karen's head like the windblown
snowflakes outside her window. The office seemed stuffy and con-
fining. The only advantage the old section of Shoreview had over
the new wing was that the old section had windows that could be
opened and closed. Karen unlatched the window and pushed up
on the sash. It stuck for a moment and then opened with a bang,
driving a lone sparrow from the branches of the sugar maple.

The cold air blowing in made Karen's eyes water and stung her
nostrils. She took a few deep breaths and blinked, as her vision
cleared and she looked out at the hospital parking garage and
the Traymont apartment building across the street. Below her
was the front entrance to the hospital. A seed of suspicion
implanted in her brain. In an instant, it sprouted and grew into
a satisfying hypothesis. Another blast of arctic air caused her to
take a half step backward and close the window.

For the first time in almost two weeks, Karen felt her favorite
feeling of all. She felt *right*, and she felt it all the way down to
the soles of her feet.

In the time it took her to cover the distance from the window
to her desk chair, she mapped out a course of action. She picked
up her telephone receiver and dialed.

"Anne Delaney."

"Annie, I'm so glad you're in the office on a weekend. Do you still have the security camera tape from the weekend before Larry died?"

"No, I returned it to Max. Karen, my telephone console tells me you're calling from your office. I thought you were out of here."

"Almost, but not quite. Annie, I need you for a couple hours. Stay put until Max Schumacher gets to your office, then call me back. Have you still got the videotape player in your office and the chronology you prepared when you watched the tape from the day Larry died?"

"Yeah, sure. What's going on?"

"A little experiment, Annie." Karen lowered her voice to a near whisper. "If I'm right, in a couple of hours we'll know who killed Larry."

"Hayes, you're giving me the heebie-jeebies."

"Under the circs, Delaney, heebie-jeebies are completely appropriate. Sit tight."

"Security. Schumacher."

"Max, it's Karen Hayes."

"Oh, yeah, Mrs. Hayes, I just got off the phone with your husband. Funny guy, he told me a good one. What do you get when you cross a donkey with an onion?"

"Max," asked Karen, nonresponsively, "why were you on the phone with my husband?"

"You asked me to call you with the name of the owner of the pickup truck." Karen had forgotten. "Anyways, most of the time you just get a smelly vegetable with long ears. But sometimes, just every once in a while . . ."

"I'm sorry, Max, I don't have time right now. Max, I need you to get all of the security camera tapes for the week Larry Conkel died out of safekeeping and take them down to Anne Delaney's office, okay?"

"Okay." Max sounded hurt. "We don't keep all of them, you know. Just the ones we have a reason to keep."

Karen said that would be enough.

"Don't you even want to know," asked Max, "the name of the guy with the pickup truck? I went to a lot of trouble."

"Sure, Max, I'm sorry. What's the name?"

Max assumed a magisterial tone. "The vehicle in question is registered to one Vincent H. Bernard, a resident of the city of Jefferson."

Karen was not surprised. "How lovely," she commented. "A family that preys together."

"How's that again, Mrs. Hayes?"

"Max, on Monday, check into whether Vincent Bernard is related to Dr. Edward Bernard of our medical staff. Like maybe brothers."

"You think so?"

"I'd lay money on it."

"You want I should call the officer who took the report on your Volvo break-in and have him check out this Vincent Bernard? He might still have your stuff in the truck. We shouldn't wait too long."

"It can wait, Max," insisted Karen. "Security tapes. Anne Delaney's office. Now."

"Okey-doke, Mrs. Hayes." Max still sounded broody. Karen relented.

"All right, Max. What do you get, every once in a while?"

His voice brightened. "A piece of ass that brings tears to your eyes."

Karen's phone chirped. Anne was on the line, reporting that Max had arrived at her office with the security camera videotapes. Karen asked Anne to put the tape from the morning of Larry's biopsy into the videotape player and cue it up to the place on the tape where the time display showed 4:57 A.M. Then Karen asked to be put on the speakerphone.

"Okay, Karen," said Anne, "we're looking at November 21, 4:57 A.M., and rolling."

"Good. Now Max, does your watch have a digital display?"

"Sure."

"Good. Set it to 5:00 A.M. and leave it there without starting it for a moment."

"Gotcha."

Anne's voice interrupted. "Hey, there's you, Max, coming to unlock the cath lab."

"Jeez, that can't be me. I gotta lose some weight."

Karen spoke. "Now, Max, when the time display on the videotape turns to 5:00 A.M., start your watch. Got it?"

"Check." All three were silent for two minutes and several seconds. "There it is," said Max. "She's going."

"Okay, guys," said Karen, "here's the deal. Max, you watch the time display for any irregularities. Anne, watch the picture and note the time the people in your chronology make their appearance."

"This'll be a rerun for me," said Anne. "How long are we supposed to watch this?"

Karen said two hours.

"Two hours!" protested Anne. "Boy, you're going to owe me big time! What are you going to be doing while Max and I are spending the rest of our Saturday afternoon bored out of our minds?"

"Playing computer games," replied Karen. "Stay alert, now. I'll call you back in exactly two hours."

Late Saturday afternoon, Dr. Edward Bernard left the office of his travel agent, tickets to Aruba in hand, and climbed into his white Jaguar sedan to head home to his wife and son. Paula Conkel decorated an enormous Frasier fir tree in her living room with glass ornaments and colored lights. Joe Grimes watched the Hartford College basketball team on cable television; the team was losing badly to Southern Illinois University. Dr. Carson Weber rested in a patient room on the third floor of Shoreview Memorial Hospital, where he had been readmitted two days earlier, suffering from bacterial pneumonia. Karen's secretary, Margaret, was feverishly cramming clothes into a suitcase and cursing her boyfriend Marty, who had just broken up with her. Jake Hayes got out his acoustic guitar and began to compose the tune to go with the lyrics he had just written for a new song, which he had tentatively titled "Karaoke Bites." Karen Hayes sat in front of the large folding table in Unit 207 of the Traymont apartment building and switched on Larry Conkel's computer.

CHAPTER
28

The computer in Larry Conkel's apartment was connected via modem into Shoreview Memorial Hospital's central computer files. The menu intimidated Karen. It seemed to go on forever. Her own office computer offered her a choice of word processing, electronic mail, an appointment calendar, a Rolodex of names and addresses, and a calculator. The central computer, to which the terminal in Karen's office did not have access, had dozens of menu choices, including an Internet service, medical records, anti-virus scan, medical library, Nexis news service, purchasing files, financial records, contract directory, billing histories, personnel records, and, as Karen had anticipated, one called "Security System." She scrolled to it and pushed "Enter." The monitor read:

"ENTER PASSWORD"

Karen had no idea what Larry's password was, nor was she certain Larry's password would be authorized to access the most sensitive functions. But she knew a password she figured would work on anything in the hospital's system. She entered: "MEM CEO," Joe Grimes's password. The words on the monitor moved up one line, and a new prompt appeared:

"ENTER ACCESS CODE".

Karen had already searched Larry's studio apartment, but then she had been looking for a large reddish-brown folder. Fortunately, the apartment was small enough that now it took her only forty-five minutes to determine that nowhere in the place was a notebook or piece of paper containing a list of access codes, although she did notice that the check to Emergency Medical Services from the Jefferson Clinic was no longer in the coffee mug on the wall-mounted shelf where she had seen it on her first visit. There was no point in searching Larry's office for a list of access codes. If Larry kept such a list in his office, it would take months to find.

Karen decided to try a different approach, which she knew was a long shot. She went back to the menu and entered Larry's Rolodex. Possibly Larry kept his access codes right in his computer. That would have been convenient, if uncharacteristically cavalier. Not finding the list in the Rolodex, she entered Larry's word processing software. Word processing programs like the one used by the hospital were set up to permit the user to store documents prepared on the computer in files, for retrieval at a later time. Larry could have stored his access codes in his word processing files for easy reference.

Karen scrolled through the names of Larry's word processing files, finding nothing that looked like it might be a list of access codes. She did spot one file name, however, that stopped her in her tracks: "L. CONKEL TRUST." She pressed "Enter," and the first page of the trust document that Ben McCormick said he was looking for appeared on the monitor.

Karen turned on the printer and read the screen while the printer warmed up. When the printer was ready, she printed out a copy of the trust document, stuffed it in her jacket pocket, turned off the computer and the lights, and left.

"This is the stupidest damn thing I've done in a long time," said Max. "Sittin' here watchin' numbers change on a TV screen. 6:09, 6:09, 6:09, the suspense is killin' me. Woo-ha, there it is, 6:10. What a relief. Mrs. Hayes is a smart lady, but sometimes she can act a little tetched in the head."

Anne sat attentively, pen in hand, her eyes glued to the screen. "I'm sure she has a good reason for making us do this. She's not one to waste other people's time."

Max challenged her on the point. "Oh, yeah? Thursday she had me get the cath lab key out of safekeeping, run down to the cath lab and lock it, just to open it up again with the key. Then, she has me lock it again to open it up with the other key, then lock it again to try to open it with another damn key, even though I told her there's only the two keys. Then she has me watch these damn tapes to get the license number of a pickup truck, use up a favor with the police department to get the owner's name, then she drops the whole thing. Now this. 6:11, whoo-pee. I tell you, she's tetched."

Anne watched the monitor as Joe Grimes walked the length of the hall with determination, passing the cath lab without the slightest pause. She noted the time, put the end of the pen in her mouth, and gnawed.

"It does seem a bit excessive," she said. "At least she let me watch the Saturday night through Monday morning tapes on fast forward."

"Hey, maybe we could do that with this one," suggested Max.

"No, Max," asserted Anne. "We've stayed with it this long, we can make it another forty-five minutes."

Max corrected her. "Forty-nine minutes. Whoops, there's 6:12. Forty-eight minutes. Say, Annie, do you know what you get when you cross a donkey with an onion?"

As twilight yielded to darkness in the city of Jefferson, Vincent Bernard gave up trying to repair the muffler on his twelve-year-old pickup truck. The epoxy patch would not do the job; he would have to replace the muffler. Paula Conkel's friend Lisa Fuller sprayed her blond hair in preparation for a Saturday night date with a married veterinarian. Dr. Leonard Herwitz sat in the doctors' lounge of Shoreview Memorial Hospital, reading an article in a medical economics journal about investing in dotcom IPOs. Ben McCormick and his wife sat down to dinner at the Palmer House in Chicago with a county judge and his wife. Dr. Norman Caswell sat in the video room of his suburban tract mansion, watching a rerun of *Bewitched* on cable. Elizabeth Decker sat at the dining room table in her apartment, addressing Christmas cards and sipping a double Old-fashioned. Her daughter Karen sat at the computer in Joe Grimes's huge office, scrolling his word processing files for a list of access codes.

Joe had very few files in his word processor, and nothing on his Rolodex. Karen wondered if Joe ever did any actual work. She used his password to check his e-mail. The list of messages was immense. Joe apparently never deleted messages, possibly never read them. She skimmed the messages. One caught her eye. It was dated November 29, sent by "EMS." It confirmed "the availability of needed venture capital within estimated 120 days." Karen forwarded the message to her own terminal and shut off the computer. She skimmed the hospital telephone directory next to Joe's telephone console. Nobody in the hospital with a tele-phone extension had the initials "E.M.S." As Karen finished scanning the directory, she heard footsteps in the hall, approaching Joe's office. She immediately switched off the com-puter and froze, her ear to the door. Her stomach knotted, and cold sweat formed on the backs of her hands. The footsteps got louder until they were coming from immediately outside Joe's office. Karen stood and faced the door, her chin raised.

"I don't care if it's Jack the Ripper," she said, through clenched teeth. "I'm not going back in that urn."

CHAPTER
29

"6:59, 6:59, 6:59, 6:59, 7:00. That's it, I'm outa' here. I wish I knew what the hell that was all about."

"Wait, Max," said Anne. "Karen will call soon, then we'll find out. Believe me, she knows what she's doing."

"Really. Well I heard her say she'd call back in exactly two hours. Where's the call? Who knows what she's up to? She and her husband do some kooky stuff, I tell you. Besides, I got better things to do than . . . Hey, what's the matter, Annie?"

A tear trickled down Anne's cheek. She pointed at the monitor.

"Look, Max, it's Larry on the tape. He must have come down early from Admitting, like they tell you to. The big goof, he works here for years and still follows the rules like any other unsuspecting patient. Now he'll sit there for an hour and a half while they set up. The fatted calf waiting patiently for the slaughter."

"He don't look any fatter than I do," said Max. "Now, Annie, if you don't mind, my wife is gonna have a hemorrhage if I don't get home. We've got Bulls tickets for tonight."

Anne's telephone console chirped. "See?" said Anne, sniffing unselfconsciously. "I told you Karen would call soon. But, wait a minute, my console readout says it's not her extension calling."

"Whose is it?" asked Max.

"Yours," responded Anne.

The caller was a security guard, who asked to speak to Max. Anne put the call on the speakerphone.

"Max, it's Billy. I just detained a female, about age forty, five foot two or three, say one hundred pounds, dark hair, blue eyes. Caught her prowling around in the CEO's office. She claims she's the hospital attorney, but she has no ID badge and, frankly, I don't think she's no lawyer."

Max grinned from ear to ear and winked at Anne. "What makes you doubt she's a lawyer, Billy?"

"For one thing, she didn't question my authority to detain her. For another, she's wearing white pajamas."

Six feet away from the receiver, Karen could hear Anne laughing. She picked up an extension.

"Annie, try not to injure yourself. Max, would you ID me so your storm trooper will back off?"

Max chortled. "She sounds dangerous, Billy. Better put the cuffs on."

"Max! So help me God . . ."

"All right, all right. Sheesh, where's your sense of humor? Go back to your rounds, Billy, she's who she says she is. She had permission to be in Grimes's office. Karen, stay on the line."

After Billy left, Max asked Karen what she was doing in Grimes's office. Karen said Joe's palm tree looked like it needed some water, which was true enough. She changed the subject abruptly, asking Max how the security cameras were controlled. Max said they could be controlled from the cameras themselves, which required entering a locked steel panel in the wall to which there were only two keys—one of which Max kept, and the other of which was kept in safe deposit. The cameras could also be controlled from a master panel in his office where the live-action monitors were located, or through the hospital's central computer from a terminal with the right software, if the user had an authorized password and the access code. Max said he, the CEO, and the CFO all were given the access code.

Anne interrupted. "You should see this, Karen. Larry is on the tape, reading a magazine, waiting patiently. Poor guy."

"Annie, did you watch the tape from 5:00 A.M. to 7:00 A.M. continuously?"

"Yes."

"Notice anything unusual?"

"No."

"You noted the times when each of the people on the tape appeared?"

"Yes."

"How frequently do people walk down that hall at that time of day on a Monday?" asked Karen.

"Well," explained Anne, "it varies. As 7:00 A.M. approaches, people walk by every few minutes, sometimes there's two at a time. Early on, especially near 5:00 A.M., there's long stretches of time when there's no activity at all."

"Uh-huh. Max, you still there?"

"Yes, ma'am."

"Did you watch the time display from 5:00 A.M. to 7:00 A.M. continuously?"

"Sure did. And it was the only thing I've ever watched on TV that was more boring than golf."

"Notice anything unusual?"

"Nope."

"What's the time on the videotape right now?"

"7:19 A.M."

"What's the time on your watch?"

Max paused. Anne noticed a slackening in his facial muscles. Karen prompted him. "Max?"

"Well, I'll be dipped in shit."

"What's the matter, Max?"

"My watch is eight minutes slow. Damn. This is supposed to be a good watch."

"It's a great watch, Max. Has it got a stopwatch function?"

"Sure, it's got everything. Want to know what time it is in Paris?"

"No thanks, Max. But I do want one of you to back the tape up and time the length of the minutes after 5:00 A.M. A bunch of them are shorter than sixty seconds."

"Come again?" said Max.

"Sometime after 5:00 A.M. someone paused the security camera," Karen explained, "and restarted it eight minutes later. Then he advanced the time display to the next minute in less than a full sixty seconds, repeatedly, to make up the missing time. You see, if he advanced the time display one digit every fifty seconds, in forty-eight minutes the security camera would be back in sync with the real time, and with the rest of the system."

"Wait a minute," said Anne. "Wouldn't we have noticed if the camera went off and back on? We watched the whole two hours."

"It would only be noticeable if something moved or was added to or removed from the scene on camera while it was shut off. If the hall looked exactly the same when the camera was restarted as it did when it was put on "pause," the interruption would be virtually undetectable. Especially if you weren't looking for the seam. That's how they make things disappear on television shows. If our security cameras recorded sound, you might notice the break, but without sound, it would be hard to spot. Might just be a slight blip, like the blink of an eye."

"Not even that much," said Max. "Those are real good cameras. No offense, Mrs. Hayes, but so what? Now we know how somebody got in and out of the cath lab undetected. It doesn't tell us who it was."

"It does," said Karen, "by inference. After you confirm the shortened minutes on the tape from Monday morning, do the same experiment on the tape from the security camera on the main entrance from 10:30 P.M. to midnight Thanksgiving Day."

"Holy shit," remarked Anne. "I just got it. Hayes, you're brilliant. Max, you can go home to your wife. Enjoy the game. I'll take the tapes home with me and review them tonight. Karen, I'll call you as soon as I've confirmed the missing time. By the way, you know he's in the hospital right now? He was admitted two days ago."

"Who?" asked Max.

"Where is he?" asked Karen.

"New wing, third floor," said Anne.

Karen paused. "Max," she said, "I need one more favor from you tonight. How many security guards do you have on the hospital campus right now?"

"Just two," said Max. "One in the jeep and your friend Billy patrolling on the inside."

"Before you leave," said Karen, "post them both on the third floor of the new wing for the rest of the evening."

"Roger. As head of Security, do I get to know why?"

"There's a patient up there who might sometime this evening become a danger to himself," said Karen, "or to others."

CHAPTER
30

The nurses at Shoreview Memorial were trained to forewarn visitors that the patient they were visiting might look worse than expected. Often, the first time a spouse, child or parent saw a loved one after surgery, a serious accident, or the onset of some abrupt illness, they were emotionally unprepared to witness the facial edema, bandages, transparent tubes bubbling with tobacco-colored bodily fluids, open wounds and other indices of pathology or trauma. Sometimes the visitor would faint on the spot and sustain an injury from the fall that required medical treatment. So Anne Delaney arranged to have the nurses trained to say things like, "Your wife might not look the way you are used to seeing her. You might want to prepare yourself."

Of course, no one spoke to Karen before she walked into Carson Weber's hospital room. Visiting hours were over and she was not a family member or friend of the patient. But that did not prevent her from being startled by his appearance. The thin, handsome young man looked frail and sweaty, and his pale skin had a bluish tinge. His gray eyes appeared murky and dull. His green hospital gown was wrinkled and damp. He stared blankly at a television set, his right hand holding a remote control. He had an IV tube in his left arm. It was a small, private patient room. The Venetian blinds on the single window were closed.

An uneaten plate of hospital food sat on the tray adjacent to his bed, next to a deck of cards laid out in a hand of solitaire.

"Come on in, counselor," he said to Karen. His voice was thin. Speaking seemed to be an effort. "I can't believe," he said wheezing slightly, "there are people who actually enjoy these Martha Stewart Christmas specials. I mean, does anybody really spend hours making elaborate Art Deco designs out of sugar cubes and butter frosting? The woman has no shame."

Karen sat down in a guest chair facing the patient bed. "I'd like to talk with you, doctor, if you don't mind."

He pressed the "mute" button on the remote control. "Not at all," he said. He coughed hard and swallowed. "I heard you were out to get my staff privileges. Is that what you want to talk about?"

"No. I want to talk about Larry Conkel," said Karen.

Weber raised his eyebrows. "What about him?"

"To start—your relationship with him. How long had you and Larry been lovers?"

Dr. Weber's breathing got louder. "What makes you think we were lovers?"

"For one thing, this," said Karen, extracting the folded copy of Larry's trust document from her jacket pocket. "He made you one of the beneficiaries of his trust, along with his children. All his assets and the proceeds of his life insurance went into the trust. From that I conclude you were pretty important to him."

Dr. Weber turned his head slowly away from the television and looked directly at Karen. He mopped his forehead with the sleeve of his hospital gown.

"So, you know. Yes, I was very important to Larry. And he was just as important to me."

Karen returned his gaze. "Maybe so, doctor, but for different reasons. You took advantage of Larry. You exploited him. He shared something with you and you turned it to your personal advantage. You know what I'm talking about."

230

Dr. Weber stared at Karen with narrowed eyes. "Suppose you tell me, counselor."

Karen told him about the check from the Jefferson Clinic, payable to Emergency Medical Services, which she had seen in Larry's apartment. As she told the story to Weber, she claimed to have made a photocopy of the check before replacing it in the coffee mug.

"Larry told you about his investigation into the Jefferson Clinic's billing fraud. In fact, you were the only one he told. If he'd had any idea that you had told Dr. Herwitz about it, Larry would never have gone to a clinic cardiologist for his biopsy. Larry knew better than anyone that those files could destroy the clinic and the careers of several clinic physicians. He also knew that the big shareholders at the clinic would do almost anything to prevent that from happening. You knew that, too. That's how you were blackmailing them. Emergency Medical Services is your service corporation."

Dr. Weber picked up a plastic cup from his bed stand. He coughed and spat into the cup. The effort seemed to exhaust him.

"You figured all that out from one check?"

"Not really. I knew something was going on under the table when the Medical Executive Committee didn't yank your privileges after the patient assaults. It was out of character. Oh sure, the docs will tolerate a physician who pinches nurses, or even one who now and then amputates the wrong leg. But a homosexual assault on a patient? They would have bounced you in nothing flat if you hadn't had something on them. The committee vote was three to two. The three clinic docs voted to go easy. The other two were ready to suspend you without a second thought."

Dr. Weber smiled weakly. "You're very sharp. I like that. If I were into women, I'd ask you out. You're right about the medical staff being hostile to gays. But you know, you'd be surprised how many

231

of them—even ones with wives and children—shine around every now and then," he looked Karen straight in the eye, "to take it in the ass."

Karen blushed. She crossed her legs and straightened her posture. A nurse entered the room to take the patient's temperature and blood pressure and to place a white sleeping pill on his tray with a cup of water. Karen sat silently until the nurse left the room.

She slid her chair closer to his bed. "At some point Larry told you he was going public with his investigation, didn't he?"

Weber looked at the television screen. Martha Stewart was dressed like Mrs. Santa Claus, standing in front of a cardboard sleigh while cornstarch fell gently from above.

"He mentioned it," said Dr. Weber, pressing the "volume up" button on the remote control. "Pah-rum-pah-pum-pum" blared from the tinny TV speaker. "I hate that crappy Drummer Boy song," said Dr. Weber.

Karen walked to the television set and pushed the power button. The picture went black. She sat back down in the guest chair and leaned toward Dr. Weber.

"That's why you killed him. So he wouldn't end your blackmail operation by exposing the clinic. Once he did that, you'd have nothing to threaten Dr. Herwitz with anymore."

Weber clenched his teeth, lifted his head, and glared at Karen. For a moment, his eyes showed energy. "That's not true! You don't understand. You couldn't possibly understand."

Karen leaned further forward and put her hand on the side rail of the patient bed.

"Help me, doctor," she said softly. "Help me understand."

Carson Weber looked away and settled his head back on the pillow. His breathing was labored and noisy.

"Larry's death was an accident. A defective catheter. One of the techs made a mistake and resterilized it, probably."

"That's what it looked like," Karen acknowledged. "But it wasn't resterilized. It was deliberately heated to a point where it would fall apart during the procedure. Tests performed by an engineering consultant showed that. And it wasn't random. Someone removed all of the other catheters from the cath lab cart and left the sabotaged one there so Bernard would be sure to use it on the first procedure scheduled that day. Which was Larry."

Dr. Weber craned his head up and coughed. The bluish cast to his skin seemed to darken. Karen pushed the button on his bed to raise the upper part of the mattress. He settled back, panting. "Thank you," he said. "I would imagine any number of people could have planted that catheter on the cart, if that's in fact what happened."

"No, Dr. Weber," said Karen. "The cart was fully stocked Saturday afternoon. Then the lab was locked until Monday morning. The security camera tapes showed that no one entered the cath lab from the time the head nurse left on Saturday until Bernard arrived Monday. The bad catheter was brought in after the cart was stocked on Saturday. It was added to the total number of catheters in the hospital, brought in from the outside."

Dr. Weber stared straight ahead. "Wouldn't that point to Dr. Bernard? He was first in the cath lab Monday. You said yourself the security tapes show that. He could have brought in the bum catheter himself. He had a motive, too, if, as you say, he knew about Larry's investigation."

"No," said Karen. "The good catheters were removed from the cath lab and ended up in a supply cupboard in your department. With the nurses arriving right after him, Dr. Bernard would have had to dump the good catheters in the waste container. He couldn't have packed them up and toted them away. When I realized that, I was frustrated, because it eliminated all the suspects. Unless, that is, someone got into the cath lab without being recorded by the security camera." Karen explained that the security tapes from Monday morning showed eight minutes missing, and how they had been restored.

Dr. Weber closed his eyes. His chest heaved. "So that just throws it wide open. Anyone could have done that."

"Not quite," said Karen. "It had to be someone with access to the system that controlled the cameras. That's Max Schumacher, Joe Grimes, Larry himself, or someone very close to one of the three of them. What narrows the field is that someone used the exact same technique to slip past the security camera on the main entrance to the hospital at around 10:30 P.M. on Thanksgiving. That's how you got back into the building to assault Dietrich Heiden after the camera in the garage recorded you leaving. After Steven Linder reported you, it was obvious Dietrich Heiden was telling the truth. It kept bothering me that, according to the security cameras, it wasn't possible for you to have been in the hospital when Heiden was assaulted. I had the exact same frustration when it looked like someone got into the cath lab when they couldn't have. When I realized the common link was my reliance on the security cameras, I knew it was you. Your mistake was using the same trick again to go after Dietrich Heiden."

Dr. Weber's eyes were squeezed shut. His mouth was drawn down in a scowl of agony. His body shook.

"I can't believe I did that. I've never done anything like it before. I never did it again, either. Steve Linder came on to me. Thanksgiving, I was upset about Larry's death." Tears ran from his eyes. "Oh God, I miss him." He began to sob, then convulsed with a spasm of coughing. His breathing became quick and shallow. He wiped his eyes with his sleeve. "I can't let myself cry. My respiratory system is compromised. A couple more days of IV antibiotics, then I can cry. It's like the song says, counselor, you don't know what you've got 'til it's gone. I never thought Larry's absence would hurt so much."

"If you had, would you have given up your second income from the clinic rather than get rid of Larry?"

Dr. Weber sat up and turned toward Karen. "That was not why I did it. I said you couldn't understand!" He flopped back and covered his eyes with his hand. "I can't cry, I told you. My lungs will fill up with fluid. Lachrymation is contraindicated." He pointed to the cup of water and Karen handed it to him. He took a sip and held the cool cup to his sweaty forehead. "I must say I'm impressed you figured out the security cameras. How did you connect me with Larry in the first place?"

Karen folded her hands in her lap and looked off to the side. "I knew Larry was having an affair. Someone, most likely Larry's lover, was hanging out in Larry's apartment after his death. Larry had coffee mugs in his apartment with prescription drug logos on them, the kind of thing pharmaceutical companies give away to physicians to promote sales, so I figured Larry's paramour was probably a doctor. I knew about your illness. When I found out Larry was HIV positive, I tried out what could have been a fallacious surmise." She looked at Weber, lifted her eyebrows and cocked her head to the side. "But when I did, everything fell into place, including your access to a computer tied into the hospital's security system, a two-minute walk from the hospital's front door. If your motive wasn't to preserve your blackmail opportunities, what was it? Larry's life insurance?"

Dr. Weber rolled his head back and forth on the pillow. His wheezing got louder, and he moaned. "No, no, no, don't you see? I didn't kill Larry that Monday morning. I killed him a long time ago. When we first met I wasn't sick yet, but I knew I was HIV positive. I didn't tell him, do you understand? I didn't tell him. I never told him. I was scared, and Larry was just the most . . . comforting person to be with. Nothing to write home about in the looks department, I know, but just the sweetest, most loving, most trusting man. This isn't about greed. It's about guilt."

235

Weber's chest jerked twice and he coughed violently for several seconds. He rested for a moment, then he rolled his head to face Karen. "I don't know how much you've heard about this disease, Mrs. Hayes, but whatever you've heard doesn't do it justice. When I started to get sick, Larry took care of me, in more ways than one. He enjoyed it. But you see, by the time he got sick, I would've been gone. He would have faced it alone." Dr. Weber smiled sadly. "It's funny, I could imagine myself without Larry, but I just couldn't bear the thought of Larry, facing AIDS, without *me*. That thing with the catheter, Mrs. Hayes. That wasn't murder, it was euthanasia. You're supposed to be the progressive thinker on the Ethics Committee."

To Karen, Dr. Weber's thinking did not seem to be progressive. It seemed deranged, but she could see little reason to debate the point. Carson Weber was clearly distraught. He may even have convinced himself that his motivation was unselfish.

"But what about all the progress that's been made in AIDS treatment?" said Karen.

"Treatment, yes; cure, no," said Weber. "I'm doomed and so was Larry. It was euthanasia."

"If you're so despondent about your prognosis, doctor, why wouldn't you have encouraged Larry to blow the whistle on the clinic? Do a little service to the public while you're still able?"

"Screw the public," he said. "I didn't really object to what they were doing. They just found some creative ways to make more money off Uncle Sugar, and when I found out about it, then I had a new way to make some money myself. What do you think Medicare is for?"

Karen cleared her throat. "I thought it was to take care of the elderly."

The doctor looked at her through hooded eyes and said, "You're naive."

Karen reached into her jacket pocket and pulled out another folded sheet of paper. It was a printout of the e-mail she had extracted from Joe Grimes's computer terminal. She opened it. "Exactly when," she inquired, "did Joe Grimes turn the tables on you? Some party with the initials 'EMS' is going to make a big contribution to the hospital next spring. I figure that's you, Emergency Medical Services."

Dr. Weber laughed, wincing from the pain the laughter caused him. "Grimes is savvy, but he's not as smart as he thinks he is. He thought he had me. That the patient assaults could ruin my career. Knew about the blackmail, too. Probably suspected I had something to do with Larry's death as well, but he didn't have any proof." Dr. Weber grinned sardonically. "I strung him along. By March, if I was at death's door and didn't need the money anymore, fine. I have no family, he can have the money. But if I had some time left, he would have come by to pick up the check and I'd have been in Key West with a new name, sipping a piña colada." Dr. Weber coughed raucously and swallowed. He seemed drained, and his eyes started to close. His voice dropped to a whisper. "I don't know what's going to happen now, and I don't much care. I guess it's up to you. I'm no threat to anybody, counselor. You gonna turn me in?"

Karen stared straight ahead. "I don't know," she said.

"You gonna turn the clinic in?"

Karen blinked. She looked at her watch. It was after 10:00 P.M. She stood abruptly. When she reached the door, Dr. Weber called after her.

"Mrs. Hayes!"

"Yes?"

Weber took a deep, wheezing breath. "I really did love Larry, you know," he said.

Karen's eyes filled suddenly with tears. "So did I, doctor," she said. "So did I."

237

Karen walked out of the room. In the hall, she pulled her dictaphone from the belt of her yoga suit. The reels were still turning. She clicked it off and trotted down the hall.

As the sound of Karen's footsteps faded, Carson Weber pushed the red button on his bed stand to signal the floor nurse. She appeared in the doorway promptly.

"Yes, Dr. Weber. What can I do for you?"

"Could you get me Dr. Edward Bernard's home telephone number, please?"

CHAPTER
31

Too late to finish the letter to the Inspector General, thought Karen, as she walked into her office, which glowed with blue light from the computer monitor. She tossed her jacket onto a guest chair and sat down at her desk. No reason to put it off any longer, either.

Karen put her Rolodex up on the computer monitor and scrolled to the telephone number of Charles Packard, Deputy Attorney, Office of the Inspector General, Washington D.C. She picked up her telephone receiver and dialed the number. A recorded voice invited her to enter the extension if she knew it, which she did. She heard a recorded male voice say, "*Charles Packard*," and then a recorded female voice said, "*is not available at this time. If you wish to leave a message, please press 1.*" Karen pressed 1 and clicked on her speakerphone, leaving her hands free to handle documents while she spoke.

"Mr. Packard, my name is Karen Hayes. I am General Counsel for Shoreview Memorial Hospital in Jefferson, Illinois. I am calling to inform you that I am in possession of documentary evidence of massive Medicare billing fraud that has been perpetrated over several years by certain physicians at the Jefferson Clinic. At least five physicians are directly involved. The fraudulently obtained Medicare payments are substantially in excess of $30 million." She went on to specify the nature of the fraud: billing for services not rendered, rendering services not medically indicated, determining the level of treatment based on reimbursement. She described the methods by which Larry Conkel had uncovered the fraud, and his careful and extensive documentation of the facts. And she named names. Caswell, Whitman, Bernard. She extemporized on the contents of Larry's file for over fifteen minutes, then concluded by leaving her home telephone number and address.

"In the event that for some reason you are unable to reach me, Mr. Packard, the facts regarding the Jefferson Clinic Medicare fraud are also known by Shoreview Memorial Hospital's Risk Manager, Ms. Anne Delaney, D-E-L-A-N-E-Y."

Karen was reciting Anne's telephone number when the odor of stale cigar smoke reached her nostrils. She rotated her chair. Standing in the doorway in a camel's hair coat and gray fedora was Edward Bernard.

"What in God's name do you think you're doing?" he demanded.

"My job," said Karen flatly. Dr. Bernard stepped toward her. Karen's hand dropped to the keypad of the telephone console and her index finger pressed 2. "And now it's done."

But she was wrong. The government office telephone answering system was the type that accommodated those with second thoughts.

"*If you wish to send the message, press star,*" said the female voice on the speakerphone. "*If you wish to leave a different message, press number symbol.*"

Dr. Bernard took another step toward Karen. His sweaty upper lip twitched. He clenched his jaw. "Press number symbol, Hayes. Press it, or you will regret it, I promise you." He took two more steps toward her. His six-foot frame towered over her.

"Stop," Karen directed, pressing her small body back into her leather chair. "Stay away from me." Karen remembered with regret that she had arranged with Max to have the security guards spend the evening on the third floor of the new wing, well out of earshot of a scream. She moved her left hand over the keypad of the telephone console. Her index finger rested on the number symbol button. Her ring finger rested on the star button.

"*If you wish to send the message, press star,*" repeated the recording. "*If you wish to leave a different message, press number symbol.*"

"Don't do anything stupid, Hayes," advised Dr. Bernard. The phrase triggered a memory for Karen. It was the same phrase the threatening telephone caller had used. Dr. Bernard's bulging, bloodshot eyes locked on the heavy cut-crystal paperweight on Karen's credenza. He took a small step to his right, reached over and placed his hand on the large, faceted globe. His fingers closed around it. He picked up the paperweight.

Karen's heart pounded. She tried to conceal her fear, but her voice quavered. "P-put that down, Dr. Bernard."

Bernard's face reddened. Veins stood out on his forehead. "Get your hand off that phone." He raised the paperweight to shoulder height and drew it back. The blue light from the computer monitor glinted in the facets of the crystal orb. "In two seconds, I'm going to give you an impromptu lobotomy. Get away from that phone!"

He took a step toward Karen. She saw him shift his weight backward, to get more momentum behind the blow. The voice from the speakerphone said, "*If you wish to send the message, press star.*"

Karen pressed the star button.

"Damn you!" screamed Dr. Bernard. He brought the paperweight down with all his force on the keypad of the telephone console, splintering its plastic shell. Karen jerked her hand away. She felt a numbness at the tip of the middle finger of her left hand. A small red line appeared under the end of her fingernail. She squeezed the tip of her finger with her right hand.

241

"The message is sent, Dr. Bernard. Smashing the phone won't stop it."

Dr. Bernard stood in front of her, his shoulders drooping. "Are you out of your mind? What makes you think I'm going to let you walk out of here?"

Karen's sudden calmness surprised her. She looked up at Bernard. "You have no alternative, Dr. Bernard. If I hadn't sent the message, there's no telling what you might have done. But now, the Inspector General has a report from me on your crimes, recorded with the date and time, concluding with a nice clear recording of your voice asking me what in God's name I think I'm doing. If something happens to me now, where do you think they'll start looking? The security camera tapes will show you entering the premises at the time in question. Dr. Bernard, I know this much about you. You always act in your own self-interest. This is the safest I've been since I found those files."

Bernard looked forlorn and deflated. Karen was right. He walked around to the front of her desk and looked out the window at the clear night sky.

"Do you know what you've done? You've taken away everything I've worked my entire life to build. I'll lose my license, my reputation. I'll never be able to practice medicine again."

To Karen's astonishment, she actually felt sorry for him. It was an involuntary reflex, this instant pity she felt for anyone who was hurting, even if he deserved it. She stood and closed her briefcase. "There are other things to do than practice medicine," she said.

Bernard snapped his head around. "Not for me. I can't accept it. After twenty years as a doctor, I can't adjust to being just another . . ." he curled his lip, "head of cattle."

Karen felt her pity evaporate. "If that's how you feel, well . . . you never really were a doctor."

Bernard sneered, his jaw muscles flexing in fury. Karen was alarmed to see he had gone from forlorn to ferocious in the blink of an eye. She had miscalculated. Maybe he had doubts himself about his fitness to be a doctor. Or maybe he just had a problem enduring defiance from a woman. In any case, Karen's instincts told her Bernard's face and posture signaled violence.

He still held the crystal paperweight in his hand. He tossed it a few inches in the air and caught it.

"You know what Shakespeare said, Hayes? 'The first thing we do, let's kill all the lawyers.' He was right."

Dr. Bernard drew the paperweight back, as if it were a baseball, a manic look in his eyes. Karen backed away until she bumped into the monitor of her computer terminal, then turned, her body against the front of the monitor.

Half of the monitor screen remained exposed. Bernard stepped forward and hurled the sphere into the glass.

Inside the picture tube of the computer monitor was a powerful vacuum. The instant the crystal paperweight broke the glass envelope of the picture tube, it imploded with prodigious force. A blinding flash of light appeared in the center of the picture tube, followed instantly by a boom that split the still, dry air of the small office like the report from a cannon. Massively thick chunks of glass were sucked into the center of the picture tube, passed through it, and kept moving with the implosion momentum. Pieces of glass from the back of the picture tube launched themselves directly into the room outside the monitor. Pieces from the front of the tube ricocheted off the inside of the monitor and sprayed out like a geyser. The office and its occupants were peppered with flying glass, which spattered against the desk, pelted the walls and window and, after a long second and a half of bouncing around, settled with a clatter to the floor. A bluish-white puff of smoke hung in the shell of the monitor, as an acrid smell permeated the office.

The room was silent for a few seconds. Karen saw Dr. Bernard, a surprised look on his face, reach down to check his genitals.

243

Then he looked at the palms and backs of his hands. A small, red trickle appeared on his forehead. A piece of glass had glanced off it, opening a small cut. He reached up and touched it, then looked at his fingertips.

"Oh my God," he said. "I'm bleeding." He turned and ran out of the room. Karen heard his heavy footsteps receding down the hall.

Karen stood motionless as Bernard's footsteps faded away. She hesitated to look at herself, afraid of what she might see. She felt no pain; that was good. Her vision was intact. She raised her hands slowly to her face and explored it with her fingertips; no apparent cuts, no embedded slivers—good. She looked at the backs of her hands, then turned them over and looked at her palms. Other than the fingertip injured when Bernard demolished her telephone, her hands were fine. Then she felt a trickle running down the inside of her thigh, and a slight burning sensation on the surface of her belly. She looked down. Five small spots of blood were growing rapidly on the front of her white yoga garment, blossoming like crimson roses on her abdomen. Two of the blooms had long glass pistils protruding from them. The other three had breaches in the cotton cloth at their centers, but no visible glass. Within seconds, the trickle on Karen's thigh became a rivulet, then a stream. The inseam of her white pants was soaked with blood.

In her lifetime, Karen had experienced fear, even terror. Panic, once. But never had she experienced the primordial sensation that came racing from her lower brain like a freight train when she realized she was seriously injured.

Shock. Shock, in the medical sense. She knew what it was, and she knew she had to resist it.

Can't lose consciousness, she thought, I'll bleed to death before anybody finds me. She lowered herself slowly into her desk chair, trying to avoid any movement that might cause the shards of glass she suspected were penetrating her peritoneum from slicing her viscera. She reached for her telephone, only to realize it was smashed and useless. The nearest telephone was at Margaret's desk. About twenty-five feet away. An impossible distance.

Try.

Karen rotated her desk chair with tiny movements of her feet until her back was to the door of her office. It was a straight shot between her desk and credenza. She pushed with small, walking movements of her feet, avoiding as much as possible engaging her abdominal muscles. She felt a wet sloppy sensation at her anus and wondered if she had lost control of her bowels. When she realized it was blood puddling in her chair, she moaned and shock bore down on her. She fought it back.

The distance to the door of her office was covered in seconds, but a raised strip of wood at the threshold stopped the casters of her swivel chair. Her little foot movements would not budge it. She would have to risk one sudden flexion of her muscles. She walked the chair forward a couple of feet, moved it forth and back by bending and straightening her knees, then forth again, then pushed back with all her strength. The back wheels hopped over the threshold, but the front wheels were stopped. She could move neither backward nor forward.

"Operator," said Jake, "I've been trying to reach a number for a long time, but I keep getting a busy signal. Could you break in on the conversation for me?"

"Is this an emergency, sir?"

"Well, that's sort of what I'm trying to find out."

"Hmph," said the operator. "I'll check the line for you." Jake waited several seconds.

"The telephone you are calling is out of order, sir."

"Thanks." Jake hung up, ran to the closet, grabbed his jacket, and ran out the front door without stopping to put on the jacket. When he reached the icy top step, his feet went out from under him and he sat down hard. "Man," he commented. "Concrete is a lot harder now than it was twenty years ago." He got up, walked carefully to the Mustang, and peeled out of the driveway.

Karen finally gave up on pushing the chair over the threshold. She decided she would do herself less harm by standing briefly, taking a few steps to Margaret's desk chair, and sitting back down before her compromised blood pressure caused her to pass out. She felt weak, but was reasonably confident she could make it. She rotated around to face Margaret's desk. She stood up and almost immediately the blood drained from her head and her field of vision got dark and full of purple splotches and little glowing dots. Three quick steps and she rolled onto the top of Margaret's desk, knocking to the floor a small vase, a stapler, and a pencil holder. She caught the telephone just before it slid off the edge of the desk. Lying on her back, she picked up the receiver with her left hand and set it down on her chest. Then her fingers found the keypad and felt around for the place where the "O" would be located.

"May I see your driver's license, sir?"

Jake promised to pay any ticket the officer wrote, if he would please let Jake get to the hospital to check on his wife, but the cop would have none of it. After what Jake considered a long enough time to write a dozen tickets, the cop was still sitting in his squad car, red and blue lights flashing like a major bust was going down.

"Aw, screw this," said Jake, as he popped the clutch and sent the Mustang squealing away.

Karen lay motionless on her back, her eyes open, whispering Jake's name. A face appeared above her, a male, African-American face, with a mustache. He was wearing blue hospital scrubs. It had been less than three minutes since she had spoken by telephone to the emergency room receptionist. The young man spoke to someone Karen could not see.

"She's conscious. Get the gurney ready. I'll get a pulse." Karen felt the young man's fingers press on her throat. He looked at his watch briefly, then looked over his shoulder. "Pulse is weak and irregular," he said. "Start a line, stat. Add an amp of Levophed to the IV." Karen concluded that the guy was an emergency room physician. A female nurse appeared at Karen's right side and swabbed the underside of her forearm with an antiseptic-soaked cotton ball. The nurse deftly located a vein in Karen's arm and plunged a thick needle into it with quick, efficient movements.

The ER doctor looked down at Karen with an expression of gentle concern. "Don't you worry about a thing, Mrs. Hayes. Everything's going to be all right. Just hang in there." Karen felt several hands slide under her back, head, hips and knees, heard the doctor count to three, and in an instant she was on a moving cart, clattering down the hallway. The nurse walked along briskly at Karen's left side, pushing a vertical stainless steel pole

247

on wheels with a plastic IV bag hanging from it. The ER physician walked at Karen's right side, pushing the gurney with the aid of persons Karen could not see. The gurney bounced onto a waiting elevator car and stopped.

Karen spoke in a raspy whisper. "Where are you taking me?"

"Try to stay calm, Mrs. Hayes," said the doctor. "We're taking you right up to surgery. It will only be a few minutes." He put his fingers lightly on Karen's wrist, monitoring her pulse.

"Take me to St. Peter's," ordered Karen weakly. A Jefferson Clinic surgeon might be waiting for her in the OR at Shoreview. "If I need surgery, I want to go to St. Pete's!"

His eyes moved down to Karen's feet and back to her face. She appeared to be dressed in scarlet from the bottom of her rib cage down. He placed his warm hand on hers. "No, Mrs. Hayes, you don't want to go to St. Pete's," he said kindly.

"Why not?" she queried.

"Because at St. Pete's," he explained, "you'd be DOA."

Jake took the steps to the basement of Shoreview Memorial three at a time and sprinted to the freight elevator. He pushed the call button seven times and cursed the slowness with which the old gunmetal gray elevator door opened. The elevator creaked as it rose imperceptibly to the second floor, while Jake paced frantically. As soon as the door opened a crack, he squeezed through it sideways and ran down the hall to Karen's office door. The doorway was blocked by Karen's black leather swivel chair, with what appeared to be a pint of limpid blood pooled in the seat. Margaret's desk looked like it had been finger-painted in red. Jake looked into the office. The telephone and computer monitor were smashed. The floor was covered with blood and broken glass. He turned away from the door and bent over at the waist as if he had been hit in the stomach, his anguished outcry echoing down the deserted hallway.

"Karen!"

The elevator stopped and the doors opened. Karen recognized the distinctive smell of the surgical suite. Dread passed through her, draining all of her remaining strength. She could feel herself slipping into unconsciousness. She noticed the doctor's name badge.

"Dr. Covington," she whispered. "Who is the surgeon on call tonight?"

He smiled reassuringly and squeezed her hand. "The best," he said. "The big chief. Dr. Herwitz."

As if through a dark fog, Karen recollected her last conversation with Dr. Herwitz. She had hung up on him. For all Herwitz knew, the report to the Inspector General that would destroy the clinic had not yet been sent. Oh no, Karen thought, as her eyes rolled back in her head and she lost consciousness.

"No pulse. I've lost the pulse. Nurse, call a code."

The nurse who had been in command of the IV cart ran to a wall-mounted telephone and pressed O. She spoke rapidly to the hospital operator. The operator switched on the hospital PA system and made an announcement that was heard all over the hospital campus. Edward Bernard and Carson Weber heard it.

Leonard Herwitz, reading in the doctor's lounge, heard it, as did Jake Hayes, standing, bewildered, in the hallway on the second floor.

"Code Blue," declared the operator. "Fourth floor, surgical suite one. Code Blue."

CHAPTER
32

By May of Jake's senior year at college, the engagement at The Mineshaft had been winding down for some time. The crowds had thinned out. Blues was going through one of its regular down-cycles in popularity. Jake's bass player, a college classmate, had announced he would be returning home after graduation to work in his father's lumber business. Jake had decided the act had become shopworn and tedious, including the gravelly-voiced alcoholic club owner's not-very-funny introduction:

"Good evening, ladies and gents, and welcome to The Mineshaft. I want to remind you cats to tip the waitresses generously, because they have children to support, and most of them are mine. Now, let's get it together for the best blues in the middle west. Ladies and gentlemen, The Mineshaft is proud to present . . . Buddha and the Lowdown Polecats!"

As Jake waited behind the tattered velvet curtain to make his entrance, the club owner had walked by, remarking slyly, "Check out front row center. Real fox." The words had rolled off Jake like water off waxed paper. He had not had female companionship since Karen's visit home from England at Christmas, but he was not looking for any, either. Karen was nearing the end of the first year of her two-year fellowship. He had made it this long, he could make it another year. He had gotten serious about meditation.

251

The band finished its introductory instrumental, and Jake dutifully delivered his opening vocal.

"Gonna rock this joint,
Yeah, gonna rock this joint.
Now I know we can do it,
So let's get down to it."

Jake had changed his leap-with-slide approach to the microphone to a less strenuous moonwalk. He arrived at the mike stand, spun one and a quarter revolutions on his heels to face the audience, and lifted the blues harp to his mouth. As he blew his first note, he observed a woman across the empty dance floor, at the front row center table. She was dressed in black and wearing a beret. It was Karen. Jake had spoken to her by long-distance telephone three days before and she had not mentioned a visit home.

Jake dropped his harp to the floor and did a seven-foot standing broad jump off the stage. Although he had lost thirty pounds in the previous nine months, the one hundred seventy pounds he still carried shook the dance floor when he landed. Karen bounded out of her chair, took one step, and jumped, spread-eagled. Jake caught her in midair, her arms around his neck, her legs around his torso. Their mouths locked. Jake spun in a circle, got down to his knees, and rolled onto his back. The audience gave them a standing ovation.

Karen ended the kiss and put her lips to Jake's ear. "I quit my fellowship," she stated. "I'm not going back."

"Thank God," said Jake. "Don't ever leave me again."

"Don't worry," Karen had said, "I won't. That's a promise."

Eighteen years hence, had Drs. Covington and Herwitz taken a minute longer to restore Karen's heartbeat, she would have broken that promise. Instead, after more than three hours of surgery and four transfusions, she woke up in the surgical intensive care unit of Shoreview Memorial. She was breathing on her own, but otherwise felt like she had been the victim of either a shark attack or a buffalo stampede, or both. She hurt everywhere, some places worse than others. Her neck screamed at her, she had a blinding headache, and someone was apparently using her belly as a pincushion. The middle finger of her left hand was throbbing. From what? Then she remembered Bernard slamming the crystal paperweight down on her phone and clipping the tip of her finger. Amazing she could feel that, with all the other pain competing for her attention. The headache was probably from the anesthesia. But what was with the neck? God, it was worse than the pain from the surgical site. Karen had observed enough surgery to know that anesthetized patients were often heaved around in a pretty rough fashion. Had the OR staff given her whiplash? Maybe she hurt her neck when she threw herself on Margaret's desk.

When she opened her eyes, she saw Jake's face hovering over her protectively, his brown eyes rheumy and haggard. He smiled.

"Hey, Alto," he said softly. "The doctors did everything they could, but you pulled through anyway."

Karen grimaced, letting Jake know that she was in no condition to appreciate humor. She looked around, moving only her eyes, having a sense that any slight movement would make the agony even worse. The room was dim and windowless. It reeked of antiseptic, and something foul and visceral Karen could not identify, but guessed was emanating from her wounds. A bag of intravenous fluid dripped steadily through a needle into her arm, and a heart monitor blipped out her cardiac status on a glowing screen. For some reason a uniformed policeman was seated by the door. Cripes, was she in that much danger? They had to post a cop to guard her? She opened her eyes wide, showing Jake her alarm at the policeman's presence.

"Oh, sweetheart," said Jake sheepishly, "this is Officer Sprague. Uh, technically I'm in police custody right now for fleeing a traffic stop. No biggie, I've got your friend Emerson on it."

"Please . . ." whispered Karen. Uttering the word cost her a stab of abdominal pain.

"What? What do you want?" Jake said, eagerly.

"Tell them . . ." Again, the pain stopped her words.

"What? What should I tell them?"

"Tell them . . ." She paused, drew a shallow breath and clenched her teeth, determined to get the sentence out regardless of how much it hurt.

"Tell them I need morphine *right now*."

Two days later, Karen was out of intensive care and into a regular patient bed. Her room looked and smelled like the inside of a hothouse, with fragrant blossoming plants and elaborate floral arrangements on every available surface, including the floor. The largest and gaudiest display was from Joe Grimes, followed by a huge but slightly more tasteful one from the law firm of Winslow & Shaughnessy. Karen expected the flowers from her parents and sister, but was astonished and a little embarrassed at the number of friends, business acquaintances, and hospital employees who had sent them. Even the sidemen in Jake's band had kicked in to send her a phallic cactus.

Karen had her first postsurgical chuckle at the card that accompanied a small wicker basket of daisies: "I don't know you, but I certainly feel like I do. You've kept me very busy this week." It was signed by the proprietor of the Jefferson Flower Shop.

She had a dozen visitors in the next three days, not counting Jake, who had become a combination hospital roommate and guard dog. He slept in a guest chair, leaving the room only to get meals at the hospital cafeteria or to run to the medical staff library to double-check the dosage, contraindications, and side effects of every medication ordered for his wife.

Pamela came to visit within an hour after Karen was out of the ICU. This impressed Karen, because it meant that Pamela must have been checking constantly, so she could arrive just as soon as Karen could comfortably receive her. Pamela had Suzanne and Dante with her, and the children appeared to be momentarily shocked at seeing their aunt in a hospital bed, bruised and bandaged with an IV line taped to her forearm, but they recovered quickly. Suzanne shuffled around the room sniffing the flowers and reading the cards, while Dante tried to amuse himself with the medical equipment. Pamela told Karen she looked great.

"Liar," said Karen. "There's a mirror in the bathroom. I know what I look like. I look like the Ghost of Christmas Past."

"Oh, that reminds me," said Pamela clapping her hands. "I got a part in the Shaker Heights Theater production of 'A Christmas Carol.' I'm going to be Mrs. Cratchit!"

Suzanne chimed in. "Mom made Dante audition to be Tiny Tim, but he couldn't remember his lines." When Pamela advised her to shut up, Suzanne slouched to the window, looked out and muttered, "God bless us, every one." Dante, meanwhile, was experimenting with the recreational potential of Karen's IV bag, giving it a few tentative left jabs while quietly humming the theme song from *Rocky*.

Jake, loitering in the doorway, offered to take the kids to the cafeteria for a treat, and his offer was enthusiastically and unanimously accepted. After they left, Karen realized that, strangely, this was the first time she had been alone in a room with her sister in almost a decade.

"Do you still have a lot of pain?" asked Pamela.

"On a one-to-ten scale," said Karen stoically, "it's about a thousand."

Pamela stiffened in her chair. "The bastard who did this to you should spend the rest of his life in jail." Karen watched her sister's eyes fill. Was she going to cry? "I hope you'll be out of the hospital by Christmas," Pamela continued. "I think Dad has something special planned."

"Oh no," groaned Karen. "I hope he's not going to go overboard again trying to outdo Mom, professional tree-trimmers and caterers and all that. I just hate to see the waste."

"He might surprise you," said Pamela. "Remember how Mom and Dad used to do Christmas? Very tasteful and authentic. Mom baked real stöllen and küchlein from scratch, they hung holly and mistletoe, and Dad would cut his own tree from the woods on Uncle Wayne's farm."

"Oh, God," said Karen, "and they'd ride us around the farm on that absurd old sleigh."

"That sleigh," said Pamela with a tone of facetious snobbery, "was a genuine antique, handcrafted in Denmark, or someplace."

"It was so heavy Uncle Wayne's horse couldn't pull it, so he'd drag the thing behind his tractor. It was ridiculous."

"It was a blast, and you know it."

As Pamela reminisced at length about Christmas at home when they were little, Karen was amazed by the clarity of her sister's memory, the way she could recall and describe their family's holiday traditions, right down to the smallest details of specific tree ornaments. She knew Pamela's memory was generally not as good as her own, but her sister was much better at recollecting this part of their childhood. Perhaps it was the children. Cookies, colored lights, and the exquisite anticipation of a debauchery of toys were all kid's stuff. Pamela had gone almost directly from a household in which she was a child to one in which she was

256

a parent. Karen had spent half her life in a childless home, where she and Jake celebrated Christmas Eve, when Jake didn't have a gig, by listening to modern jazz versions of holiday tunes and mixing up a big bowl of forty-proof eggnog. She had apparently lost the Christmas of childhood somewhere along the way, but when she thought of how those jazz-and-eggnog eves usually ended, she decided they were a sweet alternative.

"Remember Mom's hand-painted nativity set on the mantel, with all the little animals and the Magi and everything?" said Pamela.

"Yeah," said Karen, "and I remember how you and I would rearrange the pieces in goofy ways, like putting baby Jesus on the back of a camel."

"And we'd put a sheep in the manger with its legs sticking straight up in the air, and then laugh ourselves sick."

"And none of the grown-ups ever noticed."

"Like hell we didn't!" came a deep voice from the hallway. Gene Decker walked through the door with an armful of packages. He was wearing a plaid car coat and a wool cap, which told Karen he had taken the day off work. He blanched and took a half step backward when he saw his daughter.

"Gee, Tootsie Roll," he said, "you look fine."

"Dad, I look like excrement," said Karen.

Dante ran into the room, kicking over a potted poinsettia in his path, and leaped onto Pamela's lap hard enough to make her wince. "Mom," he asked, "what's excrement?"

When Jake and Suzanne showed up, both looking a little bored and exasperated, it became obvious that the room could not accommodate six people. So Pamela kissed Karen, hugged her father and then Jake, gathered her children and left. As the clamor receded down the hall, Karen was surprised to find that she felt closer to her sister and to her own childhood than she had in years. Somehow, Pamela's walk down memory lane had been more soothing than the medication dripping through the IV.

Jake stepped out for a cigarette, leaving Karen alone with her father. She asked him if he had made an appointment with the urologist in Evanston and he said that he had.

"Did you figure out what Larry's mysterious file was all about?" Gene asked.

"You were right, Dad. It was a billing summary. The hospital wasn't involved, so I went to my office and made the report to the government. One of the doctors involved caught me making the report." Karen went on to explain how she had sustained her near-fatal injuries.

"Well, I'll be damned," said Gene. "You know, when you were about four months old, I was working on a bank loan my company had taken out. I noticed that the valuation of the company's assets supporting the loan included a multimillion-dollar appraisal on some land that I knew was actually worthless due to contamination."

"Har-rumph," said Karen.

"Uh-huh. And I reported it. I barely slept for the next six months, I was so afraid of retaliation. I was sure I had goons following me."

"Was there a prosecution?"

"You bet. Company paid a fine, couldn't borrow for a while. There were layoffs, hurt growth." He bit his bottom lip and blinked hard. "The head accountant got a year in the penitentiary. That man had a family."

"He got himself in trouble; you were just doing your job," said Karen. "You did the right thing, Dad."

Gene Decker looked at his frail, wounded daughter, the bruises on her limbs and the pain and fatigue in her eyes. His jaw tightened. He touched her hand. "So did you," he said.

Before Karen could respond, they were interrupted by a voice from the hall. "Look at the flowers! Did somebody die?" Elizabeth Decker walked in wearing a bright red coat and a black fur hat.

She stopped as abruptly as if she had walked into an invisible wall when she saw her daughter. "Dear Lord," she gasped, shaking her head. "You look dreadful."

Karen raised an index finger in the air. "The only honest person in the family!" she announced.

"Am I interrupting?" asked her mother.

Gene cleared his throat and stood up, offering his ex-wife his chair. "No, not at all. I was just about to go. But before I do, Karen, I wanted to invite you and Jake to the house for Christmas." He turned to Elizabeth. "I had Christmas dinner last year, didn't I? So I guess they'll be at your place for dinner and at my place Christmas morning. Or is it the other way around?"

"Look," said Elizabeth, "it doesn't seem to me that Karen's going to be in any shape to run all over town on Christmas. If it's all the same to you, Gene, why don't I just make dinner for everyone at the house?"

Karen thought it interesting that her mother called Gene's place "the house," but she made no comment. She watched her father's reaction and found it comical.

"Uh, well, um," he stammered. Karen noticed a little color rise in his cheeks. "Oh, um, well," he said, "that would be fine." Then, as if concerned his response had been too hesitant, he added, "I mean, that would be great!" But apparently abashed that he may now have sounded overly enthusiastic, he went on, "That would be just fine."

Jake returned from his smoke and declared the plans for a unified Christmas celebration "molto cool," but said Karen needed to "take five" now. Over Karen's protests that her mother had just arrived, Jake decisively ushered her parents out the door. Karen whispered to her mother, "I appreciate what you did, Mom, but you don't have to do dinner at Dad's house on my account."

"Maybe I'm not doing it on your account," said Elizabeth with a wry smile. "Fact is, I wouldn't want to miss it." She leaned over the bed and Karen smelled face powder and stale Chardonnay. Her mother cupped her hand to her mouth and whispered, "Pammy said Gene's driving out to Wayne's farm to cut a tree. He's going to try to get that old sleigh back to the house!"

The next morning Joe Grimes came to Karen's room, looking like he had just had a facial to buff up his fading ski-trip tan. His cologne overwhelmed the wilting flowers. Karen thanked him for what she called the "Rose Bowl float."

"Hey, it's Christmas," said Joe with an expansive flourish of his arms, as if basking in his own generosity. Karen knew that when Joe sent flowers, he charged it to the hospital. "And in the spirit of the season," he continued, suddenly serious, "I'm replacing your telephone console and computer monitor, and I won't even deduct the cost from your salary."

Karen studied his face. Total deadpan. She absolutely could not tell if he was joking. She was either looking at someone with a devilish sense of humor, or the most colossal jerk she had ever known.

"Got another deal in the works," he said, more ebulliently. "Gonna need your help. I've been talking to some of the execs and board people over at St. Pete's."

"Consorting with the enemy, eh?" said Karen.

"Who says they have to be the enemy?" said Joe. "We need to start thinking outside the box. Show more vision."

Outside the box. Vision. Joe with his irritating business-speak clichés. It was making her stitches itch.

"I think I've got our friends across town interested in developing a health services coordination and cooperation venture, to create a more harmonious delivery system."

260

This made her neck start to ache like she was back in the ICU. "Could you translate that into English, Joe?"

Joe plopped down into the guest chair closest to her and hunched forward. "I'm talking about entering into an agreement with St. Pete's to stop providing the same services at both hospitals. They deliver most of the babies anyway, we could close our obstetric service. Give them orthopedics, too, they already own the spine clinic. That way we can concentrate on our heart and cancer programs, create Centers of Excellence. The beauty part is they get the high-volume stuff, but we get the high-margin stuff. Total win-win."

"Joe, you know competitors can't divide markets. It's an antitrust violation."

"It's best for everybody. The quality of care would improve if we focused on what we do best. It would unify the provider community," he said, putting his hands together, like he was about to pray, then interlacing his fingers for emphasis.

"Perhaps. But the scheme is illegal."

"It would avoid wasteful duplication of costly technology. I know how you hate waste, Karen."

"I'm just telling you the law, Joe."

He sat back. "Now there is a law against cooperation? I won't accept that." Joe stood up, straightened his tie and brushed the wrinkles out of his suit. "I imagine you're still quite debilitated from surgery. We'll talk about this when you're feeling better. You'll find a way."

After Joe left, Karen remarked to Jake that it was amazing Joe had not even mentioned her report to the Inspector General or the collapse of his pet MRI project with the clinic.

"One thing you've got to give Joe," said Jake. "He keeps on truckin'."

Later that day Max Schumacher came to report that one of his friends at the police department had recovered Karen's car battery and cellular telephone from Vincent Bernard's garage. The police had asked if Karen wished to file a criminal complaint against Vincent Bernard. Karen declined, but told Max she did want to swear out a complaint against Dr. Edward Bernard for assault.

When the police came to take Karen's complaint against Dr. Bernard, the officer reported that, according to Dr. Bernard, Karen had been the one who threw the paperweight at the computer monitor. Since he, too, had received an injury—a small cut on the forehead—Dr. Bernard had said he would be swearing out a complaint against Karen, but would not do so if she dropped her complaint against him. The policeman said it was her word against his and in such cases the police could not make a judgment as to the credibility of the parties. The police officer explained that there was no evidence at the scene to support either party's version. The traffic cop who had taken Jake into custody had reported the condition of the office to a hospital security guard named Billy Walker, who had tried to call Max Schumacher. Max had been at a basketball game, so Billy called the hospital CEO at home. On Joe Grimes's instructions, housekeeping had cleaned up the whole mess Sunday morning. Besides, the officer concluded, the police department preferred not to get involved in a private dispute that was likely to be the subject of a lawsuit.

Karen dropped her complaint.

That night, Karen spiked a fever of 103. The night nurse reached the physician on call, who ordered a change in

Karen's antibiotics and had the nurse reserve an operating suite for the next day. Karen knew that once they started going back in looking for abscesses, her recovery could be complicated and take forever. For the first time in longer than she cared to admit, Karen prayed. Jake ran to an herbalist and returned with an assortment of leaves, stems, and seeds from which he brewed a tea that tasted like bitters and iodine. The taste was still in Karen's mouth when she awoke the next morning to the touch of Jake's lips on her forehead.

"How'm I doin'?" she asked.

He smiled and replied, "You're cool as a Miles Davis solo."

Two days later, Anne Delaney came to report that Charles Packard from the Office of the Inspector General had contacted her. She said she had arranged to have the originals of Larry Conkel's files delivered to Packard.

"Did Joe try to stop you?" asked Karen.

"He gave me a line about loyalty to our medical staff, but he backed off pretty fast when I pointed out that he could get dragged into it personally if we tried to withhold the files."

"With Joe, loyalty is no rival to self-preservation."

Anne then moved on to discuss other sundry legal matters, each represented by a neatly organized file folder resting on her ample lap. Karen was distracted from the details of Anne's discourse by the unexpected comfort she derived from it. The familiarity of Anne's voice and mannerisms, the reassuring sense of normalcy from being at least a little bit back to work, the calming distraction of having difficult questions to focus on and answer were all a part of the relief Karen felt. But she was feeling something other than relief: a unique sort of connection. Here, Karen realized, was her comrade-in-arms, the person who knew better than anyone else, better even than Jake, exactly what it was she did all day long and why it mattered.

Anne had not greeted Karen with hugs or cheek kisses or a box of chocolates. Instead, Anne had come bearing a rat's nest of problems for Karen, but they were accompanied by Anne's sweet, welcome acknowledgment that they were her problems, too.

"You have a whole bunch of faxes on your desk from Ben McCormick," said Anne, "and Lou Chambers's process server has been here a couple of times."

"I'm going to let Emerson Knowles handle those suits from here on," said Karen. "I think they're under control. Anything else, Annie?"

"What are you going to do about Carson Weber?"

Karen considered telling Anne about the dictaphone tape of her conversation with Carson Weber, but decided to keep it to herself a while longer. She sat in silence, Anne's question pressing down on her, awakening the pain in her gut. She looked at the wilting flowers around her and suddenly felt like one of them.

Jake, who seemed to be monitoring Karen's visitors with a stopwatch, materialized in the room. With uncharacteristic assertiveness, he invited Anne to lunch, practically lifting her from the guest chair and escorting her out the door.

After they had gone, Karen said to herself, "I don't know."

CHAPTER

33

The evening before Karen was to be discharged, Carson Weber came to see her. He looked at least as sick as he had when Karen had last seen him, but he was dressed in khaki pants and a cotton sweater. Apparently he was going to be out of the hospital before she was. He asked Jake if he could speak with Karen privately.

"Jake stays," said Karen.

Weber shrugged and winked at Jake. Jake responded with a two-finger salute. Carson sat down and folded his hands in his lap.

"I can't tell you how sorry I am about what happened to you, Mrs. Hayes," he said. "When I called Dr. Bernard I knew you were about to drop a dime on the clinic, but I had no idea he would do anything more than try to talk you out of it. I never would have called him if it had crossed my mind that he would get violent. I guess I underestimated how much of an asshole he is."

"Hard to overestimate," said Karen.

"I'm hoping you can forgive me," said Weber.

You're hoping I won't tell the police who murdered Larry, thought Karen.

"I want you to know," he continued, "I have no hard feelings about the snooping you did into my relationship with Larry. I know it must have been you who tossed his apartment, but I'm not going to report the break-in."

Ah, there's the quid pro quo, mused Karen. You don't squeal on me and I don't squeal on you.

He continued. "I am curious, though, as to why you put so much effort into figuring out who . . ." he paused and looked uneasily at Jake.

"Jake already knows," said Karen. "When I started investigating Larry's death, it was just a matter of defending his wife's malpractice claim against the hospital. Then I learned the catheter had been sabotaged and found the files from Larry's investigation of the Jefferson Clinic. With his last words, Larry entrusted me with those files. I owed it to him to find out whether there was a connection between his investigation and the faulty catheter. Larry was a good friend. I really cared about him."

"You weren't the only one," said Weber.

"I know," said Karen.

Carson Weber smiled, crinkling the gray skin in the hollowness around his eyes. "Thank you for that," he said. "You'll be glad to hear, Mrs. Hayes," Weber continued, "that you and the Medical Executive Committee can take me off your to-do list. I'm resigning from the medical staff. Is there anything else I can do for you?"

"Yes, there is."

Karen asked Jake for her briefcase. She popped it open and removed a business card and a microcassette in a plastic box. She handed both to Weber.

"Listen to as much of this tape as you like, then call Attorney Emerson Knowles at the number on this card. He has a copy of the tape, and a third copy is in safekeeping. Knowles is handling several lawsuits against Shoreview Memorial that involve you."

"Paula Conkel," said Weber.

"And Steven Linder and Dietrich Heiden," said Karen.

Weber looked down at his feet.

"I know you've put something aside from your dealings with the clinic. Now you won't be using that money to fund Joe Grimes's MRI venture. Between that money and your liability insurance, you should be able to settle all three lawsuits, without any contribution from the hospital. Especially once the plaintiff's attorneys understand there is no way to pin any responsibility on the hospital and its deep pockets."

Weber continued to study the floor, his face gaunt and impassive. "Which they'll know because what I'm going to admit to will exonerate the hospital."

"Exactly," said Karen. "Once the attorneys understand the situation, you can probably negotiate a confidentiality agreement within the terms of the settlements."

After a long silence, Weber looked up and sighed, the vestiges of his bout with pneumonia giving his sigh a gravelly rumble. His eyelids drooped and he smiled. "I don't see I have a choice. Ah, well. Perhaps accepting responsibility and compensating the victims will help ease my conscience a little about Larry. What do you think, counselor?"

"One can hope," said Karen. She gave Weber a sharp look, confessing that she herself felt partially responsible for Larry's death, because she had talked Larry out of having his biopsy performed at St. Peter's Hospital by pointing out to him the possible adverse effect that might have on his career. Weber assured her that she had had nothing to do with Larry's decision. Larry had originally planned to go to St. Pete's so he would not have to disclose his HIV status to his coworkers.

"Once I'd set my course," Weber explained, "there was no resistance. I made sure Larry switched cardiologists so his biopsy would be done here. I persuaded him that it was okay not to tell anyone about his HIV status. He never even mentioned your comment about the effect on his career. Frankly, he wasn't that focused on his career at the time."

Karen felt a little foolish for having so overestimated the impact of her advice on Larry. She also felt the last remnants of her guilt dissolve. After Weber left, she said to Jake, "I guess it's safe for me to hand out advice. Apparently nobody listens to it anyway."

"They should," he responded. "Why, look at the way you've made all the hospital's legal hassles disappear. I don't think very many lawyers could have pulled that off so neatly. But what was that remark about a confidentiality agreement? Aren't you going to finger Weber for Larry's murder?"

Karen stared at him with a forlorn expression. "He's really not dangerous to anyone at this point, and he's going to pay for the patient assaults."

"That doesn't undo what he did to Larry."

"I think at this point he sincerely believes that what he did was euthanasia." Karen began to cry and Jake handed her a box of tissue. He reached over and touched her shoulder.

"You just can't do it to him, can you?"

"Jake, he's dying," she said.

"He's big-time sick, that's for sure," Jake said, "but I've read that with all the drugs they have now, AIDS patients can live for a long . . . what? Why are you shaking your head?"

"I see it in his eyes. It's imminent, and he knows it."

Jake stroked his wife's hair. "The quality of mercy is not strained," he said. "It droppeth . . ."

"Not up to your usual standards of obscurity, sweetheart," said Karen.

"Wait. All right, here you go. 'Mercy shines with even more brilliancy than justice.'"

"Who 'dat?"

"Cervantes."

"Not bad, Sancho Panza," said Karen. Her eyes cleared and she put the box of tissues on the nightstand. "But that isn't quite it. The fact that Weber is dying just makes it pointless to turn him in. He would die before he even got to trial. In the meantime, the investigation and the publicity would severely damage the hospital and cause a lot of innocent people grief and anxiety. It's my job to protect the hospital."

"And you want to do your job without hurting anybody," said Jake.

"Why are you smirking?" asked Karen.

"Right Livelihood!" said Jake. "Earning your living without harming others!"

"Okay," said Karen. "Score one for Buddha's Eightfold Path. It's just too bad the Jefferson Clinic docs strayed so far off it."

"And the feds aren't exactly famous for the quality of their mercy," said Jake. "What's going to happen to those guys?"

Once each day, Dr. Herwitz popped into Karen's patient room, glanced at her chart, made quick notes adjusting her medications, and briefly inspected the dressings on her wounds. There was little conversation beyond "How are you today?" and "Fine, how are you?" until the morning of the day Karen was discharged. Karen had read her own medical record, including the operative report, and thought she understood fairly well what had gone on in the surgical suite for over three hours. Repair of a tear in the inferior mesenteric artery. Removal of three pieces of irregularly shaped glass. Suturing abdominal lacerations. On his last visit to Karen's room, Dr. Herwitz sat down and talked with Karen and Jake for a few minutes.

"You'll be going home this afternoon," he said. "The nurse will give you written instructions. Change your dressings twice a day. Use an antiseptic soap and apply the Neosporin for ten days. I'll give you a prescription for a pain medication. You may not need it." He shifted in his chair and cleared his throat. "Mrs. Hayes," he said, "about your surgery . . ."

Outside the room and down the hall, a hopelessly bad children's choir from Our Redeemer Lutheran Church Sunday School launched into a barely recognizable version of "O Little Town of Bethlehem." Jake cocked his head to one side, screwed his face into a comically exaggerated expression of pain, and stuck the middle finger of his right hand in his ear.

"Somebody should tell those guys not to quit their day jobs," said Jake, getting up to close the door. Dr. Herwitz waited for him before beginning again.

"The reason your incision is so long, Mrs. Hayes. We found three large pieces of glass in your abdomen almost immediately, one of which had penetrated your peritoneal cavity, where the intestines are, and nicked an artery. The cavity was filled with blood. We had no way of knowing if there were lacerations of your intestines or other organs without examining them. We also had no way of knowing if there were additional glass fragments in you other than the three large pieces. If there were, and we left one in, it could have nicked you at any time and started an internal bleed. Consequently, I had to perform a total lower ab exploratory. Basically, this involved removing each of your internal organs below the diaphragm far enough to inspect each carefully for bleeding and glass fragments, and then restoring each organ to its normal position."

Karen made a face like she had swallowed a bad oyster. She grabbed Jake's hand and squeezed it.

Dr. Herwitz looked away from Karen. "Your mother told me a couple of years ago that the two of you were trying to have children. Are you still?"

"Like Sisyphus with his boulder," replied Jake.

"Beg pardon?" said Dr. Herwitz.

"We're trying," said Jake.

"Well, I'm not surprised you've been unsuccessful. Mrs. Hayes, you have quite a bit of endometriosis. While I had you open, I took the liberty of removing as much as I easily could without significantly extending the duration of the surgery, and without risking injury to the bowel. I don't know if it will make any difference, but you may notice that your menstrual periods are a little lighter than they have been, at least for a while."

Jake and Karen looked at each other with expressions of sad, knowing resignation.

"Well, that's something," said Jake.

"It may redevelop in a few years," said Dr. Herwitz, "but by then you'll be reaching menopause."

"Oh," said Karen. "So much to look forward to."

"Well," announced Dr. Herwitz, clapping his hands on his thighs and rising from his chair. "I did my best. If your incision turns red or oozes, or if you develop a fever, call my office." He walked to the door. As he opened it, Karen called after him.

"Dr. Herwitz!"

"Yes, Mrs. Hayes?"

Karen took a deep breath and let it out. "Thank you for saving my life."

EPILOGUE

A month after Karen was discharged as a patient from Shore-view Memorial Hospital, Joe Grimes was fired by the Board of Directors. Three weeks later he began his new position as CEO of Raasch Evangelical Medical Center at a forty percent increase in salary.

The following June, Norman Caswell, the spooky cancer specialist who had grown rich giving unnecessary chemotherapy, voluntarily surrendered his medical license in exchange for the government dropping all criminal charges and actions for forfeitures against him. He retired on the $250,000-per-year tax-free income he received from his municipal bond holdings.

Edward Bernard decided not to retire. In July he moved with his wife and son to Cancún, Mexico, to set up a practice in cardiology at the Hospital Americano.

In August, Carson Weber died of complications from pneumonia. That same month, Jake Hayes's song, "Karaoke Bites," was recorded on CD by a Chicago-based band called the Swinging Chads. Royalty checks began arriving at the Hayes household in October, the same month the Jefferson Clinic was assessed a forfeiture of $48 million by the federal investigators. No fines were imposed on any of the physicians as individuals, and the clinic was subsequently placed in bankruptcy. The government collected two-and-a-half cents on the dollar.

A year after Karen's surgery, Leonard Herwitz was the subject of a disciplinary hearing at Shoreview Memorial, based on his complicity in the fraudulent practices of the Jefferson Clinic physicians. The hospital was represented at the hearing by Emerson Knowles. For Dr. Herwitz, in a three-hour surgery in the middle of the night, had managed to repay at least part of the debt he owed.

Karen Hayes was on maternity leave.